influence

CHRIS PARKER

http://urbanepublications.com

First published in Great Britain in 2014
by Urbane Publications Ltd
20 St Nicholas Gardens, Rochester
Kent ME2 3NT

A CIP catalogue record for this book is available
from the British Library.

ISBN 978-1-909273-06-1

Typeset at Chandler Book Design, King's Lynn, Norfolk

Printed in Great Britain by
CPI Antony Rowe,
Chippenham, Wiltshire

http://urbanepublications.com

For 'M'.

Acknowledgements

Marcus Kline, the world's greatest communication guru, owes his existence to four people: Mairi, Alan, Matthew and IbA.

Mairi helped bring him to life during two fabulous weeks in France.

Alan provided great knowledge about campaigning communications and was instrumental in the selection of Marcus's hair styling.

Matthew ensured that this, the first part of Marcus's story, is now in your hands.

IbA started it all for me over thirty five years ago, when he first sparked my desire to learn how to read the lines on peoples' faces.

Also DCI Peter Jones, the great detective and Marcus Kline's best friend, and I, are forever indebted to PJ for so many vital insights shared through so many wonderful evenings.

And, finally, I would not have known how to get inside people's heads without the medical expertise of Dr Ian Campbell. Whilst I am extremely grateful to Ian for his time and support, I am certain there are characters in the book that are not.

Influence

by

Chris Parker

'The worst pain isn't physical.'

Influence

'A power affecting a person, thing, or course of events.'

'To flow into; to produce an effect by imperceptible or intangible means.'

PART ONE

Different Worlds

It starts before it starts

Let me tell you the most important thing now, before everything else, before you start thinking too much.

The most important thing is this:

Influence is the ultimate resource.

You were born with nothing. Knowing nothing. And from the moment you took your first breath the influence began.

We create our power through our ability to influence.

We create the power to understand, the power to change.

We create our world and rule our planet not because we are the strongest animal, or the fastest or the most durable. No. We dominate because we are the most influential.

And our influence is contagious.

It is contagious because influence surrounds us whether we realise it or not. It enters through our eyes and ears, whether we mean it to or not. It seeps in through the very pores of our skin.

It is contagious because our nature makes it so, because all human beings have an instinctive ability and desire to create associations and meanings.

In simple terms we see a facial expression, we hear a tone of voice, we witness behaviours and we interpret them almost immediately – so fast that we don't even recognise the process. We create the power we need to navigate life successfully through our ability and our need to create meaning.

That means we are all open to influence.

Which is why the most powerful people are those who have created meanings that most of us – meanings that you – buy into. Meanings about right or wrong. Meanings about how society is supposed to work. About how we are should relate to other humans. And how they should relate to us. Meanings about how we should look and what we should wear. Meanings about life and success and failure.

You know these things. You have your own set of meanings. You believe you created them yourself.

You are wrong. Pathetically, hopelessly wrong!

You didn't create the meanings that you spray out into the world in the same arrogant way that a cat pisses in every corner of its territory. You didn't create them – they were installed in you by others.

By the powerful people.

People like me.

They were planted in your subconscious.

Left to grow.

Think of the most powerful antenna in the world, one that never stops receiving signals. Now think – if you can – of something infinitely more receptive. Infinitely more switched on.

That is your subconscious mind!

Always open to influence.

The hidden star inside the human brain.

It runs the show – your show – without you even realising it. Forging your attitudes. Shaping your perceptions. Sparking your responses.

Even when you fall in love, it is your brain – with the subconscious pulling strings from the shadows – that directs the process.

You don't fall in love with all of your heart.

The human heart doesn't have the capacity for such a complex creation as love. No, it is the brain, especially parts of the so-called reptilian brain, the primal part of your neural circuitry, which quite literally sprays out feelings of reward and need and desire when you tell yourself that you have found your perfect mate.

Love is all in your head. Just like every other emotion.

If that hurts just think about this: your subconscious mind is at the very heart of your relationships with everyone and everything around you. It is even at the heart of your relationship with yourself.

Only of course you can't think about it. Not really. You believe you can. You might even feel that you are. Only that's the left hemisphere of your brain talking. And that's the side that does the obvious talking. It is responsible for words and logic, for naming things. It is the side that the neuroscientists call the Dominant Hemisphere.

The arrogant bastard!

Asked to name itself, the left hemisphere comes up with something that a dictator would be proud of. What makes me laugh is that the scientists haven't even realised that the left hemisphere asked the question in the first place. And then it provided an answer designed to show its control over everything. And the scientists bought into it. They didn't even realise they were being played. They didn't consider the possibility that the left hemisphere was wrong. Or that it was lying. But how could they? There is no way the left hemisphere is going to ask those sort of questions about itself.

All I ask – for now – is that you use your puny, self-serving conscious mind to focus on this one vital truth: the subconscious is the supreme, silent power source.

The subconscious stores every influence that has ever found its way inside you. And then it, in turn, influences you in more ways than you can ever imagine. It influences you twenty four hours a day, seven days a week. It influences every minute, every second, of your life.

I have seen life begin and I have seen life end.

I have ended lives.

So many different lives. I have watched the black cloud release itself. I have quite literally seen death.

Now I have to kill again. And differently. After all, what is a researcher supposed to do? How else can I further my knowledge? How else can I develop my expertise?

So, people have to die. They have been well chosen, I promise you. And they will die painlessly. I promise you that, too. I will prove my superiority. I will be neither stopped, nor caught. Instead I will fly. I will flow. I will find my way into your subconscious. I will live inside you. Influencing you. Whether you know it or not.

You see, the subconscious connects us all.

The subconscious is the deep current that runs through everything. It is the fathomless one. Happy to let the waves of consciousness crash above it. Deep in its own resolve and purpose.

Running the show.

At the very heart of us...

1.

'At the heart of everything actually. The subconscious is the silent programmer who really only wants to create associations that are best for its host. You see, every human being is being bombarded with literally millions of stimuli every second of their life. We are all dependent on this programmer sifting through the mass of information, deciding what our conscious mind should focus on, what it should ignore, what it needn't even recognise. We are dependent on our subconscious doing all of this, non-stop, getting it right without ever being noticed, without ever getting in the way of our everyday business.'

'So, in this book you are acting as the spokesman for this silent programmer?'

'That would be an excellent way of describing it, yes.' Marcus Kline leaned back against the red studio sofa and smiled in admiration at the insight and linguistic alacrity of the TV presenter. *Spokesman for the silent programmer* was exactly the phrase Marcus had wanted him to use. It had taken only three minutes to put the words into the other man's mind – his subconscious to be precise – and for them to be encouraged out into the conscious awareness of the watching millions.

The presenter matched Marcus's smile. He had no choice. His ego had just been massaged irresistibly and he was following the lead Marcus had set from before they had gone on air. Without realising it, the presenter had been saying and doing only what Marcus required of him. Between them they were, Marcus mused, acting out a metaphor for the human brain. The presenter represented the left hemisphere – obvious, sure of his control and skill, enjoying his power. Marcus was the right hemisphere – subtle, his influence hidden below the surface, the ultimate power source. Only a genius in inter-personal communications could have watched the interplay between the two men and recognised what was happening.

And the odds were stacked against that. In the minds of many of the watching audience the genius was here, in front of the cameras, his long, dark brown hair swept back, his right arm stretched out along the back of the sofa, his black Canali suit unbuttoned, his white Eton shirt open at the collar. Some of the audience – those business leaders, politicians and celebrities who were taking five minutes out of their very busy schedules to see Marcus make a rare TV appearance – had personal experience of the benefits of his genius, had been helped by him in ways that they valued enormously yet didn't remotely understand.

Marcus nodded, feigning thoughtful appreciation. 'Spokesman for the silent programmer', he repeated. 'With your permission Charlie, I might just use that myself.' As he spoke, Marcus crossed his left leg over his right and at the same time his left hand pulled briefly at the trouser crease on his left knee.

'Be my guest.' Charlie's smile broadened. The fingers of his right hand tapped unconsciously against his right knee. 'And with that it is time to say, "Thank you" to Marcus Kline, communications guru and author of "*Associations: The Secret Way We Create Our Public Reality.*" Guaranteed to be his next best seller, it is available from all good bookshops from today. Marcus, thank you. The silent programmer couldn't have a better spokesman...'

Whilst the viewing public were reminded of the latest news from their local region, Marcus let a young blond woman remove his microphone, signed Charlie's copy of the book, "With best wishes – and many thanks for a great line!" and made his way out into the bustle of the city.

2.

'Christ, it's busy!' Nic Simpson slowed the grey Audi A6 to a halt. The queue of traffic ahead looked particularly dark and dispiriting in the early November morning.

'It's the rain that does it.'

'It's not the rain that causes the queue, it's the way most people turn themselves into zombies in response to the rain!'

Peter Jones forced himself to smile at his lover's irritation. He forced himself to smile the kind of tolerant smile used only between two people who share intimate secrets. The kind of smile that says, 'I've heard you say that same thing so many times and I've seen you get annoyed like this so many times and, somehow, because it is you it makes me love you more.' Peter Jones faked the smile so well that only an expert would have identified the deception, would have recognised the tension in his gut.

'Why, for Christ's sake, does a drop of water always create such a major fuck up!' Nic's irritation continued to build.

It was, Peter knew, going to be brief, obvious and certain. He could no more change the course of the next few minutes of conversation than he could influence the weather. He knew better than to try.

'It's more than a drop and it isn't major.'

'I bet more people agree with me than you.' Nic's long, delicate fingers drummed against the steering wheel.

'Possibly.'

'Definitely. I'm telling you right now we are surrounded by a host of very angry people.'

'You wouldn't convince a jury of that.' As he said it, Peter's stomach tightened briefly. A short, sharp tug deep on his left side. Peter frowned despite himself.

'I would if they'd been in this fucking queue. It feels like the start of a Romero movie called *Drenched Zombie Dawn*.'

'Everything feels like part of a Romero movie right now.'

'By lunchtime we'll be fighting to survive against hordes of brain dead lunatics who are all soaked to the skin and desperate to get out of the rain.'

'The thing you always seem to forget is that we are part of the problem you are complaining about. We are helping to create the queue.'

'No. No, no, no, no! *They* are the queue!' A finger stabbed towards the car windscreen and the line of traffic ahead. '*We* are just the innocent victims of everyone else reacting inappropriately to a drop of water.'

'It's more than a drop.'

Above them what looked like a thick, grey quilt of cloud covered the city. Peter glanced at his watch. They were running late. Everyone who was city-based was running late. That always happened when the weather took a turn for the worse. Ultimately gridlock was just a reminder of the way everyone and everything was connected. All just part of one big system. But is it a system that society depends upon or is the system actually society?

To his left, on the pavement, a young white man no more than nineteen years old, walked past talking into his mobile phone. His younger looking mixed race girlfriend – at least Peter couldn't see a wedding ring – was a pace behind, pushing a pram. The baby was out of sight. The phone conversation was demanding all of the young man's attention. He seemed unaware of the rain or the traffic. Or his family. Peter couldn't help but wonder how he made his money. And he couldn't help but be angry with himself for the thought. Peter, of all people, knew better than to stereotype.

It's true, he mused, that every system is the result of a stream of constant patterns, but within these patterns are a range of subtle, significant and sometimes powerful differences. For the most part these differences flex within the confines of the system. Sometimes, though, they don't. And when things happen to disrupt or damage the system, professionals have to identify the source of the problem and resolve it. He was one of those professionals. He was trained to identify the sequences of behaviour that challenge expectation and conformity; that dare you to make sense of something that's different and bad; dare you to make sense of it and then do something about it. You can't make sense of things accurately if you stereotype. Good and bad, he knew, comes in all shapes and sizes.

Peter watched the young man lead his family, phone pressed to his ear, towards their undisclosed destination. He noticed a small, black tattoo of a crucifix on the back of his hand. The phone was the latest iPhone, released in time for the Christmas rush. His tracksuit was Nike's latest design. His trainers were equally expensive. Peter saw the glint of a gold tooth as the young man laughed out loud. The phone conversation ended abruptly, the phone transferred from right hand to left as he looked back over his right shoulder and spoke briefly to his partner.

The rain had increased in intensity, even during the last few minutes. Now it spiked down, bouncing off the dark blue covering of the pram, turning it an even darker hue. For Peter the sight of the young family was far more depressing than the weather. He realised suddenly that he was studying the young man for signs of a hidden weapon. His stomach tugged again.

'They'd definitely get walk-on parts in *Drenched Zombie Dawn*,' Nic's voice cut through Peter's observation. He used it to distract himself from the feeling in his gut. Nic went on, 'The parents would attack us. We'd shoot them, relax for a moment thinking we were safe, and then the baby would fly out of the pram and bite your face off.'

'I'll keep my eyes on it then, in case it contains a six month old cannibal with wings.' Peter knew the distraction would only be temporary, but he reasoned that any relief was better than none at all.

'I never said it had wings. It's a zombie film for Christ's sake. Zombies don't have wings.'

'Then how come it flies out of the pram to bite my face?'

'Zombie babies are surprisingly agile. They just stiffen up with age.' Nic's eyes were fixed on the stationary traffic ahead. 'Just like you're doing.'

'You do realise that most people in this queue are either texting work or listening to their radio. What they are not doing is imagining a zombie world.'

'I bet my students are.'

'Fair enough.' This time Peter couldn't help but smile.

'In fact, that's how I'm going to start the lecture! If I ever get there of course. I'll tell them to look out of the window at the weather, and create a name for a Romero film based on what they see. Even those with only half a brain should include the words "Day" or "Dawn" and "Storm" or "Drenched."'

'Personally, I'll be really pleased when this module has finished. I'm all zombied-out.'

'By Christmas, my love. Then we start the New Year with twelve weeks on the anti-hero in twentieth century cinema. Talking of which, did you remember to record MK this morning?'

'Of course.' He twisted very deliberately in his seat, trying to ease the tightness in his muscles, looking for the young family.

'To be fair, though, we could all just as easily be in a Christmas remake of *The Seven Dwarves* rather than at the start of the *Day of The Living Dead*. After all, we are all busy doing nothing.' Nic's mood brightened suddenly, irritation turning into silliness, just as Peter had known it would. 'So which would you sooner be – a dwarf or a zombie fighter?'

'I'd sooner be a dwarf. As long as I was Happy.' *Especially right now.*

Peter kept his gaze on the pavement despite the fact that the young family was nowhere to be seen. Images tumbled through his mind. Images in full, rich Technicolor.

Images that no cinematographer could ever show, that no audience would ever pay to see.

Busy going nowhere, eh? That would seem to be the case. Only his gut was telling him that was about to change.

3.

Marcus Kline was also busy going nowhere. He was standing with his back to the television studios watching lines of pedestrians thread their way along the pavement. People-watching was far more than just a casual way of passing the time for the author and consultant. It was practice of the very highest order.

He gave primary attention to the most obvious and yet most easily over-looked aspect of what was happening in front of him: the fact that hundreds of people were walking in both directions within the confined space of the pavement without frequently crashing into each other. Marcus's gaze followed the lines of individuals weaving patterns of movement without shouting out instructions or warnings, without pausing to decide the best route to take through the crowd.

This, Marcus reminded himself, was an activity unequalled in the animal kingdom. It was far more impressive than hundreds of ants marching in line, a lion pride hunting in unison, or even the great migration across the African plains. Here, now, there was no teamwork, no shared purpose, no primal necessity or seasonal change driving behaviour. Here, throughout the city, thousands of people were following their own path, heading towards their personal destinations, travelling at their own pace whilst working in silent collaboration with everyone around them to ensure the flow of movement continued. As people they all had much in common in terms of their biological and social make-up – what Marcus thought of as their collective DNA – but he also understood that each individual was as different from everyone else as it was possible to be.

Marcus had long-since known – and this was one of the great secrets of his success – that what he was really watching was not hundreds of different people, but rather hundreds of different individual worlds working in unison to avoid disaster.

Marcus Kline had built for a reputation as one of the most powerful experts in communication and influence in the world. His business, **Influence:** The Marcus Kline Consultancy, provided training and support for many leading international corporations. And when requested he worked personally with well-known personalities from the world of politics, sport, entertainment and business. He also worked for smaller, local businesses at greatly reduced rates, even working free of charge to help individuals and families overcome traumatic experiences, fears or addictions.

He made sure that the media were always aware of his generosity and altruism. It was an important part of the very deliberately conceived Marcus Kline brand. He didn't just want to be acknowledged as the very best at what he did, he also wanted to be recognised as one of the 'good guys'. It made building a powerful network so much easier and it dramatically increased the number of followers he had around the world. The combination of a far-reaching, influential network and many thousands – possibly millions – of followers provided the foundation for his success, enhancing the two outcomes he desired most: Profile and Profit.

Marcus's almost magical ability to understand others was based on a simple and yet profound truth that he had learnt many years before. The truth was this:

If you really want to understand another human being – sometimes more deeply even than they understand themselves – you have to give them absolute, skilled attention. You have to know, truly know, how to look and listen.

You have to do this, he told his audiences, because everyone perceives and functions differently. Everyone creates their own particular patterns of communication, each with their own distinct elements and meanings, each with their own strengths and weaknesses.

Marcus had titled his first book, the one that had given him an international profile, *"Different Worlds"*, to emphasise the magnitude and significance of these differences. In it, he had argued that, despite the uniting power of social and geographical cultures, every single human being created and then operated within their own unique world. It was a world made up of a mixture of beliefs, values and aspirations, expressed through individualised communication patterns that had, for the most part, been developed subconsciously.

The gap between people, Marcus wrote, even those people who had known each other for years, who met each other every day, was far greater than that experienced between people from different countries. If you truly wanted to understand others, he said, you had to study them with the curiosity you would feel if knowingly entering an entirely different world.

His argument for the development of what he referred to as *skilled attention* and his extravagant claim for the existence of different worlds had made the book impossible to ignore. There had been debate and disagreement; outrage from some who felt that his claims helped people justify a selfish, rather than a social, worldview. The fact that Marcus was willing on live television to demonstrate his ability to enter into, understand, and influence positively, the worlds of complete strangers, did much to strengthen his claims and enhance his growing reputation.

Now he was simply part of the early morning mass. No one paid him any attention; all too fixed on their own journey, too caught up with thoughts about the day ahead. Marcus knew that the pattern of movement playing out in front of him was being created and managed by the collective subconscious of all involved. The fact that it was a subconscious process freed their conscious minds to think about the vitally important and very obvious aspects of their lives that, for the most part, determined their mood and behaviour. Marcus watched individuals thinking of family and friends, of recent arguments, of imagined futures.

The tragedy, he knew from his years of work, was that far too many of these people were focussing on negative experiences, were imagining only the worst of all possible scenarios, were walking towards a personal future that frightened them. His skill – and a significant part of his professional purpose – was in teaching them how to break out of this vicious cycle and identify and move towards brighter outcomes.

Marcus watched the crowd, made up of hundreds of different worlds, unconsciously creating patterns of movement that, for the most part, benefitted everyone. *The power of the social subconscious at work*, Marcus mused. It was the very heartbeat of the city, powering life and movement.

He let his peripheral vision pull out one particular person. She was walking towards him from the right and was still half a dozen paces away. Marcus didn't know what it was about her that drew his attention and he didn't try to second-guess it. She had been chosen and, therefore she was going to be the focus for the next part of his practice. He let his gaze fix on and around her, let his eyes and face soften, his breathing travel down to his lower belly. He let his hands relax, felt his fingers stretch as if seeking to touch the pavement. He exhaled gently and deliberately through his nose. And then he *looked*.

She had shoulder length hair, brunette in colour, which had obviously been straightened that morning. She was in her early thirties – 32 was the number that popped into Marcus's conscious mind – and she was less than average build. She was wearing a knee length black leather dress, a white shirt, black woollen tights and ankle-high black suede boots. She was carrying a black Mulberry shoulder bag. She walked with the light yet obvious connection to the ground that was the hallmark of an athlete. She had the relaxed, very clear focus of a person driven by, and comfortable with, the need to achieve very specific goals. There was an unconscious rhythm to her movement. She was at once comfortable within the crowd and capable at the same time of moving to her own beat. So, Marcus asked himself, just who are you and what do you do?

He found himself moving towards her even before the answers had formed. When he was two paces from her left shoulder he heard himself say, 'Excuse me, Gemma?'

The woman stopped and glanced at him, a mixture of surprise and confusion flashing across her face. He saw that she was ready to move on again quickly if need be. He was clearly not quite right. Marcus ensured that he was close enough to her to be heard and to force the crowd to move around them, yet far enough away to respect her personal space. 'I'm sorry,' he said, 'Jemima.'

Now curiosity replaced the confusion. He noticed the ease and the confidence with which she changed state. He watched as she scanned her most recent experiences, searching for information about this man who she felt she knew but couldn't quite recognise.

He paused only briefly before going on, 'I'm sorry for the intrusion. My name is Marcus. We met at the party after the...' Marcus glanced back at the crowd, using it to dampen his desire to try and think what the right word should be, letting the different worlds swirling around him create the space in his mind into which the answer could be pulled from his subconscious... 'After the concert,' he said, 'Which I adored. And, if I may say, I have always been a particular fan of the...' Marcus glanced up to his right and an image of Jemima as part of an orchestra flashed before his mind's eye, '...cello.'

Jemima smiled and, despite the chill in the air, a touch of colour brightened her cheeks. It was clear that Marcus had interpreted correctly and that she was increasingly comfortable in his presence. 'Thank you! Obviously an orchestra is more important than any single performer or any particular instrument but, secretly, we all love to be recognised. And, of course, we all have a passion for own instrument.'

'I think it is the sharing of passion that creates the emotional experience that only an orchestra can give an audience.' Marcus matched her smile and moved just a half a pace closer. Jemima's shoulders were now completely relaxed.

'Yes, it is such a sharing, giving process,' she said. 'And we get emotion and inspiration back from you, too! We can feel it when an audience warms to us, when it is living in the moment with us!'

'It's what my business friends would call the ideal "win-win" situation.' Marcus let his smile broaden as he glanced deliberately at his watch. 'Anyway, it's been lovely to see you again. And to be able to say, "Thank you" once more for a wonderful evening.' He offered his right hand and Jemima took it. He matched the pressure of her grasp precisely. 'By the way, are you still managing to maintain the work-out schedule?'

'Absolutely. I was in the gym by 6am this morning as always. Five miles on the running machine, half an hour of yoga, and then I'm ready for anything.' Jemima withdrew her hand from his. Her head cocked to one side. 'How did you know?'

'It shows.' Marcus glanced briefly at the pavement, shrugging his shoulders slightly, as if offering a silent, embarrassed apology in case his comment was too personal.

'Yoga is transformative.' Jemima's breath showed in the cold air, for a second it closed the space between them, a subtle connection they both noticed. Jemima reached into her bag. 'Here.' She offered him her business card. 'It has my mobile number on it. If you are able to come to another concert, let me know.'

'Thank you, I will. Perhaps you would join me for a drink afterwards?'

'I'd love to.'

She had beautiful, white teeth and there were delicate green flecks in the dark brown irises of her eyes. Marcus estimated that her heart was beating at fifty-eight beats per minute. He had been matching her breathing pattern from the instant she had stopped walking.

'That would be lovely. I look forward to seeing you soon.'

'Likewise.'

Marcus nodded. 'Enjoy the rehearsal this morning.'

'I will. Bye – for now.'

Marcus made as if to walk away as Jemima set off towards her destination. He watched her consider glancing back and then decide against it. He saw how the rhythm of her walk had changed to a slightly faster beat, a result of the adrenaline release he had caused within her. He absent-mindedly crushed the business card between his fingers and let it fall to the ground as she disappeared from view.

Marcus was not an athlete in the physical sense, but like an athlete he had to work hard just to maintain, let alone develop, his skill. Thankfully, he didn't need to go to a gym or a track to do that. He had a world in which to practice. Or, to be more precise, he had an almost infinite number of different worlds he could visit.

Marcus hailed a taxi, asked to be taken to the train station, and settled into the back seat. Jemima was a Hebrew name, he recalled. In the Bible, Jemima was the eldest of the three daughters of Job, renowned as the three most beautiful women of their time. In Hebrew the name Jemima literally meant "warm", although because that was associated with "affectionate" the name had long since come to mean "dove". Jemima, the bird of peace.

Perhaps, Marcus thought, meeting Jemima meant that he was going to have a peaceful day. And then he laughed out loud at the fact that even part of his mind wanted to make such absurd, childish connections.

Superstitions reflected either the naivety of youth or the laziness of adulthood. The quality of your day – the quality of your life – did not depend on whether or not you wore your lucky charm, or stepped on a pavement crack, or walked under a ladder (unless, of course, something fell off it and hit you on the head). No, it depended on what you chose to do with your time and the quality of the associations you made. "It starts with creating and managing your own neural networks," he had written once, "and then it spreads out into creating and managing your own interpersonal networks." It certainly had nothing to do with a person's name. Or the so-called bird of peace.

Marcus decided to ignore the passing show and closed his eyes as the taxi made its way through the city. He was going to have a great day. It had started really well and it was going to get better. He was sure of it.

4.

Detective Chief Inspector Peter Jones was sure that something bad was going to happen. His gut never lied. It hadn't been wrong since the day he made detective. Actually, he didn't think it had ever been wrong since he'd been in uniform. It was just that back then he had allowed the voices of senior, more experienced colleagues to drown out the message he felt inside. Now, when his stomach spoke he listened. And when he spoke to his team, they listened to him. Now *he* was that senior, more experienced colleague. The man who stayed at the same rank so he could keep active in the field, rather than pursue a highly paid desk job.

Peter Jones was not a strategist or a political animal. He was a detective. He solved crimes. It was a game he knew how to play. And he could play it better than most. Especially the people he pursued. Trusting his gut was an essential part of his approach. Nic loved to refer to it as his 'almost-feminine intuition'. Their good friend Marcus Kline had assured him – in fact, over the years, he had demonstrated to him – it was actually the power of his subconscious.

'And there's plenty of research,' Marcus had said, back in the day when Peter had first shared his experiences, 'to show that experienced professionals, particularly those who work in stressful jobs and challenging situations, are capable of developing intuitive responses that are accurate and, sometimes, even life-saving.'

'It's like the instinctive behaviours of actors who lose their sense of personal identity behind that of the characters they inhabit,' Nic had said.

'Only this is reality – actually it's arguably the most powerful aspect of reality – not the fantasy creation of a film studio,' Marcus had countered quickly. 'Let me give you just one example. In the 1990s, a research psychologist called Gary Klein began interviewing professionals who had used their intuition to make instant life-or-death decisions. One of the people he interviewed was a fire chief who had taken his men into a burning single-storey house. The kitchen was on fire. The fire fighters doused the room with water as they were trained to do, but the fire did not go out. Suddenly, the chief had a feeling that there was something wrong. "Let's get out, now!" he shouted and the team followed his order without question. Seconds after they had exited the building the floor on which they had been standing collapsed. The source of the fire had been in the basement not the kitchen. His subconscious had recognized and interpreted the minute signals that his conscious mind had not. It's a classic example of intuition, gut instinct, being absolutely right.'

Back in the day Nic had not wanted to like Marcus. Indeed, back in the day Nic had actively disliked Marcus. The professional certainty of the consultant had clashed very obviously with the creative curiosity of the lecturer in media studies. After their first meeting Nic had expressed both surprise and concern that Peter could find anything loveable in the man who, according to Nic's first impression, *hid behind his face.*

Only the clash had dissolved with surprising speed. The impact between two opposing and seemingly immovable forces had, in fact, turned into a joyous merging of what Nic had come to think of as variations on a theme. Now the relationship between Marcus and Nic was as significant in its own way as that between the two school friends who had known each other for what seemed like forever. For the last three years Marcus had provided guest lectures for Nic, talking about the power of language in modern media, and, when Peter was working late on a case, Nic was more likely to spend time with Marcus than anyone else.

Peter had realised almost instantly that Nic's change in attitude had been created, managed and led by Marcus's ability to influence those around him. He guessed that it was just one of the many ways his friend had used his skill to ensure that their relationship continued without unnecessary stresses or threats. He had, after a particularly drunken evening, asked Marcus just how he had managed to win Nic over so quickly. Despite the several bottles of Rioja they had shared, his friend did indeed immediately retreat 'behind his face' and deny all charges. Peter had not pursued the conversation. Given his profession, Peter knew that, as a basic rule, the right outcome was what mattered most. The key, as he often told less experienced officers, was in ensuring that their foundations were always secure enough to support the desired outcome. They had to be layered and congruent. They had to be without any obvious gaps, without any room for doubt – reasonable or otherwise.

Although he kept the thought to himself, Peter couldn't help but wonder whether or not Marcus really did like Nic.

Nic released the handbrake as the queue began to slither forwards. The road they were on, Carlton Hill, was one of the main roads into Nottingham city centre. It was not their usual route into work, but they were returning from a very welcome, and rare, romantic night away. The Audi began to pick up pace. Somehow, for reasons that Peter or Nic would never know, the traffic was releasing itself; the delay was over. 'There's just a chance my lecture might even start on time.' Nic looked at Peter. 'What do you think?'

'Fingers crossed.' Peter faked another smile. The queue had come alive. Destinations were getting closer. The feeling in Peter's stomach twisted and pulled, tugging his mind towards the dark room, the place that could only be entered, explored and survived through the clinical and, sometimes, callous application of procedure. His stomach was offering a warning, not a solution. In his line of work Peter couldn't order a retreat. It didn't matter how much pressure he found himself under, how much heat there was, he had to keep going forwards until he had found all the answers and the story was complete. The only way he knew to do that and have any chance of keeping safe was to build a wall around himself; a wall that was cold, hard and strong and that, so far, had proved impenetrable. Peter swallowed as the adrenaline kicked inside him. His stomach said it was time to start putting the wall in place.

Sometimes, even when you're a detective, you hope like hell that you're wrong.

Nic eased the Audi up to twenty miles an hour. It felt like the city was finally opening itself to them.

5.

Nottingham is a city built on caves. There are more than four hundred built into a soft, sandstone ridge, creating a subterranean labyrinth that runs beneath and beyond the modern city centre. The caves date back to the Dark Ages and were used officially for housing until 1845, when the St. Mary's Enclosure Act banned the rental of cellars and caves as homes for the poor. The practice, although illegal, continued for some time afterwards.

In the modern city that Nic and Peter were driving through the caves had become just an unusual and entertaining tourist attraction; what were once homes for the poverty-stricken were now accessible only to those who were willing to pay for a visit, who wanted to gain an insight into how it once was.

In 2010 Nottingham had been identified by a leading travel publisher as one of the top ten city destinations in the world. It was a result that surprised Peter as much, he suspected, as it had the vast majority of the three hundred thousand- plus population. It was true that Nottingham boasted some great attractions, yet by 2006 it had built for itself the reputation as the country's crime capital, with the highest number of murders per one hundred thousand people of any city in England and Wales. Gun crime had become a significant problem too, and the ensuing press served only to damage Nottingham's reputation even further. It was a reminder that, no matter what was written in a tourist guide, the city was built on sand and underpinned by caves.

Despite that, Peter thought the situation had improved considerably of late. At least the number of crimes committed every year was reducing and the number of crimes being solved was increasing. People are always going to go out and get pissed or stoned and, as far as Peter knew, every city on the planet caters for that. So he could hardly blame his hometown for filling its coffers in the same way, even if the availability of booze and other drugs did lead directly and indirectly to a wide range of criminal activity. For the most part, though, it was the kind of activity that did not make Peter's gut tense. Only the most extreme type did that. It was the type that made him wonder, late at night while Nic was asleep and he was alone staring at the night sky, if evil was a primal force that actually existed within some human beings.

Peter didn't believe in spirits, or possession, and he certainly didn't believe in a divine, loving and all-powerful force. However he had seen enough to consider the possibility that evil was born, or created, within some individuals. He did, in his darkest moments, find himself questioning whether or not evil was a tangible entity. It seemed the only possible answer to the question that some crimes forced him to ask:

How can someone do *that* to another human being?

It was one of the few beliefs that he had never shared with Marcus. Well, not knowingly anyway.

'Fancy going to see him?' Nic eased the Audi to a halt at the traffic lights facing the National Ice Centre and gestured towards the advert for Eddie Izzard's appearance in May of the following year. 'You can't beat a good Action Transvestite.'

'Of course you can't.' Peter looked up at the row of adverts plastered across the front of the Ice Centre. It was one of the city's more recent and successful new builds. Opened by Jayne Torvill, the ice skating Olympian and local girl made far-more than good, it was home to the Capital FM Arena which had established itself as a major concert venue, attracting the world's greatest bands, comedians and acts. The people who take the stage, Peter thought, are all superstars, known wherever they go. Somewhere inside that building, though, unknown to the crowds who flock there to see a legend, are people playing mole, working to create a hole or a burrow for their family.

'So shall I try and get tickets?'

'Absolutely. I'll look forward to it.'

'You don't sound convinced.'

'I'm just thinking of all the work I'll have to do between now and then.'

'Whatever it is, it will pass.' Nic patted Peter's thigh, squeezing the muscle, offering a promise of sensual diversions.

'Time passes,' Peter heard the dullness in his voice; wished that he could fake his tone as well as his smile. 'So we'll definitely get there. I think you should get the best seats possible.'

'Leave it to me.'

The traffic lights turned to green. The Audi set off again, turning right in front of the building. Peter looked at the Ice Centre as if he had never seen it before. Perhaps, he wondered, only the infrastructure changes with the passing of time? Perhaps the things we keep below the surface stay the same?

6.

Paul Clusker had to change. He had to change so that his business could change. Paul had realised this, he told his wife, at the end of the last financial year when the numbers showed their third consecutive downturn. Incredibly, during his first meeting with Marcus Kline, he came to the understanding that he had known it on some deep level for years.

Paul was a healer. He had started his clinic, "Health Matters", in 1985. What began as a one-man operation had grown into a thriving establishment that employed three full-time and two part-time therapists and a secretary. Throughout the 90s and into the early 2000s "Health Matters" had been the city's premier centre for remedial massage, osteopathy and acupuncture. There had been waiting lists and articles in local glossy magazines and a vibrancy in the building, an energy that seemed to grow out of the many interactions that took place on a daily basis. Paul had been filled with optimism and a certainty of purpose. His bank balance had been similarly buoyant.

And then something had happened. It had not been a

sudden collapse, more a gradual seeping away. A loss of everything that made it all so special.

'It starts and ends with you,' Marcus Kline had said ten minutes into their first meeting. 'The likelihood is that you have outgrown your original business.'

'What do you mean? I'm still there every day. I'm still in charge of everything.' Paul had been both confused and, if he was going to be honest, more than a little annoyed by the consultant's sudden and swift conclusion.

'I don't doubt that you are there every day. My point is this: although you employ others, this business is based around you. You conceived it, created and managed it. You are the designer, the architect, the manager and the figurehead. You are the brand because this business was built as a reflection of your own beliefs, values and aspirations. You cannot – or rather you should not be able to – separate "Health Matters" the business from Paul Clusker the human being. And from what I've seen of you already, and from what you've said, that's the problem you're facing.

'You have evolved since you first established the business and you have not changed your operation accordingly. It's almost thirty years since you began the business. In that time you have learned new things, had myriad new experiences, clarified your thinking. Only you have not applied any of that in a business development programme. You, my friend, have outgrown 'Health Matters". In a business in which the leader is the ultimate brand symbol, it is essential that the business processes, practices, systems and communications are all synergistic with the attitudes, purposes, behaviours and values of the leader.

'"Health Matters" should, at all times, be closer to you

than your own child, because, you see, "Health Matters" is *you*. At least it was when it began. Back then it was the business personification of Paul Clusker. Now, though, there are several degrees of separation. Before we can create a new, better communication strategy for you, we first need to re-connect the business to you.'

'How do we do that?'

'By teasing out into your conscious mind what your subconscious already knows. Namely, the beliefs and values that currently drive your thinking, and the ways you can best demonstrate these through every aspect of your business practices, even the symbols – including the language – that most accurately and emotively represent those beliefs and values.'

'I'm not at all sure that I know these things.'

'Who's telling me that?'

Paul had rocked back in his chair, struggling to make sense of the question. 'I...I don't know what you mean... I'm just being honest with you...'

Paul had been both surprised and delighted when Marcus Kline had agreed to work with him. He had heard that **Influence**, Kline's world famous communications consultancy, did occasionally work for local businesses, sometimes even at a reduced rate. He had even read an article in a national magazine in which Marcus Kline had said that his company was committed to helping the Nottinghamshire economy grow by accepting regionally based clients, but he had been somewhat sceptical about the claim, considering the possibility that it was no more than a clever piece of PR.

Despite Paul's qualms the increasingly desperate nature of his situation had forced him to risk making a fool of himself by phoning the offices of IMKA. To his astonishment, after a brief chat with the young woman on reception, he had been put through directly to the man himself. Despite a stuttering and stumbling explanation of his concerns and needs, Marcus Kline had agreed to work with him – and at a price that was far less than Paul had ever imagined.

'You sound surprised,' Marcus had said, a hint of amusement in his voice. 'Actually, to be completely accurate, you sound surprised and just a little embarrassed.'

'Well, to be honest with you…'

'-You might as well be.'

'Yes.' Paul had paused as the implication of Marcus's comment registered. What was the point, he wondered, of trying to hide something from a man who was world famous for his ability to read people, to identify what they were really thinking and feeling no matter what they said or how they behaved? It was a realisation that also highlighted the downside of spending time with such a person: there was nowhere to hide. Most relationships, even the most intimate and long lasting, offered opportunities for at least some secrets. If Marcus Kline was anywhere near as good as he was supposed to be, lying to him would be pointless. He would see straight through it. So the question was, did Paul want to engage with a genius who worked with some of the most important people around? The fact that he could afford to pay for it was more than he had expected; the fact that he would lose his privacy was something else altogether.

'So,' Marcus returned to his original question, 'What part of you is telling me what it doesn't know?'

'I, er, I guess it's my conscious mind.'

'Indeed. If you can't yet trust yourself, do trust me when I tell you that you know more that you realise. As I said, my job will simply be to help you bring into conscious awareness what your subconscious already knows, and then to help you shape it into a compelling communications strategy.'

'You make it sound so straightforward.'

'In one sense it is. Although you will still find yourself on a journey that will have more than a few loops and backtracks in it. For the change you need to make to be as positive and powerful as possible, you will need to tell me what is going to happen; not the other way round. The rebranding of your business has to come from inside you just as it did when you first started, not from my external perspective. Does that make sense?'

'I think so. I'm guessing that it will make more sense as I go through the process.'

'That is how most things tend to work.' Marcus opened his diary. 'Let's schedule our next three sessions together and then I will tell you what I need you to do for homework.'

It had been a task that was at once challenging and intriguing, inviting Paul to explore the deeper levels of his current attitudes and thinking. Simply, Marcus had asked him to write down why he worked as a healer and his beliefs about the nature and purpose of healing. Marcus had waited until Paul had jotted down the required activities, before asking, 'As a healer, do you make people *better* or do you simply aim to return them to the state they were in before the problem occurred?'

It was the second time in the meeting that a question had rocked Paul's senses. Only this time Paul heard his answer come firing back. He spoke without preparation or hesitation. His voice seemed to have the same strength and flow and awareness that his hands did on those magical occasions when he was truly connected to a client; those rare moments when it felt as if his fingers were actually listening to another person's body.

'I live to make people *better*! I live to help them realise that a problem state – any problem state – can be transformed positively and contains within it the seeds of learning and growth. Doctors with their inappropriate willingness to hand out antibiotics and all manner of other drugs simply want to end the problem. It seems to me that most of them don't have the time or inclination to do anything more. When they see a patient the first question they tend to ask themselves is, "What is the best drug I can give?"

'My starting point is completely different. When I see a patient I want to understand the totality of their life. I want to gain insights into the relationship they have with their body. I want to know about any pressures and stresses they are experiencing. I always tell my clients that the human body is like the planet: the way it is performing, the ways the different and yet interconnected systems and processes are operating, is ultimately a reflection of the way we are treating it. "Health Matters" exists to make people better, to improve them in significant ways, to move them on, not to simply take them back to how they were so that they can make all the same mistakes again.'

When he finished speaking, Paul realised that his heart was hammering in his chest and that his face was flushed. His back had straightened and he was acutely aware of the natural curve of his spine. His feet were pressing into the carpet on the office floor. He hadn't felt so alive in years.

'Happy writing,' Marcus had said, bringing the meeting to a close.

Now, as Paul Clusker walked through the city in the direction of his clinic, face down against the oncoming rain, he looked forward to his second meeting with Marcus Kline. It was due to take place from 3pm to 4pm that afternoon. He couldn't help but wonder what he might hear himself say this time.

It wasn't just because of the way he was looking down to escape the rain that Paul Clusker failed to notice the grey Audi A6 as it passed him. It wasn't because of his preoccupation with the forthcoming meeting that he ignored the man in the dark green raincoat looking up at the clouds as if welcoming the cleansing rain on his skin; the man who was actually keeping his eyes open letting the raindrops hit his pupils, blurring his vision before running down his cheeks like tears. The man who was actually *looking* at the rain.

Paul didn't notice that man at all. He was wrapped in his own thoughts, insulated against all that was happening around him by his own imaginings. Paul had not been conditioned to give others attention unless, or until, they appeared at his clinic. As committed as he was to his work, Paul had long ago learned the importance of knowing how to distance himself from the stresses of his work, of being able to take time out to ensure his own wellbeing.

There was such a thing, he told his clients, as appropriate selfishness. It was, he said, the ability to do those things necessary to look after yourself without causing harm to others in the process. Appropriate selfishness meant finding time, even if it was only brief periods, when you just did what was best for you. He suggested to everyone who would listen that it was more basic and more important than any form of clever, communications technology. For Paul, walking to and from work was a crucial part of his own time.

So, he walked past the man who was letting the rain spike into his eyeballs. He had no more sense of him than he did the buildings that towered above them both. Right now he was no more likely to consider the man in the green raincoat than he was to pause and look up at the higher floors and the rooftops of the buildings. Only a tourist would stop to study the architecture. Only a professional who had an unhealthy obsession with their work would fail to create personal time.

If asked, Paul would have said that creating this time was an essential way of maintaining one's own sanity. The challenge for anyone working in the service of others – particularly those who, like Marcus Kline, were the very best at what they did – was in ensuring that that whilst they were making things better for others, they were also making things better for themselves. Brilliance, Paul knew, came at a price. Clients usually had to pay large sums of money to be associated with such brilliance. Too often, though, those who were brilliant got their work-life balance wrong and the price they paid was even more significant.

If asked, the man in the green raincoat would have agreed. If asked, he would have said that there was always a price to pay. He would have said that nothing ever came for free, that payment and accomplishment was one of the most basic and powerful forms of association. It was not as primal, of course, as left brain and right brain connectivity, but it was pretty close to it. Only the laziest and weakest backed their hopes of a successful future on a weekly lottery ticket. The truth was the more you wanted to get back in life, the more you had to give out. The man closed his eyes and felt the rain sting his eyelids. And if you don't give it out, he thought, you have to make someone else do it for you. Sometimes that is the best and only option.

7.

'There's always another option,' Marcus Kline said as he walked across the Market Square in the very heart of Nottingham. 'The problem Simon, is that you haven't identified that option yet.'

Marcus heard Simon Westbury sigh. It was followed by a brief silence. Marcus found it easy to imagine Simon moving his face away from the phone, looking up to his right, shaking his head in bewilderment as he considered the best response.

Marcus waited.

After several seconds, Simon had gathered his thoughts. 'But the client is wrong! I don't see why I just can't tell them that. After all, they pay us for our expertise don't they? They come to us because we know more about this sort of stuff than they do. So why not, in this case, just tell it like it is. I know that what I'm recommending is right, because you've told me it is. I know, therefore, that his alternative idea is bollocks. Why waste time –both the client's and ours – pussyfooting around? My granddad used to say that if you don't call a spade a spade, you never know which tool to bring out of the shed. I really think it's time to bring out the spade.'

Marcus chuckled. He thought of Simon Westbury as his protégé. The twenty- three year old had been with him for a little more than a year. Simon had first approached Marcus when he was midway through a Masters degree in Strategic Marketing at Nottingham Trent University. Simon had emailed and then phoned asking for part-time, unpaid work experience. Marcus had agreed to meet the proactive young man and had been immediately impressed by his overwhelming passion for a career in communications and influence. During his work placement, Simon had shown such promise that Marcus had created a full-time post for him when he graduated.

The appointment had come as a shock to Emma, his totally reliable PA and receptionist, who until then had been Marcus' only employee. 'I thought you said this was always going to be a one man band,' she commented. 'I thought the point was that there could only ever be one Marcus Kline, that clients only came to us so that they could be helped by the great man himself.'

'That is, indeed, true.' Marcus had bowed his head in acknowledgement. So far he had managed to build himself a global reputation and a hugely successful business using only Emma to answer his calls, organise his diary, and act as a bridge between himself the and rest of the world; and two independent researchers he employed whenever he needed detailed background information relating to current or potential clients. 'Think of Simon's appointment as just another example of my extremely charitable nature,' he said. 'I'm not only helping a young man to fulfil his dreams, I'm also paying for him to do so.'

'Nonsense!' Emma snorted. 'I think of it as a man in

the early stages of thinking about his legacy. After all, the problem with a one man band is if the one man goes, the music ends.'

'I have no intention of going anywhere. And, as I've told you before, the best music is yet to come.'

'Aah, but who's going to be playing it? Will it be you or will it be Simon?'

'I will treat that question with the silence it deserves.'

'The peace and quiet will be most welcome.' Emma's nose crinkled as she smiled.

Marcus shared the humour and then left her to her paperwork. She was right, of course. His motives for employing Simon had been purely selfish. He didn't need a helping hand. **Influence** was *the* Marcus Kline consultancy. Given his unique skill set it would have been detrimental to have a team of consultants working on his behalf. In *his* name. Clients came to work with the very best, not a substitute. And the same clients were inevitably hugely grateful – and very willing to pay whatever was asked – when they got access to the very rare commodity that was Marcus Kline.

No, Marcus didn't need to expand his team. He had taken Simon on because he wanted to know just how good a communications consultant he could create out of someone who, despite his clear desire to learn, had not been born with the innate instincts he had. It was a challenge he relished. One he now couldn't imagine being without. One that might be showing the first traces of a future legacy.

Simon Westbury was very different to Marcus in just about every way that mattered. Simon's passion, like his heart, was worn on his sleeve. Whilst Marcus had grown up sensing the need to operate from behind a protective shell, Simon had no such reserve. Marcus had always found it easy to adopt the disassociated state working with clients required – particularly when working with individuals to help them overcome tragic personal experiences, fears, anxiety or any of the other potentially debilitating factors that limit human potential.

Marcus had known from the very beginning that the best way to help people was from a detached perspective rather than an emotional one. If love and compassion were the prime ingredients for creating personal change in others, then all people would have to do was turn to friends and family for help. And many did, at least in the first instance. The fact that it rarely worked should have come as no surprise. After all, as Marcus was fond of pointing out to a client, if you needed heart surgery who would you choose to perform the operation – a member of your family who loves you and is trained as a postman, or a qualified and successful specialist surgeon who cares more about his success rate and his reputation than he does anything else?

The truth that underpinned successful communication and influence was a simple and profound paradox: if you really wanted to understand and influence others, if you were genuinely committed to helping them make the changes they desired, you could only do so by disassociating yourself emotionally from them. Emotion blurred the senses. It fired neural networks that actually limited the ability to influence positively. If Simon was ever going to become a truly great communicator, he would first have to stop caring so much, so easily.

'I hear you,' Marcus said into the phone. He stopped

walking and positioned himself with his back to the nearest building. 'So let me share this particular spade with you: I agree, the client is wrong in wanting to change the strategy we have suggested. You, however, are equally wrong in thinking that your straightforward honesty will be of great benefit to them; so don't even think of pursuing that approach. You might be sure that it will work, but remember that I am right in these matters nine times out of ten. That's why the business is so successful. Whilst being obvious and straightforward is occasionally the best approach, I very much doubt that it is in this instance.

'As Lao Tzu said the best teacher is not even recognised as such by those they teach. The best teacher finds ways to allow students to discover the answer for themselves. In that way, the student takes ownership of their learning and gains confidence in their own abilities to solve problems. So, how can it make sense to call a spade a spade when the best teachers are not even called teachers?'

'But everyone calls you a genius. Does that mean that you're not really as good as they think you are?'

'Either that or I'm even better than they know.'

'And the prize for the World's Most Humble Man goes to…'

'I'll be in the office in fifteen minutes. And then the World's Most Humble Man will continue to explain to the World's Most Naïve and Excitable Man why he needs to become a master of his emotions if he wants to become great at influencing others.' Marcus shivered. He didn't mind being out in the rain, actually he enjoyed it, but the chill in the air was cutting through his raincoat. He glanced at his watch and began to walk again.

'I can't wait,' Simon said dryly.

'You are going to have to. And under no circumstances contact the client. Do you hear?'

'Loud and clear.'

Marcus rang off and immediately made the call that couldn't wait.

8.

There was only one particular type of waiting game that Peter Jones hated. It was waiting for the feeling inside him to stop. And that only ever happened when the crime revealed itself and he could begin to do something. Even if that something was not of immediate value. Even if meant that sometimes, for a while at least, he just had to go along for the ride.

His colleagues nicknamed him "Jonah". On the most obvious level it was a simple play on his surname of Jones. However, to those in his team, and to those who had heard the stories about his many successes, it was an oblique reference to his incredible patience and his willingness to do everything that was ethically possible in pursuit of the desired result.

The Old Testament character Jonah had willingly acknowledged his responsibility for a storm that threatened the boat he was travelling on. He urged the sailors to throw him overboard in order to save themselves. He had subsequently been swallowed by a whale and had lived, patiently, inside it for three days before being cast ashore to pursue his cause.

Peter's team knew that he was meticulous, dogged and selfless in his resolve to win. He had his own set of values and a sense of professional pride that combined to create a quiet, unflinching strength and a cast iron commitment. Even if – *especially when* – it seemed that a case was so complex it would swallow the investigating officer whole and reduce him to pulp, Peter not only came out in one piece, but with the desired result. Which was an arrest leading to a conviction.

Peter knew that the best detectives and the most professional criminals were game players. They knew the rules, the risks and all the tricks of their respective trades. He was well aware that patience was one of his strongest virtues. Sometimes his bosses and the media wanted to suggest that a particular game had a specific – and inevitably limited – time period, but Peter knew that the result was all that mattered. And some games just lasted a lot longer than others. There was a world of difference between knowing you were right and being able to prove it so convincingly to a dozen strangers that they could find no reasonable doubt in the story you told them.

Storytelling was not Peter's forte, but there were several excellent barristers who created and told those on his behalf. He was outstanding at finding all the relevant details and linking them together. Even if it did take longer than some journalists and office-bound bureaucrats liked.

Peter knew that the deeper meaning of his nickname was meant as a compliment from his colleagues. Most people, they said, simply did not have the level of patience that he did. They saw it as a rare strength. Peter, on the other hand, found that patience came easily as long as he was able occupy himself doing something useful. As long as there were lines of enquiry that could be checked, theories that could be proved or disproved – and, for Peter, disproving something was as exciting as actually discovering part of the truth – he was always motivated, calm and focussed.

Learning, he had been taught as a child, happened one step at a time. It was an incremental process that sometimes required you take one step forwards and two steps back. In his opinion too many people wanted quick and easy answers. They wanted real life to be like cheap and tacky newspaper headlines that made quick and easy associations, linking an effect to the most obvious or the most readily available possible cause. The truth was usually more complex. A crime was simply a highlight event in a system of activity. If his good friend Marcus Kline identified, influenced or created patterns of communication, he, Peter, identified and interpreted the patterns of behaviour that rippled out from a crime scene.

Peter believed that if he and his team had great systems of their own in place and if they followed those systems accurately, resorting occasionally to some additional creative endeavour if the game called for it, they would inevitably identify the system, the behaviour-chain, which would lead to the guilty party.

So Peter did not regard himself as simply a patient man. Rather, he was an accomplished game player with an innate curiosity and an unquenchable thirst for the next challenge. He always wanted to make progress as quickly as possible but, importantly, he knew how to direct and motivate both himself and his team especially when the pace of progress was frustratingly slow.

What Peter couldn't stand was the waiting game he was being forced to engage in now. It was the game in which there was nothing he could do but wait. There were no lines of enquiry, no avenues to explore. Not yet. Although his stomach forewarned him it gave him no information that he could act upon. Peter was not remotely fascinated by the intuitive sense that tugged at his gut. He didn't care what caused it or why it was always so accurate. He just hated the fact that there was absolutely nothing he could do but wait until it – whatever *it* was – became known.

Peter Jones was a detective. Pure and simple. He just needed a starting point. He just needed something to detect. And then, once that something had revealed itself, Jonah, the so-called Patient Man, could begin to ask questions and instigate systems that he did understand and that he could control.

Peter stood outside the building that housed his office for several minutes after Nic had driven away. He was so lost in his thoughts that he didn't notice the rain. He only realised that his phone was ringing because he felt it vibrating in his pocket.

9.

Marcus's offices were in the area of the city known as the Lace Market. During the days of the British Empire this part of the city had been the very heart of the world's lace industry. Now the quarter-square mile with its nineteenth century industrial architecture and quaint streets housed offices, bars, restaurants, museums and shops.

Marcus waited for a tram to pass and walked over Middle Hill onto Weekday Cross. Nottingham Contemporary, one of the city's newer art galleries, was hosting an exhibition titled, Kafou: Haiti, Art and Vodou. Marcus had visited the exhibition when it first opened in October. The mixture of paintings, sculptures and sequin flags provided a representation of Vodou in Haiti from the 1940s to the present day. It was, according to the marketing material, a reflection of Haiti's historical experience through the supernatural.

Vodou or, as it was more commonly spelt in the West, Voodoo, was a spiritual belief system that was followed by the vast majority of the Haitian population. Marcus had been aware of its origins and practises before he visited the exhibition. Religion in its different forms had long been a fascination of his.

Voodoo was rooted in West African religions and incorporated aspects of Catholicism, Islam, European folklore and even freemasonry. In Marcus' opinion Voodoo, like all religions, was man-made, born out of a mix of social and geographical influences to serve a powerful and primal purpose. He had always viewed religion as one the most significant – if not *the* most significant – provider of *meaning* ever created by human beings.

And Marcus knew that those people who created meanings that were shared and accepted by the masses shaped both the present and the future.

Shared meanings led to shared behaviours, agreed rules and a sense of belonging. Shared meanings created and underpinned society. They were an essential and very powerful form of influence. Whenever a politician convinced the electorate that he or she shared their common values and understandings, that politician always increased their power base. When the man on the street said, 'Do you know what I mean?' and his audience nodded in agreement, a community, no matter how small, was being either built or reinforced.

What most religious believers failed to realise, Marcus felt, was that meaning was both created and shared through human communication. There was no divine message. And, therefore, there could be no divine messengers. An Almighty God had not created the world; rather great communicators had built it over centuries of carefully planned, and often selfish, influence.

Every generation in every culture always had a need for special, talented influencers who could operate in ways that were not understood by the rest of their society. Prophet.

Magician. Shaman. Whatever the label, the meaning and the role were the same: to influence, shape and lead the masses. Voodoo was no longer a powerful force in most parts of the world because its leaders had not known how to adapt. Now it was confined mainly to art galleries and lecture halls. The most powerful modern-day shamans did not perform ancient rituals or sacrifices. They wore Canali, Armani, or Boss.

They were people like him.

Marcus glanced at the art gallery as he passed. He could see only three people studying the exhibits. Last week Simon Westbury had said, 'Words are the real Voodoo!' and everyone in the office had chuckled in appreciation. Once upon a time Marcus might have said the same thing. Now he knew that the real Voodoo, the real God or whatever else people wanted to call it, was the Subconscious. The ultimate universal power lay within those parts of the brain that were still beyond the understanding of even the greatest neuroscientists. Space travel, he thought, whilst providing interesting information, was going in entirely the wrong direction. The real journey of discovery was inward, into the human brain. It was a journey that would eventually reveal what human beings were truly capable of, how communication created the neural networks, the associations, which shaped experience and defined and developed our world.

Marcus smiled at the fact that an exhibition of Voodoo art was surrounded by the traditional Christmas symbols and greetings that had taken over the city. 'Tidings of zombies and joy," he thought to himself as he walked up High Pavement.

Influence: The Marcus Kline Consultancy was based on the south side of the street within a Grade II listed building that dated back to the late eighteenth century. High Pavement was one of Nottingham's earliest city streets. In the Georgian era High Pavement had been one of the most fashionable places to live in Nottingham. Now it was essentially a place of work or pleasure, with The Lace Market Hotel, modern and trendy, reflecting the upmarket nature of the area, and providing accommodation for business people and tourists alike.

Accommodation of a very different kind was also offered by the oldest building on High Pavement. It was the Church of St Mary the Virgin, with a mention in the Doomsday Book and a history tracing back to Saxon times.

Marcus loved the street. He loved the way it looked, the mix of buildings, the way it was fashionable and relevant just as it always had been. He loved its situation, close to the very centre of the city and yet removed, part of a discreet area with its own sense of identity and value.

For Marcus, High Pavement was an architectural reminder that, if you were skilled enough, you could always see the experiences and lessons of the past, etched in the lines of the present. The street was like a lined face, all its secrets hidden in plain view. Every time he walked to his office Marcus looked at it anew, as if for the first time. It was another part of his daily practice.

As Marcus neared the Galleries of Justice a group of students came out of the building, congregating on the pavement ahead of him. Their teacher followed them out. 'Leave space on the pavement, please,' he said as he saw Marcus approaching. The man's voice was soft and hesitant, his tone rising slightly at the end of the sentence.

Marcus automatically moved onto the road. The students, as he expected, stayed where they were.

The raised inflection meant that the teacher had made a request rather than given an instruction. His hesitancy had made it at best a very weak request. Given the excited chatter of the group nothing less than a clear order was ever going to move them. Marcus passed by on the cobbled road, nodding in acknowledgement at the teacher's raised open palm of apology.

Less than a minute later he was stepping into the reception of his offices. Emma greeted him with the same, genuine smile that she had for the last three years. Wonderfully, the greeting she gave to total strangers was only slightly less genuine. Marcus found himself, as he always did, returning her smile and feeling immediately very, very good at being back in his professional home. He had no intention of going into his office without talking to her first. Rituals were an important part of every person's and every organisation's life, and spending two or three minutes chatting to Emma when he first entered the office was one of Marcus's more obvious workplace rituals.

'How are you this fine winter's day, Em?'

'Slightly poorer since I came to work, thank you for asking.'

'You and everyone else I hope.'

'Indeed. Payments to the charity box all duly made.' Emma flipped open a notebook on her desk. 'That takes the total from the office and associated folk to £1,480 for this calendar year. Overall, with all the other contributions you've persuaded people to make, we've raised just over eighty thousand since January. At this rate the school will be built and up and running on schedule.'

'I never doubted it. And I bet we can get the office intake up to at least a nice, round one thousand five hundred in the next five minutes.'

'Oh dear.' Emma closed the notebook. She tried to resist asking the question and gave in almost immediately. Marcus's decision to establish a charity with the sole purpose of raising money to build one new school every year in the most deprived parts of the African continent had been made the previous Christmas. It had come as no surprise to Emma who found the charitable part of his nature a compelling counterpoint to what others often referred to as his arrogant genius. 'Go on then, what's the bet?'

'That I know exactly how Simon has spent the last five minutes or so.'

'And he hasn't already shared that information with you?'

'Nope.'

'And you didn't leave him a list of things for him to do this morning.'

'Nope.'

'So...?'

'So if I'm right you and Simon put in a tenner each and if I'm wrong I'll put in forty.'

Emma sighed, picked up her phone and keyed in a single digit. In an instant Simon appeared through the door that led into the main office. He reddened when he saw Marcus.

'Yes...Yes, boss?'

'Ah, so polite now that we are face-to-face.' Marcus flashed a grin and went on quickly. 'Simon, I'm sure you will be pleased to know that The World's Most Humble Man is taking yet another minute out of his frantic schedule to raise even more money for charity.'

'I paid my tenner even before the interview started!' Simon looked to Emma for support. 'Honest! That poor TV interviewer – what was his name, Charlie? – never stood a chance. He was always going to say whatever you wanted him to.'

'I wasn't talking about the interview. However, now that you've mentioned it, how precisely did I get him to say that I was the spokesman for the silent programmer?'

Simon shook his head. 'I don't know. Yet. I haven't had time to really study the recording. To be fair, though, I think it was one of your more one-sided bets. I know it's all for a good cause, but this time I think you should have offered odds.'

'Then you'll be delighted know that for the current little wager Em has just volunteered you for, I am offering odds of two to one.'

Emma frowned and shook her head in denial.

Marcus continued, 'The bet is that I mysteriously and miraculously know how you have been spending the last five minutes. Which, of course, would seem to be an impossibility given that you haven't shared that information with me.'

'You haven't, have you Si?' Emma asked.

'Of course not. Why would I help him win?'

'Fair point.' Emma nodded, her gaze fixed on Simon. 'Then why are you so nervous? Even I can see that you look like you're guilty of something.'

'The question,' Marcus said, 'is what exactly is young Simon feeling guilty about? And, I'm delighted to say, the answer to that question is the answer that wins me the bet.'

'What have you done?' Emma's gaze hardened on Simon.

The young man's face flushed. 'I…erm…I've just been

on the phone.'

'He called Dean Harrison,' Marcus said, 'one of our oldest and most beloved clients, to explain to him what a spade is.'

'I beg your pardon?' Emma's attention was suddenly all on her boss. 'Why would Simon want to talk to the owner of a law firm about garden tools?'

'A spade in a manner of speaking. Simon actually felt the need to have a full and frank conversation rather than let Dean work something out for himself.'

'How can you know that?' Simon blurted. 'Has Mr Harrison called you?'

'How could he? I'm guessing you'd only just finished talking to him when I got here.'

'Then you can't know, because...because...' Simon spluttered.

'Because what?' Emma demanded.

'Because he told me not to call him under any circum-stances.'

Emma switched back to Marcus. 'So how did you know he'd ignore you?'

Marcus shrugged. 'Do we agree that I have won the bet and that you both owe the charity box another donation?' The pair nodded. 'Excellent!' Marcus rubbed his hands. 'Let's be cheerful people! After all, the Christmas season is the season for giving. And that's precisely what I did with Simon when he phoned me about Dean's predicament. I gave him some very powerful instructions.'

'To not phone Mr Harrison,' Emma said.

'Quite the opposite. I actually told him to make the call. Under the guise of directing him to say nothing, I gave his subconscious very clear instructions to pick up the phone and have the conversation. I then very quickly called Dean myself, warned him that Simon would ring, explained that it was all part of our young man's education, and promised to pay for our New Year dinner at Harts, if he would just go along with it all. Fortunately, Dean and I go back a long way and he thought that giving up a few minutes of his time was more than a fair trade-off to help Simon learn – and, of course, for the price of a great meal.'

Simon groaned. Emma looked down at her desk, shaking her head. In many ways Marcus was a great boss. She wouldn't have stayed with him for so long if he hadn't been. Yet he was also the most challenging and contradictory human being. He was the most generous person she had ever met. He was generous with his time, his money and his skills. And he was a genius. And he knew it. And he made sure that everyone else did too.

It was incredibly demanding being around someone who could make you do things without you realising it and who, Emma felt, could see your deepest secrets.

In her mind, Marcus was special and that meant the normal rules of human engagement didn't apply. He could understand and influence people – anyone, she believed – in ways that were normally the reserve of individuals in the closest of relationships, and yet there was always a sense of distance about him, something that seemed untouchable and unfathomable. Something that, despite the fact she felt a most appropriate love for him, made her feel an emotion that played around the edges of nervousness whenever she felt he was focussed solely on her.

Marcus watched the play of emotions on the face of his two employees. He gave them just long enough to make sense of what he had said and then went on, 'No harm done with the Harrison account, Simon. Just a learning experience and we can never have too many of those. So let's go into my office and deconstruct our conversation. You need to understand the language patterns and covert commands that I used to get my wicked way with you.'

'Yes, boss.'

Marcus crossed the reception, clapping the young man on his shoulder as he passed. 'Give your money to Em and then we'll get started.'

Simon waited until the door had closed behind Marcus before taking out his wallet and handing over another ten-pound note.

'You know that he'll more than make it up in your Christmas bonus, don't you?' Emma said as she took the money.

'I almost wish that he wouldn't,' Simon replied. 'I wouldn't want to work anywhere else and I feel bad saying this, but sometimes you want the unbeatable to lose just once – or at least come close.'

Emma patted the back of Simon's hand. 'You can't expect him to be perfect.'

'I know. It would just be nice, though, if he didn't know how good he was.'

'Then he wouldn't be the boss.'

'Or he might just be a different type of boss. Instead of being…' Simon's voice trailed off for a second before he spoke again, punctuating each word with a movement of his hand as if placing them in the air. '…Simply Marcus, Unbeatable Genius.' He lowered his hand. 'Or smug, for short,' he said with a wink.

10.

Peter Jones took the phone out of his pocket. He recognised the number. His stomach tingled and twisted with a feeling that was one part anxiety and several parts excitement. One hundred per cent adrenaline, Peter reminded himself as he put the phone to his ear.

'Hi Mike.'

'Morning Jonah.' Mike Richards was the Senior Controller in the Force Control Room. He was an experienced, reliable guy, with a voice that held a constant pace and pitch no matter what information he was sharing.

'What have you got for me?' Peter felt the tingle move up the length of his spine as he asked the question.

'A very unusual dead body tied in a chair. I've informed SOCO. Two uniforms are there.'

'How did we find out?'

'An anonymous phone call. I'll forward the address.'

'Ok. Thanks.'

Peter Jones hung up and gave instructions for his team to be assembled there. Then he looked at the address Mike had sent. It was nearby. In fact, he and Nic had driven past it only a few moments ago. He dialled his office.

Peter returned the phone to his pocket. There was a very real chance that this was the *it* he had been waiting for. The fact that Mike had already alerted the Scenes of Crime Officer and that he had just described the body as unusual meant that the initial report back from the uniformed officers on the scene was clearly indicating foul play. Not that Peter would make any presumptions. He never allowed himself to do that at the scene of a crime or any other step along the way. He observed, asked questions – sometimes creative, challenging questions that no one else would have thought to ask – and let the answers and the evidence speak for him.

Peter knew how to control his adrenaline rush. He knew how to consider and explore all possibilities in an organised and sequential way. He knew that imagination had to be directed and managed, never allowed to run free, and only ever used to open up avenues of enquiry that could be justified by the information currently available.

Peter stood still for a few more seconds, looking up into the rain at the grey, dense cloud cover. He felt his shoulders relax.

Whenever he could Peter always took just a moment to prepare himself, controlling the desire to rush in at the start of what might turn into a major investigation.

'The controlled calm before the possible storm,' is how he had once explained it to Nic.

'And what if there isn't a storm?' Nic had asked.

'Then it's just good practice. And you can never have too much of that.' It was an answer that satisfied his partner and steered the conversation away from the fact that violent crimes were as much a part of the landscape as a change of weather. The important difference was that everyone noticed the weather and everyone was touched by it in equal measure. The worst of what Peter and his team dealt with was kept away from the general public as much as possible. It was better that way.

Peter Jones knew the importance of keeping the reality of his work out of the public eye. Much of what he said and did was based on a need-to-know basis. Sometimes he even applied that rule when talking to senior officers. He always applied it to the general public, the people who paid him to detect.

Peter wiped the rain from his face. To his left the steady stream of traffic continued its way into the city centre. He ignored it.

It ignored him.

Peter took one deliberate breath and set off towards the possible storm.

11.

The address was a late nineteenth century terraced house in one of the few city side roads that had not been converted into offices or shops. The street was a community in miniature. At its best, it was a city village. At its worst, just a collection of properties in which people did whatever was necessary to survive without any thought for those around them. In all likelihood, the truth of the street was somewhere in-between: a mixture of people with their own motives, experiences and expectations. Some of whom hoped to move on, some who lived only for today. And one who wasn't even going to do that.

The death had occurred inside number fifteen. Or, to be more accurate, all that Peter knew for certain right now was that the dead body was inside number fifteen; that didn't mean that the death had necessarily taken place there.

The ambulance parked outside and the uniformed police officer standing by the door marked out the house. As Peter approached he was aware of faces peering through windows that were already bright with Christmas decorations. He could see the ambulance crew waiting patiently for instruction inside their vehicle.

The officer straightened slightly as Peter neared.

'Sir.'

Peter nodded briefly. 'What we have we got?'

'Male. Presumed dead. In the dining room taped to a chair.'

Peter stepped inside, straight into the lounge. He saw it all in a second. He allowed himself a few seconds more for the interpretation, the *learning*, to sift into his consciousness.

A black, leather two-piece sofa and a matching armchair faced an enormous flat screen television standing between the fireplace and the front window. Between them these three pieces dominated the room. Several piles of dvds were stacked beneath the window sill. A calendar with pictures of naked women was hanging above the mantelpiece. Miss November had extremely large, false breasts and her legs spread. The look on her face was no doubt meant to show a mixture of willingness and gratitude for the interest being shown in her deliberately produced body. It was meant to say, 'This is for you, boys. And thank you for wanting to look at me, wanting to do things to me.' The look didn't reach her eyes though.

Peter flared his nostrils. The room smelt most obviously of alcohol and stale curry. Behind that it smelt of something else. It was something that Peter couldn't put a single word to. It was the smell that existed somewhere between machismo and despair. Peter put both of his hands into his jacket pocket and walked through into the dining room.

He was greeted by two sets of eyes. The ones he noticed first were grey, glazed and as dull, despite the secrets they held, as only the eyes of the dead can be. The others belonged to the second, younger police officer. They were filled with unspeakable fear. It was obvious why. The carpet immediately underneath and around the body was soaked in blood. There was blood too on the wall to the right of the body and on the ceiling. Peter's instinctive assessment was that at least one artery, but in all probability several, had been cut.

More horrific still, the victim had been scalped and the top part of his skull, the cranium, had been removed and placed on the carpet. The young officer was struggling to keep his eyes off the dead man's exposed brain. He looked at the Detective Chief Inspector with welcome relief. He was clearly struggling to keep the contents of his stomach down.

Presumed dead? Peter felt his face become the professional mask behind which he performed best. *God bless police protocol.*

'You haven't touched anything, have you?'

'No sir.'

'And you haven't been any closer to the body?'

'No sir.'

'Good lad.'

Peter was sure that the older officer on the door had managed the young constable's behaviour. The only way you could develop junior talent was by giving responsibility. The risk, though, in doing that was that an officer made a mistake and a crime scene was ruined. It was another of one of those unspoken truths: police officers, just like any other professionals, could only improve by being given opportunities to practice and develop their skills. Unfortunately, their most productive training ground was a crime scene. Junior officers had to be trusted. And they had to be left alone. If you wanted to progress you had to learn how to deal with increasingly unpleasant situations. In Peter's experience, you learned best by watching how far more experienced colleagues behaved and by then being trusted to do it yourself.

He stepped past the uniformed officer, making sure that he stayed at least two metres away from the body; making sure that he avoided contaminating the information in front of him.

He was looking at the dead body of a male, probably in his mid-thirties. He looked to be just less than six feet tall and he was not carrying any excess body weight. He was wearing black jeans, a white tee shirt and a black leather waistcoat. On his left forearm there was a simple, dark blue tattoo of a crucifix. It was simple cheap rather than simple refined. His wrists, ankles and chest were strapped with brown heavy-duty tape to a tall-backed wooden chair. His crotch bulged against the cheap fabric of his jeans. His mouth hung open and his tongue showed, resting against his lower lip. His eyes looked nowhere and said nothing.

One thing Peter Jones did know for sure, though, was that this man hadn't strapped himself into the chair. Someone else had done that. And they had killed him here.

Peter felt another surge of adrenaline squirt inside him. His professional face didn't even twitch. Instead he reached into his pocket, took out his phone and called the control room. Within a couple of minutes he had notified the on-call Detective Superintendent and asked for a Home Office pathologist to attend the scene.

Waiting was easy now.

Game on.

12.

Marcus Kline wanted to make learning happen as quickly as possible. He believed that those who *knew* and taught were obliged to speed up the learning process for others. He felt that they should be impatient for change and intolerant of delay. He believed that teachers – helpers, healers, and counsellors, whatever label people wanted to use – should be committed to creating the speediest progress possible. After all, the rate of change always increased. Human understanding was growing faster than ever before. Even though it was true to say that most of that development was in the realm of technology, there was still an underbelly of increase in the study of the so-called *soft arts*: the nature and power of influence, the dynamics of human interaction, the power of the *word* and, beyond that, the role of the subconscious.

Marcus Kline wanted to make sure that all of his employees developed their communication skills. He particularly wanted to speed up Simon's progress. He believed that the young man had the potential to become outstanding in the field and he felt both an obligation and a desire to help him. The greatest challenge was in teaching him how to disassociate.

'We learn best from experience,' he said to Simon. 'If we get a chance to think, feel and do, we are far more likely to develop quickly and appropriately than if we only hear, read or talk about a topic. That's why I like to create opportunities for you to experience things first hand.'

'Even if that means that I make an arse of myself?' Simon scowled. 'Any credibility I had with Dean Harrison has been taken away. Surely you could have provided the lesson without embarrassing me?'

'Embarrassment isn't real. It's just an illusion created by the ego. If you truly want to be brilliant at understanding and influencing others, you've got to learn that. In our work there is no place for embarrassment, fear of failure or concern for how others regard us. When you put your *work head* on, your ego should fade and, by extension, so should any possibility of feeling embarrassed. We can't really focus on someone else if even a small part of us is still thinking about ourselves. I've told you this before, Simon, if you want to associate with another fully you have to first disassociate from yourself.'

'That's easier said than done.'

'Of course it is. That's why there are so few people who can do it. That's why we can charge so much.' Marcus grinned. 'That's why clients like Dean Harrison are willing to be supportive.'

'I still feel like I was being played rather than being taught.'

'Get over it. You need to learn how to step away from your own unnecessary emotional responses as much as you do those of your clients. If you keep wearing your heart on your sleeve, it will come off in the wash. And, anyway, you haven't been taught yet. You've had the experience. If you're going to learn something from it, you need to spend time reviewing what happened and then you need to ask the right questions.'

'OK.' Simon sank back in his chair and closed his eyes. He remembered something that Marcus had said on his return to the office. It seemed like a good starting place for his enquiry. 'I want to ask you about covert commands,' he said. 'You mentioned that you used these to make me call Dean even though it seemed that you were telling me not to. So, what I want to know is, what covert commands did you use and in what order?'

Marcus tipped his head in acknowledgement of a good question, well formed. He reminded Simon of a well-known TV chef who always made a similar gesture when tasting food that impressed him.

'As you know,' Marcus began, 'a covert command is an instruction that is not stated explicitly. It is embedded into a sentence and delivered through a subtle shift in pitch and tone of voice. If covert commands are delivered well the recipient gets the message without ever consciously realising that they have.'

'Hence your Lao Tzu reference when we were talking? When you said that the best teachers are not even recognised, you were telling me precisely what you were doing – that you were influencing me without me knowing.'

'Absolutely. Now, let me reveal precisely how I did it. And whether you can remember these lines or not, what I am going to share with you now is precisely what I said during our phone conversation. I'll just put them altogether now, without your responses included. Ok?'

Simon nodded.

'Good. I said, quote: "You, however, are equally wrong in thinking that your straightforward honesty will be of great benefit to them, so don't even think of pursuing that approach. You might be sure that it will work, but remember that I am right in these matters nine times out of ten...Whilst being obvious and straightforward is occasionally the best approach, I very much doubt that it is in this instance...Under no circumstances contact the client. Do you hear?"

'Is that it?'

'Yes. Did you hear the covert commands this time?

'Some of them I think.' Simon frowned. 'I definitely heard the way you emphasised certain phrases.'

'Exactly!' Marcus clapped his hands. 'When I said, "Your straightforward honesty will be of great benefit to them" I stressed *will be*. When I said, "Don't even think of pursuing that approach" I emphasised *think of pursuing*. In other words, I directed your attention towards that behaviour whilst seeming to request the opposite. Then I told you that you could *be sure it will work*. And when I said that being obvious and straightforward is only occasionally the best approach, I went on to stress *it is in this instance*. I followed that with the instruction to *contact the client*. Even my final comment, "Do you hear" was a command rather than a question; I lowered my inflection as I said it, which your subconscious would have recognised immediately as a direction. As you know, when we ask questions our inflection naturally goes up. When a Sergeant Major barks out an order, however, his tone goes down. We are conditioned to distinguish automatically between questions and commands – and you did. So, when I said "Do you hear" I was, in effect, telling your subconscious to recognise my commands.

Simon nodded thoughtfully. 'Anything else?'

'There were a few bits and pieces. I gave you scope to doubt me which, given that you were already convinced you were right, made it all the more easy for you to do your own thing.'

'To do my own thing, that was really not my own thing.'

'It was your idea in the first place. You went first on this occasion and I just piggy-backed the ride.'

Simon lapsed into silence again. A moment later he said, 'When you told me that you were right nine times out of ten and that you very much doubted that I was right, you were encouraging me to take action?'

'Absolutely. And last, but by no means least, the phrase "no circumstances contact the client" was another instruction to the deep well of your subconscious. The word 'no' is a homonym. It is a word that can be spelt in different ways and have different meanings but that always sounds the same. I spoke the phrase as an instruction, so your subconscious had to make an instantaneous decision about which type of the word 'no', it was hearing. Given my inflection, it had to conclude that it was 'know', relating to knowledge, as opposed to 'no' meaning 'you can't' or 'don't'.

'So you were really telling me to know the circumstances in which I should phone Dean? And you had already helped me establish those circumstances...'

'Indeed. Make sense.'

Simon chuckled. 'I've got the point. Your inflection lowered just then, so you weren't asking me if it all made sense, you were telling me to make sense of it all. That was another covert command.'

'And this time you heard it. I think you can call that progress.'

Simon's smile broadened. 'I still don't fully understand how your mind is able to compute all of this whilst still holding a conversation.'

'It's called practice. Practice and...' Marcus glanced down at his desk. He paused briefly, just long enough to grow Simon's curiosity. The young man leaned forwards and Marcus continued, his voice just a fraction quieter than before, his gaze low, '...And a willingness to take responsibility for achieving the best possible outcomes. As I've said to you before, we have to be more alert, our senses have to be brighter, than those around us. Remember, being a so-called communication expert – a master of influence – is not a job that someone does, or a role they occasionally play; it is who they are as a human being. It's a twenty- four-seven commitment.'

'No time off for good behaviour?'

Now that would be criminal,' Marcus said, lightening the mood. 'And we don't want to be criminals now, do we? We're the good guys, remember?'

13.

Three Scenes of Crime officers arrived just a few minutes after Peter. All three were covered head-to-toe in white suits, with gloves on their hands, what looked like plastic bags on their feet, and masks on their faces. Peter watched as one took photos whilst another filmed the entire scene. It was vital that everything, including the carpet, was recorded, bagged and removed if necessary, and made available in pristine condition for future examination. A mistake at this stage of the process, whether it was the result of inattention leading to the missing of a detail, negligence that caused the contamination of evidence, or inappropriate haste that meant a procedure wasn't followed properly, could prove to be crucial at a later date.

Peter was standing next to the senior of the three officers. His name was Barry Long. They had worked together on numerous occasions. Barry was capable and efficient and, like most team leaders, he preferred to be in charge. Peter understood that tendency and respected Barry's skill. Ultimately, though, he was the operations manager on this case. Whilst his Detective Superintendent had overall control, he, Peter, was the man on the ground that had to lead and manage the practical process.

'Watertight as a duck's arse, Jonah,' Barry murmured. 'That's how this is going to be.'

Peter very deliberately raised an eyebrow. 'Is a duck's arse actually watertight? Doesn't water just go up it, swirl around like a natural bidet and then run back out again?'

'Might do. To be fair I'm not an expert on arses. I am good at making sure nothing escapes us though.'

Peter grinned. 'That's all we need Barry.'

The officer with the camera was squatting down next to the corpse taking photos of the detached cranium and the bloody scalp. For a second everyone's attention focused on the body parts.

'Makes you wonder what the hell was going on here,' Barry said. 'It can't have been meant as torture. You don't scalp somebody in an attempt to make them talk.'

'Maybe the perpetrator was looking to see if he was hiding something in his head.' The photographer suggested, grim-voiced.

'Or perhaps,' the other Scenes of Crime officer proposed, 'we're after a trainee hairdresser who just had a very bad home visit.'

'Or maybe it's just someone who likes boiled eggs in the morning,' the first officer countered, mimicking slicing the top off a boiled egg with the edge of his right hand.

Peter smiled along with the others. There were two essential questions he needed to answer. One, who had done this? Secondly, why? A good detective knew how to manage questions. Question asking and evidence gathering were the cornerstones of great detecting. The skill in the former lay in knowing how best to construct questions and when precisely to ask them. Timing was everything. And this wasn't the right time to ask any questions. The focus now was on evidence gathering. So Peter said nothing.

Barry turned to Peter. His eyes were emotionless above his mask. 'Well, Detective Chief Inspector,' he said, 'it looks as if you've got a headline act.'

'Could be.' Peter offered the obligatory smile and moved on to the equally necessary one-upmanship. 'I think, though, we have a case of skulduggery.'

Barry chuckled despite himself and Peter joined in. Both men knew that behind the humour, behind the need to downplay the situation, something very bad had happened here. Right now, they just didn't know why.

14.

A radio interviewer had once asked Marcus Kline if he knew of anyone else as skilled as himself. When Marcus had admitted that he didn't, the interviewer had asked if he ever felt lonely.

'Why should I?' Marcus had questioned.

'Because you don't have anyone you can share with on an equal level; because you are different from the rest of us – and those people who know you, know that you are.'

'First of all, if you dedicate your life to being the very best at something you are actually aiming to be different. You can't be the best and have people you can share with on an equal level. In one sense what you call loneliness is one of the key measures of absolute success.

'Secondly, I have a very good friend who has a job that seems at first glance to be very different from mine and yet in many ways is very similar. He is a detective. He says, "There is no such thing as normality." I agree with him. There are no two people who are exactly the same. We are all different. It just makes life and relationships easier to manage if we think that our obvious similarities bind us more closely together than they really do.

'You see, there is a gap that exists between all people –
even the closest of lovers, the best of friends, or the most
committed of family members. It is a gap created by the
fact we all perceive the world differently and because we
all communicate to ourselves and to others differently. I
suspect that some part of every human being is either lost
or misinterpreted in that gap. In one sense, then, we are
all alone. It's an integral part of the human condition. The
difference is that some of us are alone because of our level
of expertise.'

The interviewer fell silent for a second, looking down
at the floor, his shoulders slumping. Marcus pointed very
deliberately at the microphone. The interviewer suddenly
remembered his listeners and forced himself to straighten
and speak. He said what was clearly on his mind, 'That
sounds a dispiriting assessment of the human condition.'

'That's an interesting interpretation and response,'
Marcus said quickly. 'We need to remember whenever we
are communicating that words are only sounds – sounds
that we have agreed as a society to give a basic level of
shared meaning to. Given that, we have the personal power
to choose how to respond to those sounds. If we deny this
power, we are saying that other people determine and
control our emotional states and associated behaviours.
That cannot be a positive way to live, can it? Surely the
most important skill we can ever learn is how to control
our responses to external stimuli?

'On one level, then,' Marcus continued, 'you are making
a decision, albeit perhaps a subconscious one, to feel
dispirited by what I said. And the fact that you chose to
describe the way you are feeling as "dispiriting" is really
interesting. Why, for example, didn't you say that you felt

"saddened' or "upset" or even "angered"? Why, I wonder, did you instinctively say that you were "dispirited"? Tell me, what does the word "spirit" mean to you in this context...?'

Marcus was sitting alone in his office. Simon had left just a couple of minutes ago. When Simon had first written to Marcus asking for work he had described himself as "naturally high-spirited". Marcus had asked him what he meant by that and Simon had replied, 'It means that nothing can ever get me down and keep me there. I've created my own approach to life. And if the Hindus are right and we are reborn, it's the approach I'll use for a hundred lifetimes! It's really that cool. I call it the Limbo Philosophy.'

'The what?'

'The Limbo Philosophy. Under pressure I'll bend as much as I need to and no matter how low I go, I'm going to come straight back up again!'

It had been the answer that had convinced Marcus to invest in the young man. Flexibility, adaptability, continual movement towards a specific outcome, these were all qualities he valued highly. Given that, perhaps Limbo was the perfect metaphor for great communication? Perhaps he should insist that they have a limbo competition at the Christmas party?

Marcus realised that he was tapping the desktop with his fingertips. He was meeting his best friend Peter Jones for dinner tonight. As professionals they had come to realise that their respective roles had much in common. They both sought to identify and make sense of patterns. They both had to *detect*. They differed only in how they responded to the patterns they identified and in the desired outcomes they sought. The greatest similarity they shared, though, was that they both knew the absolute importance of disassociating from the people they set out to understand. They both knew that when you put your *work head* on, you had to leave your emotional self behind.

Peter had told him once, 'If you are a criminal Detective Chief Inspector Jones wants to get so close to you that he can see into your mind and heart – whilst at the same time being so far removed that you can't touch him in any way. The man who is just Peter, who doesn't have to confront the detritus of the city, he just wants to be left alone to enjoy a decent glass of wine.'

Marcus admired the way Peter could turn into the Detective Chief Inspector in the blink of an eye. Or maybe it was the other way round? Maybe the Detective Chief Inspector turned into Peter? Either way, in Marcus's eyes, he was a consummate professional. And the very best possible friend. In the final analysis though, he still didn't read patterns and understand people as well as Marcus did.

But, then again, who could?

15.

The source of the Detective Chief Inspector's professional self-confidence was two-fold. Firstly, every challenging situation he entered into had been started by the criminal activity of someone else. He didn't go looking for trouble. Society only needed detectives because some people were willing to abuse, damage or destroy others for personal pleasure or gain. Bad stuff didn't just happen; people created it. Take them out of the equation and there was nothing left to detect. Peter had always believed in the adage that *right makes might* and he was always, *always*, in the right.

Secondly, and perhaps even more importantly, Peter's ethical might was supplemented by the support of the biggest and best team in the country. Some criminal gangs were undoubtedly powerful and some were part of a network that extended across countries, but the police *gang* and its associated network was more significant still. It was made up of far more than the myriad professionals who were trained and paid to solve crime and maintain order; it also incorporated a range of other experts and an equally complex network of informants. In Peter's experience right was most likely to have might when those in the right outnumbered and were better trained and better prepared than those they were up against.

Some of the criminals Peter knew were amongst the cleverest people he had ever met. They could have been hugely successful business leaders – in fact, some of them were. They knew how to strategise and influence. They knew how to motivate, delegate and enforce. They were resilient under pressure and were ruthless in pursuit of their goals. Sooner or later, though, someone who worked for them would break ranks, or some new evidence would be found, and Peter and his team would have their breakthrough. It wasn't inevitable, but it was the most likely outcome as long as everyone did his or her job right.

The perfect crime was dependent on a complete lack of evidence. And that was a very hard thing to accomplish, for even the most clever and ruthless of individuals. Sometimes just one verifiable fact created an opening, a crack in a wall of silence and, as Peter's *gang* applied their pressure, the crack widened, more evidence appeared and the previously hidden pattern of events was exposed.

The officer who was technically in charge of this new investigation was Detective Superintendent Michael Briggs. Peter knew him well. Briggs had proven himself to be a competent detective and an astute politician, with a clear intention to reach the highest levels of power. Peter had no such aspirations and was well aware that Briggs regarded him as a useful asset who offered no competition or threat. Peter was as skilled at managing his boss as he was at managing his team. He regarded those as the basic skills that allowed him to detect. And, just like the criminals he hunted, he was never involved in only one target at a time. That was one of the reasons why he needed a team that he could trust.

As a young constable Peter realised he wanted to have responsibility for identifying and arresting the most serious and dangerous criminals. He shared his dream with his far more experienced Sergeant. The advice he had received had been succinct and of enormous value. The older man had paused for several seconds, staring into his beer as if somehow it contained every hard earned lesson from the previous twenty years, and then said, 'Be your own man and pick the best to have around you.'

Peter Jones had already learnt to be his own man. He hadn't known that much then about policing, but he knew the importance of being true to himself. He had realised as a teenager that everyone was different and that life's greatest challenge lay in finding the courage to be expressly and uniquely yourself in the face of the social need for conformity. The best detectives, and the most creative of human beings, knew how to distance themselves emotionally from the twin dragons of expectation and consequence, the two seemingly irresistible pillars of social pressure.

Expectation, Peter had come to appreciate, blinkered perception; it not only tempted you to go looking for what you believed to be true, it also brought in its wake the likelihood of regret or despair whenever the expectation was not met. Thoughts of consequence, on the other hand, often introduced fear into the equation. Fear of failure or retribution. And for some people, Peter realised, fear of success, which was the only fear he had never been able to really understand.

Peter's philosophy that there was no such thing as normality had been forged long before he had joined the police force. It had begun taking shape as a teenager when he had been forced to learn that you cannot take responsibility for the expectations of others. As years passed he had also come to realise that consequence is never anything more than one link in an on-going pattern of events. Consequence was a footprint pressed more deeply than most others, a mark in time, nothing more.

Several hours ago someone, as yet unknown, had created their mark in time. For whatever reason, they had presumably taped a man to a chair, scalped him and then cut off the top of his cranium. Now Peter was en route to the Queens Medical Centre where the post mortem would be carried out. The hospital was the largest teaching hospital in Europe, with six thousand staff. Soon a handful of those staff would study, dissect and record the body with the sole purpose of determining how precisely the man had died.

The factors that had led to this death were still a mystery. The consequences that the death would create were yet to unfold. Peter was prepared to bet, though, that he could accurately predict one of them. He would track down the person responsible. You can't leave a clear footprint without providing clues about where you came from and where you are going. And Peter had spent years following the advice of his old Sergeant. He had picked the best people he knew to work with him. He led a team of keen, willing and capable detectives, supported by experts, including forensic scientists, scenes of crime and family liaison officers. And an office team led by an experienced manager who knew how to receive and record information and provide advice to Peter and his fellow detectives.

He also had one very special, and secret, source of support.

Marcus Kline.

He was quite literally the very best at what he did. He was also always willing to help. So, whenever a crime scene presented an unusual challenge Peter shared the details with his friend. He asked Marcus to read the scenario as he would read a human being, to look below the surface and find the hidden pattern. It was one of Peter's great professional secrets: he could call on the insights of a genius.

He was planning to do that again if the mad rush of the first few days of investigation did not unearth the culprit. He would, he reasoned, be mad not to.

16.

Paul Clusker had found tapping into his subconscious both challenging and, if he was to be completely honest, *frightening*.

At the end of the day and with his wife gone to bed, he settled down in his favourite armchair with a pen and paper in his hands, ready to uncover and record the hidden knowledge. His heart began to pound. His mind sprang into action, turning into an unbidden and unwanted instructor, bombarding him with orders and criticisms. He heard his harsh internal voice – a mixture of his own and his dead father's – barking out directions whilst also reminding him of past failures. The voice was made up of disappointment and frustration, background notes that combined to create an overriding sense of anger. Paul sat in the armchair, drawn into his internal world, dominated by the voice that always made him feel like a child.

Paul sat there, staring, with nothing inside his head but the language of missed opportunity and obligation. The voice was scathing, talking always of what he *should* do, *should* have been, *ought* to prioritise, *ought* to have done, *must* become, *must* overcome, *must* honour... must...

ought…should…if only, if only, if *only!*

And as the voice returned time after time to the same, *same* messages and conclusions, his pen began to circle on the page; increasing speed, pressing harder, filling in the space inside the circumference, black ink blocking out the whiteness of the paper with staccato, angry movements that finally proved too much and tore a hole.

'What do you do to make the voice stop?'

'I'm sorry?' Paul realised with a start that, as he had explained the experience to Marcus Kline, he had begun reliving it.

'I asked you what your strategy is for shutting the voice up.' Marcus Kline didn't blink. His breathing was barely perceptible.

Paul could feel his heart thumping inside his chest. 'I don't have one.'

'The evidence clearly shows that you do.' Marcus shifted in his chair, pushing down with both hands against the brown, leather arms, his body straightening then leaning forwards slightly. 'After all you don't hear the voice all the time, do you?'

'Well, no. But that doesn't mean that I have a strategy for stopping it.'

'It doesn't mean that you have a conscious strategy. However, you clearly know when enough is enough. You couldn't fall asleep if you didn't, let alone focus on your clients well enough to heal them.' A brief pause; just long enough for the message to be recognised. And then, 'Perhaps you silence it when your heartbeat reaches a certain level?'

'I, erm…Do you think so?'

Marcus smiled gently. 'It's what I see.'

'You really see what happens on the *inside?*'

The response was a brief, curt nod. The smile disappearing like a playing card beneath a magician's open palm. 'And I am always working very intently on being able to do it even better.'

'Yes, but....that level of insight...' Paul splayed his hands as he searched for the words. 'I...I can't imagine what the world must look like to you.'

Distanced. That was the answer that no client ever wanted to hear. *Far enough away for me to have the perfect perspective.*

'Given that I don't need healing, you don't need to worry about it,' Marcus replied. 'What you do need to focus on, however, is the fact that you create every voice in your head and you abdicate all of your personal power if you think otherwise. '

'But my father was always so critical, so sure that I would never amount to anything.'

'And he's dead. For a long time now, you told me. And given that he isn't an invisible spirit living on your shoulder, whispering in your ear, we are left with the only conclusion available to us: that your thoughts are your own creation.'

Paul slumped back in his chair, looked down at his feet. It felt suddenly as if there were no words inside him, nothing that he could find to say.

'Listen, there are three aspects of time,' Marcus' voice was lower now, softer, drawing Paul's attention. 'They are the past, the present and the future. Everyone knows this. The bit that most people get wrong – and it is the crucial bit – is that they believe they can influence the present and the future but not the past. This is a serious error, one that explains why people keep repeating the mistakes of their past. After all, if you believe that you can't change the past you are condemned to relive it and its effects endlessly.

'But…but the past has happened, how can you change something that has already taken place?'

'It's true that the events have happened, which is why they can now only exist as memories. And memories are created by, and contained within, the human mind. It's impossible for a memory to be an accurate record of what actually took place, because it's impossible for a person to ever identify and focus on everything that happens at any one time. We are selective in the way we give our attention and so, by extension, we are selective in the content and meaning we give to our memories. When we create and then revisit a memory we delete, embellish, or distort the details of it, just as we do every experience that happens in the present.

'Given that,' Marcus continued, 'we can actively choose to delete, embellish or distort to suit our needs and purpose. Memories are like interactive paintings and we are the artists. Often our memory-paintings incorporate sounds, especially voices, and with a little practice we can learn how to change their volume, their tone, even the words they say. Ultimately, if we choose to, we can silence a voice completely. Even if it was the voice that once belonged to a dead parent.'

Something in the certainty of Marcus's voice and the very words he used made Paul feel as if his head was spinning. He realised that he was trying to recall his father's voice, to hear it as he had only a few minutes earlier, and he could not. He felt as if a part of him was scurrying around the edges of his mind, searching for the place where that particular voice was stored, seeking to unhook it from its hiding place, to expose it.

For some reason the memory of a childhood holiday in Spain flittered through his awareness. Paul had been a young boy under a bright blue sky in a tall, gothic city. He was standing at the entrance to a cathedral, staring into its beautifully sculptured emptiness. He had felt that the great power of the place lay not in its architecture, its religious symbols or its art, but in the ability of the space to hold the history and beliefs of generations. He had heard himself whisper the word, 'Echo' with reverence and awe in acknowledgement of something so profound that he could not put any other words to it.

He realised suddenly that neither he nor Marcus had spoken for – how long? It felt, quite literally, like ages.

Paul looked Marcus in the eyes and that was the cue for the consultant to start talking again.

'Too often, for those people who are not skilled at managing the past, memories are pulled from their resting place by stimuli they encounter in the present."

'Can you help me – teach me – how to manage those memories, the voices?'

'I'm already teaching you, aren't I?'

Paul felt the internal space again. 'Yes. I just don't know how you are doing it.'

'You are paying me to help you change, not for you to understand the process.'

Paul saw the same smile, the one that suggested some deep remembering and knowing, come again. It reinforced the immeasurable difference between him and the man opposite.

Marcus shifted in his seat. "However, as I have already

said the only aspect of time that we cannot take by the scruff of the neck and lead wherever we choose is the future. The challenge is that we have to create the future amidst a mass of opposing and apathetic forces. Only the rarest of all individuals can control the future.'

That idea added further to Paul's sense of shock. 'Control the future! Who are the people that can do that?'

Marcus Kline looked up at the ceiling. 'I would call them modern day Shamans,' he said.

17.

Anne-Marie Wells was unsure whether she wanted to rush time along and jump quickly into her future, or freeze time and stay exactly where she was. To fast-forward would be to know the answer to the question that was tugging at her mind and stomach in equal measure. To freeze-frame would mean never needing to know, to be able to relax with things as they were because they could never change.

Anne-Marie looked out of her kitchen window at the large weeping willow that spread out over the furthest corner of the garden, leaning inwards slightly towards the house, reaching down to brush the grass as if gently caressing the earth with its tears.

The tree was at least seven metres tall. Samuel, who had tended the garden for far longer than Anne-Marie had lived in the house, told her that it was eighteen years old and had been planted by the previous owners. Anne-Marie was drawn to it more than any of the garden's other inhabitants. Even as a young girl she had dreamed of one day owning a house with a weeping willow in the garden. She didn't know why. She thought occasionally, that it might be related to some childhood experiences or stories that, although long-forgotten, had influenced her in some deep and lasting way. Or perhaps it was because she found something almost spiritual in the fact that, no matter how tall it grew, the weeping willow always reached back down to the earth, to its roots. Ultimately, though, Anne-Marie was happy to simply accept the attraction without needing to be able to explain or justify it. She believed, as much as she believed anything, that learning and connection and growth existed most obviously and immediately in the silence of experience and not in the description or labeling of that experience through language.

Anne-Marie was a professional photographer. Or as one journalist had described her recently, a philosopher with a camera, a seeker behind the lens. Despite the lack of clarity about her love of weeping willows and, indeed, many other things in her life, Anne-Marie was absolutely clear about the moment when she discovered her life path.

It had been November 1995. She had just turned twenty-one, had completed a teaching degree and was filled with the shocking emptiness that came from realizing that she didn't want to be a teacher. It wasn't just that she had spent three years learning how to do something only to discover that she could never possibly apply that learning. It was more to do with the realization that she didn't just want a *career*. She wanted an absolute and unbreakable synergy between who she was and what she did.

Anne-Marie didn't want to teach in the way that her lecturers and her fellow students understood the role. She wanted to structure and present experiences and through them provide opportunities for others to interpret, emote and decide. Real teaching, she believed, came about through creating opportunities and not simply providing answers. Unfortunately, such certainty had only served to prevent her from joining a profession; it had not helped her to identify what she should do.

And then she had seen, quite by accident, the November issue of The New Yorker magazine filled with the photo essay titled 'In Memory of the late Mr. and Mrs. Comfort', shot by the great photographer – in the eyes of some, the greatest ever photographer – Richard Avedon. The beautiful, violent, humorous fable was open to interpretation on every level. It spoke to her in a way that words never could. It made the base of her spine tingle. It made her appreciate that the emptiness inside her was just an open road waiting to be travelled. In that one morning, through those pages, Anne-Marie not only saw how she would live her life, she also felt that for the very first time she had come face-to-face with her true purpose.

From that day on she had immersed herself in the world of photography. Over the years she had come to develop her craft, build her reputation, and appreciate that no matter how skilled she became or how honest her intention, she never managed to share an experience in all its absolute completeness with her audience. Something changed the instant the camera recorded the reality before it. Some things were lost and, equally, some things were enhanced. Now she understood precisely what Richard Avedon, her inspiration, had meant when he said, 'The moment an emotion or fact is transformed into a photograph it is no longer a fact but an opinion. There is no such thing as inaccuracy in a photograph. All photographs are accurate. None of them is the truth.'

The search to capture that truth had become one that captivated her. She had begun her work delighted by the fact that people could draw their own interpretations from her images. Over time she had increasingly become obsessed with the idea of taking one photograph that captured a shared truth, a photograph that created a common, deep-rooted response in all who saw it.

According to her husband, Marcus Kline, it was an unachievable goal. He said that every interaction was so multi-layered and every individual perspective so state dependent that it was impossible to create anything, let alone a photograph, that could produce the same reaction and provide the same insights in everyone who experienced it.

And so Anne-Marie had found herself searching to achieve something that according to arguably the greatest photographer of all time and the world's leading communications guru was impossible. To make matters worse, the communications guru was the man she had been living with for nine years. She, more than anyone else, knew how incredibly skilled he was and how rarely he was wrong. She also knew that, for all his personal desire for success, he was equally committed to supporting her. Only in this case he had been unable to. 'It isn't as if we are talking about taking the perfect photo', he had said. 'The pursuit of perfection is a noble cause even though, by definition, it is unattainable. No, here we are talking about trying to transform one thing into another – in this case a tangible experience into a photograph – without anything being changed through the transformation. To produce a photograph that only influences in one universal way.'

Marcus had shaken his head in bewilderment and then stroked her hair as he offered his final assessment. 'Not even I would go in search of something that is so far over the horizon. And you know that when it comes to setting new standards I'll go further than anyone else.'

That should have been enough to rein in Anne-Marie's desire. After all, you would have to be stark raving mad to ignore Richard Avedon's comments about the nature and, by implication, the limits of photography, and Marcus Kline's analysis of communication. Only for some reason, as inexplicable as her attraction to the willow tree, their words had only strengthened her resolve.

Anne-Marie believed that, for all their differences, people were, at heart, far more intimately connected than was commonly acknowledged. She thought it was far more than a shared social, or group, consciousness; more significant than the power of crowds. There just had to be *something*. Anne-Marie didn't know what precisely.

One less label.

One less barrier to have to see through.

One very rare opportunity to prove the genius she loved wrong.

Anne-Marie felt the faintest of smiles cross her face as she looked out at the willow tree shivering in the breeze. Samuel, the gardener, had told her that the willow was one of the nine so-called sacred trees mentioned in Wicca, the pagan religion of witchcraft. He explained that the willow had several magical uses and played a role in guiding the dead to The Summerland, the Wiccan term for the afterlife.

Anne-Marie had been both surprised and fascinated by the old man's knowledge. 'How do you know these things?' She had asked immediately. 'Are you a follower of...' she hesitated, searching for a word that sounded right, '...of Wicca?'

Samuel had grimaced. 'No, Miss Wells. I'm not one for following man-made traditions about such stuff. I've worked the soil all my life. Nature doesn't have any rituals the way people seem to need them. Seems to me she's too busy getting on with the process of living to have time for anything else.'

Getting on with the process of living…

Anne-Marie turned away from the window and looked at the clock on the wall. It was 12.10. She would have to leave very soon. The appointment was at 12.45. Her right hand was unconsciously hovering over her lower stomach. Her photos – the ones that had made her rich and famous – captured images of things that happened beyond and around her. Today she would get the results of some very different images; images that showed what was within. Her right hand began to tremble and she moved it away from her stomach, picking up the white coffee mug from the table and placing it by the sink. Just shifting things around. Everyday stuff. The process of living.

Now Anne-Marie longed for the emptiness in her stomach that had once signaled that a creative and exciting journey lay ahead. Now her stomach was knotted and tight; gripping hard, pulling in around itself like a castle surrounded by enemies, refusing to allow easy access, seemingly impenetrable in its grim determination. Only her fear was that her stomach was too late, that the enemy had already taken hold within.

She would know soon enough. The pictures had been taken. Perhaps these images would speak the truth.

Anne-Marie left the kitchen and went to the bathroom one last time. Then she put on her Kenneth Cole quilted coat, protection against the increasing winter chill, and keyed in the burglar alarm. She picked up an umbrella from the stand by the front door and walked out of the house, locking the door behind her. She put her keys into the simple, red Radley shoulder bag that contained nothing else apart from her iPhone, turned her back on the willow tree and walked out of the garden.

She left her camera at home.

18.

They will have found the body by now. The wheels will be in motion. The great process of detecting. The systems, the teams, the procedures. The well-oiled machine, greased and spurred by my first public connection.

I wanted it to start on a day like today. The rain is symbolic. It represents a system of transformation. Just as my action does.

There will be fall out.

Only rain cannot choose to create itself. It forms because of the conditions. It falls because the height of the clouds and the prevailing temperature determines that it should be rain and not snow or hail. Rain is the product of a system. It is one part of an ongoing, cyclic recurrence. Air rising, changing, returning. From the earth to the heavens, bringing back hope. Salvation, even.

Here, when it rains all people can do as they rush from place to place is keep their heads down against it. Unwilling to look up in case reality pierces their eyes.

So blind. So lost in their lonely, disconnected worlds.

Imprisoned.

Within themselves.

On the other side of the planet people who understand drought know better. They look up to the skies desperate for the first sign of clouds. They know what it means to live in a barren wilderness. They know how it feels to be truly parched. Yet still they understand their connection to it all. They welcome the rain for what it is.

The Great Nourisher.

When I look at the rain I see more than anyone else ever could. I see every colour of the rainbow. I see connections.

We are all born connected. More so than we ever imagine – and far more than most people ever think.

There was a time when we all knew this. It was the time before we created the language of separation.

Have you ever considered that fact, that ours is the language of separation? Do you realise the tragedy of this? Do you acknowledge the part you play in it?

Language, like the rain, was meant to connect us. Only as you built your vocabulary, much as you built your societies, increasingly more complex and insular and distinct, you lost the ability to look and listen.

Now, in our so-called Communication Age, you stare into a screen with intensity, you learn the intricacies of the latest technology so that you can send meaningless platitudes to people you call your friends and yet have never even met. This is where you choose to focus, living in a world that has no substance, giving those real people – including those you say you love – nothing more than a casual glance.

How many can truly stand within a crowd and see who is around them? How many even try?

The fact that I can – the fact that I do – means that I influence with ease. I choose how to make people behave, to make the associations I want them to, when I want them to.

I can see inside you.

I will re-establish our primal connection.

I will influence you in ways you cannot even imagine.

I promise.

PART TWO

Looking

19.

Marcus Kline knew how to look.

He knew how to *really* look. He had trained himself –
continued to train himself – how to see with clarity, how
to achieve *insight*.

From his perspective the vast majority of the population
lived their lives either blind or blinkered. No matter how
significant the scene in front of them, the best that most
people could achieve was a casual glance. That, Marcus
believed, was one of the primary reasons why society was
littered with miscommunication and misunderstanding. It
was why so many people couldn't even recognise how their
own partners were feeling most of the time, why teachers
and healers caused such unintended harm, why strangers
populated the world.

As a young man Marcus Kline realised he had an innate
talent to, quite literally, capture images in the blink of
an eye. He had discovered that if his mind was empty of
thoughts and if he then looked at a subject swiftly, briefly,
then blinked before instantly turning his gaze elsewhere,
the image stayed in his mind as clear and detailed as a
photograph. The mental image was as permanent as that

captured in an album or saved on a phone. Not only that, whenever Marcus revisited the image he could see more than just the shapes, the faces, the colours or the detail.

He could see below the surface.

He could see the thoughts in a person's mind, the emotion they were trying to hide, the motive they kept secret, the fear they denied. And it had led him to the realisation that the word *insight* offered a literal representation of the ability to really see. For whenever Marcus really looked he saw what was *inside* his subject. He actually got under their skin. It was a skill that enabled him to select and direct his communication in ways that no one else could.

Although he had been born with a natural insight Marcus had, over the years, developed a very deliberate training regime to develop it further. He had done so because of a very simple revelation. It was simple and yet of enormous significance. It was simple and yet beyond the scope of everyone else he had ever met.

It was simply this: people speak, think, and converse in response to a stimulus. That stimulus is usually something they see or hear. It followed therefore, that before a person could have any chance of saying the right thing, of using the right words in any given situation, they needed to be able to see and hear with absolute clarity and precision. Marcus determined that in order to become the world's greatest communicator, he would first need to develop his senses to an even higher level than they naturally were. Only then would he address the use of language in all its many forms.

He had begun by placing an everyday object – the first had been a silver pencil sharpener – on a desk in front of him and simply *looking* at it. His practise had been to empty his mind and sit, in silence, looking at the sharpener for five minutes at a time, three times every day. His starting point had been to forget everything that he knew about the object. He had found this surprisingly easy. His aim was to see it as if for the first time, every time.

Over years of practise he had been amazed by the ever-increasing change and depth of his perception. He had become used to the way that, as soon as his silent observations ended, his brain would offer unbidden evaluation and judgements about the simple object, after which it would invariably tell him that there really was now nothing more to see. Marcus ignored it. He ignored it the way a bodybuilder ignores the screams of pain in broken-down muscles and forces out one more seemingly impossible repetition. He ignored it because it was an illusion. And, eventually, through the force of his will, Marcus made the greatest discovery. He discovered that there was always more to see.

Insight could not be fathomed.

There was always another layer, a deeper level. And the deeper Marcus travelled into his subject the more he found the silence and stillness from which his journey had begun. And the more he felt detached from the object of his study. Even when they were people.

There were still people he loved, obviously. Although he occasionally wondered if his notion and sense of love was at all the same as that of others.

Now, as had happened several times in the past, his best friend had asked him to observe a film. He wanted Marcus to see those things that were below the surface. He wanted him to provide an insight.

There was only one answer that Marcus could give. It was the answer he always gave when those few people with whom he shared his life asked for his help.

'Of course I will.'

20.

Three nights and four very busy days had passed since Peter Jones had been called to the murder of the man who had been scalped and had the top half of his head cut off.

In that time much had happened and very little was proving of immediate use in identifying the person responsible. Peter had been pulled off his other cases by D. S. Michael Briggs, and told to focus solely on the crime that was already being referred to by officers as the work of the 'Boiled Egg Killer'. When his most experienced Detective Sergeant had insisted that this was a case that just had to be cracked, Peter had raised an eyebrow and saved a smile for the security of his office.

Those people who argued that some subjects were too serious, too sensitive or too important to be the source of humour had never spent their working day in a room transformed and dominated by death and bloody violence. And that, of course, was how it should be. He and his colleagues were paid to do that (and keep the much-needed dark humour amongst their own), so everyone else could be spared that aspect of human nature, so they could become righteously enraged whenever a social sensitivity was even slightly offended.

Peter's own team of two Detective Sergeants and eight Detective Constables had been strengthened by additional officers and they had all been working flat-out since the murder had been confirmed. It was an expected and a necessary part of the job.

For the first three or four days after a crime all the possible evidence is still likely to be available, all the information still fresh in the minds of witnesses. With the passing of time, daily routines and new events filter the consciousness of all the non-professionals involved. The certainty with which witnesses share their accounts immediately after the crime is inexorably replaced with creeping and relentless doubt. The phrase that became increasingly common as the days passed, that Peter and his colleagues really didn't want to hear at the beginning of a statement, was 'I think'. If at a later stage that witness appeared in court, the phrase 'I think' was an open invitation for defence counsel to create and cast doubt over everything that followed.

So the team had been focussed on door-to-door enquiries, learning everything they could about the victim, his lifestyle, family and friends, building up a picture of what he had been doing in the twenty four hours leading up to his death, keen to find anyone who might have had a motive to kill him. They had also contacted the Research Department at the Police Staff College to see if someone else had been killed in the same, or even a very similar way, anywhere in the world. An unsolved crime with the same modus operandi in Poland, for example, would immediately have had Peter and the team searching for any Polish connection to the victim. So far, though, there had been nothing forthcoming. This was, it appeared, a unique crime.

'Although I'm not going to tell you what it makes it so different,' Peter said to Marcus as he prepared to play the film of the crime scene. 'You know how this works.'

'Yes. The only way you feel that you can trust my insight is if you've given me nothing to go on in the first place.' Marcus smiled and glanced across at Nic who was sitting silently in an armchair, a glass of Rioja held absent-mindedly in one hand. 'Your policeman-partner is always so cautious when he shows me one of his grisly films.'

'It's not caution,' Peter replied quickly. 'It's necessity. Just because you are the best doesn't mean you'll be right every time. Besides, if I tell you things it's likely to create a bias, to lead you into interpreting things in a certain way.'

'It's Nic who can't resist you,' Marcus's smile widened. 'I'm used to letting what you say fall on deaf ears. Anyway, let's get on with it. Let's see what your murder victim has got to tell me.'

The film began with a view of the street. It showed the parallel lines of terraced houses before an obvious and professionally clumsy edit switched the focus to the door of number fifteen. A few seconds later and the view shifted again as the cameraman entered the lounge and filmed a steady panorama, a circle-sweep of the room, high to low and back again.

Marcus watched in silence, blinking once as every new scene presented itself. Occasionally his nostrils flared. His head cocked to one side briefly as he looked at the black, leather settee. When the scene shifted to the dining room and the dead body, seated and tied, Marcus straightened slightly. It looked to Nic, who was watching him rather than the film, that a ripple of energy, a discernible current, travelled up the consultant's spine and was breathed out towards the screen.

The camera showed the body from every angle, from distance and from close up. It showed the room in its entirety. It was graphic, sterile reportage; a life reduced to a poorly made silent film, devoid of emotion or explanation. Nic found it impossible to watch. Marcus stared, his pupils dilated, still as a big cat implacable in its strength.

The final scene showed the post mortem and Marcus visibly lost interest. Peter, though, pointedly let the film run to its conclusion. Only then did he switch it off and turn very deliberately to face his friend.

'Well?'

'Better than the man in the chair.'

Peter smirked. When first confronted with a violent scene of crime Marcus had immediately adopted the policeman's dark humour; Peter couldn't help but wonder how deliberately he had done so.

'What did you see?' Peter asked.

'Time running out. Only I don't know what that means yet. There was something about the rooms that spoke of some sort of countdown, a deadline fast approaching. The only food in that house, for several days at least, will have been cheap takeaways. The DVDs hadn't been touched for a similar period of time. That suggests that the victim had something else on his mind. And it would have to be something really significant, because your man would have watched them daily under normal circumstances. I doubt he has any family living nearby, but those people who saw him on a regular basis – I'm guessing you would find most of them in the local pub – will have noticed the increasing sense of nervousness about him recently. He hasn't got a girlfriend, and won't have had for years, but there will be a woman, or more probably a teenage girl, still at school I suspect, who he will have been pestering. Find her and you might get some more insights.'

'What about the state of the body?'

'Aaah, now that's where we learn something about your killer rather than your victim.'

'Which is?'

Marcus sipped at his wine. The urgency in Peter's voice made the Spanish red taste even better.

'Stop playing games!' Peter leaned forward, his hands clasped as if in prayer.

'It looks as if the victim was tied up so that he could be tortured, which would then suggest that he had some information the killer wanted. That part at least is true. The torture and interrogation element is not. Whatever it was that caused the victim to be so stressed for the last few days of his life, whatever he was expecting to happen, it wasn't this. And it certainly wasn't this killer. In all probability the victim didn't know the man who killed him – and I'm certain it was a man. However the killer definitely chose him, which doesn't mean, of course, that there was any preceding social connection between the two of them. I'd guess that the killer picked him for some other reason, because he fitted some sort of predefined criteria. I just don't know what that is yet.'

'What else do you know?'

'Why he killed him. In one important sense at least, I know the killer's motive.'

'Which was?'

'He was searching for something.'

'You mean drugs or money?

'No, nothing like that at all.' Marcus drank again. 'Something…something very different.' He frowned. 'I know where he was looking, I just don't know why.'

'Where was he looking?'

'Inside.' Marcus's smile lacked humour. 'That's why he removed the top of the head. For whatever reason, your killer was looking inside the victim's brain.'

21.

Anne-Marie Wells had always believed that there were two types of expert. The first type was the researcher and consultant. The person who studied a topic, making it their life's mission to get to know more, to be the first to learn something new, to be able to talk and write about their subject with the authority and, often, in the language, that marked them out as being different from the crowd. Whenever they applied their knowledge they did so in a remote, self-contained fashion. Their role, essentially, was to be *the* expert.

And then there was the second type, the person who knew all about something because they actually experienced it. They might never think, or talk, of themselves as an expert – usually because they were too busy living the *thing*, whatever the thing was – but they had a practical understanding, a sense of connection, an emotional bond, that was the very opposite of that sought by the researcher.

Academics and surgeons were the most obvious examples of the first type of expert, whilst great artists, performers and sportsmen and women were examples of the second. As a photographer Anne-Marie had always felt that she existed somewhere between the two, combining elements of both. She believed she was all the more rounded as a human being because of this. As a photographer she had a technical expertise and a professional eye capable of seeing a story in a single frame, of knowing how to use or manage light and create perspective. Yet she also sought to connect with her subject, to understand their world, to see the situation through their eyes, to feel and reflect their emotional state.

In recent months Anne-Marie had become an amateur-expert in another, very specific subject. Secretly using the Internet to find out everything she could about the topic that had increasingly filled her mind. She had learnt facts and figures, statistics and possibilities, signs and symptoms. She had forced herself to read every article and every forum. She had experienced for the first time in her life how words on a screen could invade your mind and body, creating feelings of dread and nausea, daring you to come back tomorrow and read some more.

Anne-Marie had forced herself to read more. She had read the same pages dozens of times searching for a new interpretation, looking for even the tiniest glimmer of hope. Some nights – some wonderful nights – she had gone to bed believing that she had found it, only to re-read the pages the next day and see nothing but a cold, clinical reality.

And she had told no one of either her study or, more importantly, her reasons for it. Why she had decided to keep it a secret from Marcus she wasn't at all sure. She did know, however, that it felt completely the right thing to do. Even in the dark, loneliness of night when he slept beside her, when she had found herself gripping the duvet in the way, she imagined, that a person terrified of falling gripped the cliff edge, even then she maintained her silence. And she would maintain it, she knew, for some time yet.

The expert Anne-Marie had met had belonged to the first type. He was detached, detailed and technically thorough. She had been obliged to ask him on three separate occasions to explain himself more simply. She had ordered him to look her in the eyes when he spoke. Ultimately he had told her nothing about the illness that she had not already learnt. The difference, though, was that he had real expertise and, even more powerfully from Anne-Marie's perspective, he had the pictures to prove that what he was saying was, indeed, true.

Anne-Marie had ovarian cancer. And it was at an advanced stage.

Ovarian cancer is the fifth most common cancer in women and yet GPs on average tend to see only one case every five years. The reason for this is essentially two-fold. Firstly, many of the symptoms reflect other less threatening conditions and are therefore largely ignored. Secondly, cervical screening tests do not help detect the illness. If diagnosed at an early stage the chances of a positive outcome are good. However, as the consultant noted, too often the diagnosis was not reached until the cancer was in stage three or four, by which time it had spread into other parts of the abdomen. The problem, he explained, was that the symptoms were just so vague that neither the sufferer nor her GP recognised the risk soon enough. That, Anne-Marie had read, was why ovarian cancer was once referred to as the *silent killer*.

'I am afraid that is the situation you now find yourself in,' the consultant said finally. 'You need to prepare yourself for surgery. I will only be absolutely certain how far the cancer has spread, once I have...once surgery is underway. You do need to understand, though, that I will most probably need to remove both of your ovaries, your fallopian tubes, your uterus and the omentum, a fatty layer of tissue within the abdomen. I might also need to remove the lymph nodes from your pelvis and abdomen.'

Anne-Marie found herself nodding silently. There were no words in her mind, no thoughts, no questions. Not then. And since the meeting her mind still felt as if it was for the most part frozen.

Three times since she had left the consultant's office, Anne-Marie had screamed an undecipherable bellow that had been followed immediately by uncontrollable tears.

Overall, however, she felt nothing other than the cold, deep, silent knowledge that her body had built a cancer.

The only decision she had been able to make was that she had to get away for just a few days. She needed to be on her own. She had managed her self-imposed isolation up to this point and she needed to do so for just a short while longer.

She left Marcus a note saying that an unexpected job had come up and that she was leaving immediately for a remote part of Kenya; it was unlikely, she wrote, that she would be able to contact him for several days at least. There was, she assured him, no need to worry.

In truth, she had booked a cottage in Devon on the edge of Dartmoor and had somehow managed to drive there safely. She had taken her camera and all other relevant equipment with her. Whatever happened in the coming days, weeks or months, whether she lived or died, Anne-Marie was going to record it all. She was going to make her own homage to the photographic essay that had started it all: Richard Avedon's 'In Memory of the late Mr. and Mrs. Comfort'.

Although right now, for her, comfort was in very short supply.

22.

Peter Jones shook his head in bewilderment. 'The problem I've got is that there was no damage to the brain. As far as we can tell, after the cranium was removed there was no further contact between the killer and the victim. There are no indications that the killer was trying to get inside the actual brain.'

'That's what makes this so interesting, isn't it?' Marcus brightened for the first time since the film had been played. 'I know I'm right and yet none of it makes any sense. If the killer's motive really was to look for something in the brain we would expect to see clear evidence of brain damage. Only, as the desperately dull post mortem confirmed, there isn't any.'

'So maybe you're wrong.'

'You know I'm not.'

'I trust that you're not. I'm a policeman remember? I only know what the evidence proves.'

'And I only ever know what I see or what I hear. And I know what I saw – the killer was looking for something.'

'How can you be so sure?'

'Because my intuition tells me I'm right. And it's always accurate.'

'That's no use to me in a court of law.'

'You're a million miles away yet from getting a conviction on this one.'

'And reminding me of that is meant to help how exactly?'

'It's meant to stop you getting ahead of yourself. Remember the research that shows highly experienced professionals develop a powerful sense of intuition they can, and should, trust – particularly in challenging situations? Well, I am the most highly experienced professional in my field and you can – and should – trust my intuition. When I watched the film my subconscious saw something, possibly a number of cues that were far too subtle for my conscious mind to register, and it is sharing that information with me in the form of kinaesthetic feedback that, over the years, I have come to recognise and act upon.'

Peter sighed. 'How long, then, before you can make some sort of conscious sense of what you have seen?'

'That's impossible and, therefore, totally inappropriate for me to answer. You can't force that sort of thing out of your subconscious. It's not like an orange or a lemon that you just squeeze the juice out of.'

'What about hypnosis?' It was Nic who asked.

'Good question.' Marcus raised his glass in salute. 'A really good hypnotist can absolutely help a client to access and use subconscious resources to create change or resolve a problem. They can also empower them to remember things they cannot consciously recall.'

'So why not hypnotise yourself, or get someone else to do it to you, so that you can consciously identify those hidden cues?' Peter took up the questioning again.

'Because I don't believe there is enough there at this stage to make it worthwhile. I'm picking up the tiniest scraps of information, so even if we release them from my subconscious they won't give us anything concrete to work on; there simply isn't enough right now.'

'Then we're back to square one: how can you be so sure you are right?'

'Because I'm me.'

Peter Jones took a long, slow drink of his wine. When he stopped Nic poured more into his glass.

'Right now this is a private conversation between two friends who just happen to extremely good at what they do. Right?' Marcus's voice slowed, his tone becoming softer and yet even more compelling. 'My task is to identify associations that everyone else will miss and that will lead you to your killer in the fastest possible time. And that's what I can do. I recognise and, when necessary, make associations. It's what I'm best at. What you don't want me to do, and what I can't afford to do, is make assumptions. Let's be clear about this. The skill in using one's intuition to its full lies in being able to recognise in an instant the very specific feeling that tells you you've seen something accurately. You have to be able to acknowledge the feeling and then hang on to it in a glimmer of a second. There is literally no time for hesitation. This is the crucial thing. If you are just a millisecond too slow your conscious mind will automatically second-guess the message your subconscious is sending and – bingo! – you will create your own assumption rather than acknowledge a genuine association.

'Assumptions are dangerous,' Marcus went on, 'not only because there is a very real possibility they are inaccurate and we then base our communication and behaviour on them, but also because they act as blinkers. Once we assume something to be the case, we go looking for the feedback that supports the assumption; we rarely actively seek to challenge it. So over time the assumption becomes stronger and is accepted as part of our reality.

'Real associations differ because they are based on fact, even if these are facts that we only recognise and act upon subconsciously. The bottom line is, that the quality of our life experience – and that absolutely includes our problem-solving capabilities, Detective Chief Inspector – is determined by our ability to identify and manage associations.'

'Yeah, of course it is.' Peter turned towards his partner. 'I assumed that's what he would say.'

Nic laughed and ran his hand through his hair before addressing Marcus. 'I always said that you should be the lecturer and not me.'

'I don't think so,' Marcus chuckled. 'I only want to work with worthwhile clients, really committed, skilled and enthusiastic learners and, naturally, sarcastic and ungrateful policemen. The associations between me and the general student population would, I'm sure, become negative very quickly.'

'Fair point.' Nic had long regarded Marcus as more of a pre-eminent professor who had no interest in teaching the masses than a lecturer like himself, committed to education for all. 'It's a shame, though.'

'The real shame,' Marcus countered, taking the conversation back to its original topic, 'Is that I don't have any more to offer yet about the identity of the killer.'

'Maybe there won't be any more,' Nic suggested. 'Maybe the killing is a one-off.'

Peter felt his heartbeat quicken. That was his secret hope at every murder scene. *Maybe this is a one-off.* And often it was. And in those cases the culprit was usually found quickly and close to home. Peter's dread – every senior detective's greatest fear – was that a single murder proved to be the first act of a serial killer.

When the murder was a one-off and the killer was never caught, at least no more lives were lost. When dealing with a serial killer though, the consequences were infinitely more severe, the game was for the very highest stakes. Another death and the responsibility would, in part at least, be on Peter's head for not making an arrest quickly enough. And if the killing spree continued...

Peter shivered slightly and hoped that Marcus Kline hadn't noticed. The awful truth – the terrible hope that every detective clung to when a second killing occurred and a series was identified – was that the second crime scene offered some new and compelling evidence; that a second death made the process of detection easier. *If only,* Peter thought, *society knew how we are obliged to think. What would they make of us?*

'This isn't a one-off.' Marcus's voice cut through Peter's contemplation even though it was directed at his boyfriend. 'I'm afraid this isn't going to end quickly or, I suspect, easily.' Marcus turned very deliberately to face the detective.

'How can you be so sure?' Peter felt the question pulled out of him by the intensity on the other man's face.

'Because, as I said earlier, this guy is looking for something and he isn't going to stop until either you catch him or he finds what he's looking for. And he didn't find it with his first victim.' Marcus's eyes softened. 'So I am afraid my friend – and I hate to say this – your film marks the first act in what I am sure is going to turn into a nightmare.'

23.

Anne-Marie was desperate to sleep. She didn't actually feel tired despite the long journey from Nottingham to Devon; she just *wanted* to fall asleep. In truth, she hadn't felt remotely tired since the consultant shared his bleak news with her.

And, she reminded herself again as she tossed and turned in the bed and stared up at the pitch black ceiling, she hated how words lied in the way that photos never did! Sure, sometimes you staged a photo, but you only ever did that to bring out a greater truth, to make the point more obvious, more attractive, more challenging, more… appropriate.

Words, though, words could be used like wallpaper, they could cover and disguise a multitude of sins. Words could distract and dissuade and deny. They were too often self-serving little bastards that created in their user a feeling of superiority and in the listener a sense of doubt or despair or, perhaps even worse, inappropriate certainty!

Try as she might Anne-Marie couldn't remember the consultant's face. She could remember how he refused to look at her when he spoke the most damning words, how he kept hold of his pen throughout, occasionally dotting the sheet of paper on his desk as if punctuating his delivery with unwelcome full-stops. She could remember how incredibly polished his black brogues were and the very precise crease in his pinstripe suit trousers. She could even remember the sound of the wall clock ticking, how obvious it was in every awkward silence. She just couldn't remember his face. And that, like so many things at the moment, was really, *really* annoying. It was just one more thing that should have been under her control and wasn't.

And he wasn't a *consultant*! That was just another of those word-lies that she hated so much. He didn't *consult*. He didn't engage in a genuine two-way process. He didn't ask any genuine questions. In fact, as far as she could remember, he didn't even listen. He was just a faceless expert who understood biological processes, medical procedures, statistics and likelihoods, who spewed out facts and hopelessness in equal, uncaring measure. And if she could just remember his damned face Anne-Marie was sure that she would, finally, be able to sleep.

In an ideal world everything, she had come to realise in the short time she had been alone in her country cottage, had its own time and place. And when everything stayed within its own time and place the world ran smoothly. Nightmares belonged in your sleep. Sleep was not only their proper home it also provided the escape route. People always and inevitably woke up from nightmares that assailed them in their sleep. It was the nightmare that had broken out of its designated time and place to wreak havoc through the waking hours that could really destroy you. Waking nightmares knew how to keep you prisoner. It was simple. They refused to let you enter the sanctuary of sleep.

So Anne-Marie stared up at the ceiling and tried like hell to remember the so-called consultant's face because that would mean she was regaining some control and that, in turn, meant she would remember how to sleep. And sleep would give her at least some limited escape from her waking nightmare.

Anne-Marie sighed with impatience and rolled onto her left shoulder. The alarm clock on the bedside table showed 1.26am. She wondered where Marcus was right now and what he was doing. Somehow, she found it easier to imagine that he wasn't asleep either.

24.

Marcus chose, as he always did when alone, to walk home from Peter and Nic's large, detached house near the Queen's Medical Centre. It was a walk that took him just over thirty minutes. It was a time he used for the silent practice that was central to his ability to look with clarity and communicate with both elegance and impact. He particularly welcomed the opportunity to walk silently late at night when the city was for the most part quiet and still, the very opposite of the bustling, energetic daytime.

The evening had threatened to not end well, with Nic becoming extremely concerned by Marcus's prediction of an impending nightmare. Nic had wanted to know just what Marcus imagined would happen, and what the risks were, and why he was so certain. Peter, for his part, had simply nodded and remained silent for some time, lost in his own thoughts as Marcus worked to calm Nic's anxiety. Only when Marcus had worked at least some of his magic and Nic had demonstrated a return to his usual state, had Peter looked at him and smiled and offered his own assessment.

'This isn't the first time I've faced a new and potentially challenging situation. You need to remember that it's not only what I'm paid to do, it's what I'm trained to do. And it's what I'm good at. The nature of the killing might be unusual and, if Marcus is right, the motive equally so, but the actual game we are playing is the same as always. Someone commits a crime and I have to detect and prove who did it. I have a great team around me and beyond them I have the biggest gang in the land at my disposal if I need them. Even without Marcus the odds are stacked in my favour, but with him...well, we are an unbeatable double act.' Peter paused for only a half-beat as he saw Nic's eyebrow raised questioningly in what was clearly meant to be a sign that he had regained his composure. 'An unbeatable *professional* double act at least,' he added, reaching out to squeeze the other's hand.

The three men had shared another glass of wine and talked about the latest cinema releases for a good fifteen minutes before Marcus had decided that it was time to leave.

As he made his way up Derby Road, Marcus replayed the internal film he had created of Peter seeking to convince Nic that this killer was no different from all the others he had hunted and caught. To Marcus, Peter's internal state had contradicted his assertion; the clues were unmistakable. In his mind's eye he watched again as Peter paused just before he claimed that the odds were overwhelmingly on his side, he saw the briefest glance down as the Detective reached for Nic's hand, he heard the slightest of tremors in his voice. Everything revealed an unnecessary adrenaline release; a sense of doubt at best and of fear at worst. Marcus had never seen his friend so obviously lacking confidence.

Marcus blinked and the film returned to its place in his subconscious. He had walked barely another half a dozen paces when unwanted and unexpected thoughts of the killer disrupted the calm of his mind. The intrusion brought him to a halt. It was the first time he could remember that he had been unable to control his mental processes. He stamped his right foot repeatedly on the pavement as if trying to shake the thoughts free. They simply expanded in response, filling his consciousness as if to make the point that any attempt to remove them would result only in a more compelling invasion.

What the hell are you looking for? The voice in his head asked a killer he could not yet visualise. *What did you need to find when you revealed the brain? What is the compulsion that drives you?*

A police car drove past, the driver looking pointedly at the unmoving pedestrian. *The biggest gang in the land*, that's what Peter had said. Sometimes, though, size is a hindrance not a help. In the right environment it is safer to be small, disregarded even; if you don't want to be identified, it is essential that you are never really seen, never recognised for who – or what – you really are. Sometimes, Marcus acknowledged, invisibility can be the greatest of all attributes.

For now the killer was invisible and unknown. That was his advantage. Yet Marcus found it impossible to believe that he wanted to remain that way. The nature of the killing was bound to attract media attention once details were leaked and beyond that there was something – something he had seen in the film, something that he couldn't quite bring out of the shadows of his mind – that told him the killer wanted to be known.

The question is what do you want to be known for?
The unwanted voice in his head asked unbidden. *And to
whom do you want to be known?*

Marcus growled at his lack of self-control and set off
again, walking a faster pace, using his movement in an
attempt to create a pattern interrupt that would silence
his mind. To his anger and surprise the voice stayed with
him every step of the way asking questions that he could
not hope to answer, that he would never normally ask at
this stage in the process. Marcus began to sweat. *Is that
because of me?* The voice wanted to know. *Or is it because
you are going too fast for yourself?*

Marcus stopped dead and looked up at the night sky.
The cloud cover was low and dense. He could see neither
the moon nor any stars. This time he knew precisely
what the voice was referring to. And, no, he wasn't going
too fast. If anything he had been too slow in making the
decision that he had finally, and irreversibly, come to on
the very same day that the killing had happened.

Decisions, Marcus taught, were the planning equivalent
of full stops. When a person told either themselves or
others that they had made a decision it had to mean that
the process of information gathering, questioning and
evaluating was over. A decision, properly made, brought
with it an end to the previous internal chatter. A decision
meant that one process had ended and another was going
to begin. Decisions signified finality. They were the dot that
marked the gap between Alpha and Omega.

In Marcus's experience too many people claimed
to have made a decision and then went on to ask for
advice, or took some additional time to re-examine the
conclusion they said they had come to. Marcus applauded

thoroughness; attention to detail was something he insisted upon from his staff at **Influence**. The key, though, was to avoid ever misusing the word: only ever say that you have made a decision when you are certain that the full stop has been placed.

And Marcus Kline *had* made a decision. The full stop was clear and definite and it was followed by as yet unimaginable challenges and opportunities. For all concerned.

Even though he had nothing to say right now, no one to tell, no reason to glance down as he shared his decision, Marcus still felt himself swallow. His hands still trembled slightly.

When Anne-Marie returned from her current assignment, he would find the right time and share his decision with her. He would tell her that he was going to file for divorce.

25.

Peter Jones waited until Nic had gone to bed and then he began to pace the length of the open plan lounge-dining room. Ten paces from one end to the other. Ten. Not more, not less. Ten even paces, not counted, just felt. Ten paces and then turn round and repeat. Ten paces so well grooved they created freedom rather than restriction. Ten paces that Nic, in his fake film trailer voice, loved to refer to as 'The walk of thought.' Ten paces all far more real and meaningful and necessary than cinema films that were intended to engage and distract the imaginations of the populace. Ten paces that were only ever taken when real monsters were at large. Ten paces associated with thought and commitment and decision-making, all of which were focussed on saving lives.

Peter always lost track of time when he paced the room. He just let the movement release the images, events and statements of the previous twenty-four hours and, as he remembered them, he sought to find connections he had missed. Tonight his task was even more difficult than normal because of Marcus's talk of an impending nightmare. Peter had never heard his friend be so certain and so pessimistic, as if he had recognised something that he was unable to share. What made it even more challenging and debilitating for Peter was that Marcus had gone at least some way to verbalising his own intuitive feeling about the killing.

There was something different about this murder that went well beyond the simple fact that he had never before seen a man scalped and with the top of his head cut off. There was some sense of *purpose* that Peter was sure Marcus had felt – as he had – that changed the very nature of the game. It was a sense of purpose so obvious and profound, if as yet unexplainable, that it had stopped Marcus from asking the most basic and human of all questions:

Who was the victim?

His name was Derrick Smith. He had a criminal record for a range of minor crimes associated with drugs and low-level violence. Under normal circumstances his killer should have been easy to identify as a member of his criminal circle. Only Derrick had seemingly turned his back on crime after his most recent release from prison. According to those who claimed to know him best, Derrick had found God during his latest incarceration. He had been trying to break away from those people with whom he had previously worked. He was trying to become a new man. Whilst Peter couldn't help but doubt his chances of success, the evidence did indicate that Derrick was not under threat from any of his previous associates.

And that was bad news.

It supported Marcus's perception that this was a killer unlike any other, a killer with a very specific agenda. *Unique* was the very worst description any policeman wanted to hear about a person they were pursuing. *Unique* meant that there was nothing in the data banks that could help, that motive was going to be very difficult to determine. Worst of all it meant that in all probability more crimes were likely to be committed before an arrest could be made. And when those crimes were murders it meant that he, Peter Jones, would be almost as responsible as the unique killer.

Surely there had to be something? Something he had missed?

The great benefit of asking Marcus Kline to help him was that he had privileged access to one of the world's greatest minds. The downside was that he had to be able and willing to ignore his friend's interpretation when the evidence did not support it. His friend was a genius. And Peter was a detective. They both understood and appreciated the power of intuition and insight. Only a detective couldn't spend public money in pursuit of an instinct when the facts did not support it. And a successful court case was built on enough evidence to create a compelling story. Not even as powerful a communicator as Marcus Kline could persuade a jury to convict unless sufficient facts were available.

The problem for Peter was that he knew just how good his friend was. Marcus was rarely wrong. That meant that when he couldn't act on Marcus's advice there was a very real chance that he was going in the wrong direction. Despite that he had no choice. Swings and roundabouts. Ups and downs. What Marcus referred to as 'trade-offs,' the balancing acts that real life created.

Unless you were a Detective Chief Inspector in which case the trade-offs were deaths not life.

Peter mentally reviewed everything he had learnt about the life and death of Derrick Smith. The fact that Marcus had sensed there was something hidden just below the surface, that he had actually felt his subconscious attracted by an as yet unidentified stimulus, surely meant that there was something of significance they were all missing? Unless, of course, this was one of those rare times when his friend was wrong. And as Marcus told him frequently, no one can achieve perfection. Although he invariably then went on to stress that he did get as close as anyone ever could.

'It might surprise you all to know that I am happy to declare myself imperfect,' the consultant said once to a fascinated group at a New Year's party, 'However, you probably won't be surprised to hear that I much prefer to spell and say the word the way it was clearly intended – for me at least.'

'And how is that?' Marcus's pause had drawn the desired question almost immediately.

'I'm perfect,' Marcus said, joining in the laughter as his audience recognised the clever wordplay. 'Well, that's what I want my clients to believe and how I train my staff to think of me.'

The memory flittered through Peter's mind. Sometimes he couldn't help but wonder just how lonely his friend really was. Despite Marcus's marriage to Anne-Marie, their almost lifelong friendship, his fame and reputation and his powerful network of contacts, the detective had always felt a sense of isolation surrounding the great communicator. He had even mentioned it once, carelessly, after several glasses of red wine too many. 'I think if John Donne had ever met you, he might never have written his most famous line.'

'If I am an island,' Marcus replied quickly, "I do at least have some very significant bridges connecting me to the mainland. Although if you are really asking me about the philosophy of John Donne, I'm more inclined to agree with his notion of shadows than anything else.'

'Shadows?'

'Yes. He wrote:

"These three hours that we have spent,

Walking here, two shadows went

Along with us, which we ourselves produced.

But, now the sun is just above our head,

We do those shadows tread,

And to brave clearness all things are reduced."

As far as I can see, the only thing as certain as the inevitability of associations is the fact that ultimately "to brave clearness all things are reduced."'

'Right now I could do with things being reduced rapidly into a clearness that shows me the way forward.' Peter stopped in his tracks as he realised that he had, for the first time ever during the "walk of thought", just spoken out loud.

The shock reverberated through him. Peter was the Boss of his team. He set the pace, the tempo, the direction and the attention to detail. He controlled those he led completely and he did it, in part, by demonstrating his own high-level of self-control. Only now his self-control had just slipped. And in his world there was no such thing as a minor slip-up. Even if no-one else was aware of it.

It took Peter several seconds to clear his head. He was helped by the fact that his mobile phone began ringing.

26.

The caller was Marcus Kline. He sounded both nervous and excited.

'Peter! I've got something!'

'Something from the film?'

'No! It's more direct than that – far more personal.'

'What are you talking about?'

'It will be best if I show you. I need you to come to the house. Now.'

Eight minutes later Peter turned the Audi between the stone pillars that marked the entrance to the drive. Marcus was standing on the front lawn in front of the willow. Both he and it were clearly lit by the lights placed deliberately to highlight the tree. The sight made Peter think of a lonely entertainer waiting in the spotlight for his audience to arrive. He parked by the side of the lawn and strode over, aware of a sense of urgency that he never normally felt when arriving at a scene as Detective Chief Inspector Jones. But, then, he was here as much as a friend as a detective.

'What is it?' He asked. 'What's happened?'

'This.' Marcus pointed to the ground. A length of branch had been cut off the tree and was lying, pointing towards the house. It looked as if it had been sprayed with a dark paint. Peter squatted next to it. 'It looks like it's...'

'...Purple.' Marcus stepped back a pace. 'Someone has very deliberately removed the branch and painted it purple.'

Peter straightened. 'I'm not sure why you asked me here. Unless the house has been burgled?'

'No. This is not about vandalism or burglary.'

'Then what is it about?'

'Communication. It's a message. A message for me from the person you're hunting.'

'You think the killer did this?'

'I'm certain of it.'

Peter found himself shaking his head and glancing into the shadows at the same time. 'What makes you think that?'

'I'm a communications specialist.'

'So?'

'So if you want to send me a message and eliminate everyone else from the communication you send it in a cryptic form that only someone like me would be able to read. That way you not only get my attention, you speak clearly in a language that most others can't and, by extension, you test my ability.'

'And what language is this?' Peter gestured to the branch.

'Symbolism. In order to read the message you have to understand something about both the willow tree and the meaning of purple.'

'And you do?'

'Of course. The willow tree has been steeped in symbolism and meaning throughout history. It plays its part in Wicca, or witchcraft, but its significance has crossed cultures and centuries. For example, when Orpheus journeyed to the underworld intending to bring back to life his wife, Eurydice, he carried with him willow branches for luck and protection. The Victorians believed that flowers and plants had a language of their own. For them, the weeping willow represented mourning and sadness. In eighteenth and nineteenth century art, the same tree symbolised immortality and rebirth. This was most probably because of its ability to grow swiftly even when cut. If the roots of the willow are unharmed a cut tree can re-grow sometimes by as much as a metre or more in a single season. Today the image of a weeping willow standing on a riverbank with its branches reaching down to the water symbolises life, death and rebirth.'

'What's the significance of colouring it purple?'

'Throughout history purple has been associated with nobility and prestige. It symbolises mystery, magic and power. It is the colour of kings, leaders, wizards and magicians.'

Peter stared down at the cut branch as Marcus spoke. The light turned the purple into a dark, muddy hue. 'So, if I'm understanding you correctly, you're saying you know it's the killer who did this because the willow represents death and all associated aspects? And he knows that you will realise this, and is identifying you as some sort of magician by painting the branch purple and pointing it at your front door?'

'Something like that.'

'Did you hear how ridiculous that sounded when I said it?'

'I heard you describe something that is highly unusual, not ridiculous.'

'It's beyond ridiculous! You're not a magician! We are not Victorians or ancient Greeks. There is no underworld. A tree is just a tree – and an act of vandalism is not some incredibly subtle and personalised communication from a killer who cannot know that you are in any way involved in this case!'

'You only know that hieroglyphics are a language because someone has convinced you of that, not because you can read it.'

'This…' Peter gestured angrily towards the branch, '… is not a language!'

'Everything is a form of language in one way or another.'

'For God's sake, Marcus, save it for your clients!'

'You are my client right now.'

'No! I am a professional detective who is secretly enlisting the help of an expert who also just happens to be his very close friend. And right now the professional detective is telling the expert that he has nothing here that can be acted upon. I cannot commit resources to investigating a…a fairy tale!'

Marcus was silent for a moment, nodding as much it seemed to himself as to Peter. A thin smile crossed his lips. 'You are right. Of course you can't. And that is precisely what the killer would expect: I read the message to you, you ignore it because it's in a language you cannot comprehend, and so it becomes a competition just between him and me. You are obliged to take yourself out of the equation and I am, at that point, immediately isolated and forced to deal with him on my own. I think we have both been played rather beautifully.'

'That's bollocks!' Peter's words barked out into the cold night air. 'First of all, you seemed to have missed the point that I'm the detective! It's my job to deal with this case, not yours. You offer advice and I decide if, how and when I can use it. The odds against this killer actually targeting you for some reason are millions to one – and to date we don't have a scrap of evidence to suggest that we should revise those odds! And you know…' Peter pointed at his friend's chest, '…you absolutely know that if I thought for one minute that you were at risk I would do whatever was necessary to keep you safe.' Peter felt his anger ebb as he stared into the unreadable shadow of Marcus's eyes. The outburst was over and his voice calmed. 'This time my friend, you've got it wrong. We all do from time to time. Even the very best of us.' A smile splashed across Peter's face as he heard the words in his mind a split-second before he said them, 'You don't need a detective tonight, Marcus, you need a gardener.'

Marcus returned the smile, but there was hint of resignation in his face as he looked back the willow. 'No. The tree will take care of itself. It will have already started. It doesn't need any help at all.'

The two men fell silent for a moment, their breath showing as mist in the cold night air. Then Peter said, 'Look, I'll tell you what I'll do. I'll arrange for a Crime Prevention Officer to come round tomorrow and install a panic button by your bed. If you ever have reason to press it the call will come automatically through to us and officers will be with you within minutes. I'll create a legitimate story for why it needs to be done. For God's sake, though, when the guy's here don't tell him it's because someone trimmed your willow during the night.'

They both grinned again. Peter shook Marcus's hand and turned his back on the light. He glanced at his watch as he walked back to the car. It was 2.25am. He knew that Nic would have woken when he left the house. Although his partner was used to the demands of living with a senior policeman, he never slept well whenever Peter was called out at night. At least if nothing else happened there would be three hours of peace together before the next working day began.

Peter got into the Audi, put it into reverse and began to ease his way out of the drive. To his left Marcus Kline was standing facing the willow as he had been on Peter's arrival. The tree shivered in the wind. The man was still. The light held them both as if an island in the darkest of seas. Around them the night offered no promise of the morning.

Two hundred and thirty miles away, alone in her cottage, Anne-Marie Wells was taking a photo, a self-portrait, of her tear-lined face.

27.

Nic barely stirred when Peter lay down next to him. The movement of his left hand, reaching out to rest on Peter's forearm, the only sign that he recognised his presence. Peter relaxed his body, letting the weight of his head sink into the pillow. He thought again about what Marcus had said and his reaction to it.

Decisions, he reminded himself, had to be made based on the information available at the time. Or on instinct of course. The type of instinct he had felt and trusted prior to the killer's first murder. And tonight, in the garden, looking at the branch, listening to Marcus's explanation, he had neither seen compelling evidence nor felt an intuitive conviction. The installation of a panic button was above and beyond what he should have done in that situation – what he would have done for anyone else. And if it had been anyone else he wouldn't be reviewing the situation now. He would have been asleep within seconds of his head touching the pillow. Only it wasn't someone else. It was his genius friend. And yet despite that, the odds were still millions to one against him being right. They were lottery odds. The sort you could play all your life and never beat.

The sort you only had to beat once to change your life forever.

Peter forced himself not to think about the most recent lottery winner and told himself instead that both his mind and his body needed to rest. It was an easy argument to make. He was asleep within minutes.

The nightmare began gently: a dream barely one step away from reality, as comfortable and easy to enter as a bed already warmed by a sleeping partner. It began in the living room, with Peter, Marcus and Nic sitting, drinking wine, waiting for the DVD that Peter had put into the player to start.

The first scene in the film showed Peter asleep, un-moving, with Nic next to him. 'I can wake any time, in an instant, when I'm on a case,' Peter said. 'Nic doesn't understand how I can do it, but it's simply a matter of con-ditioning. And it's nothing unusual. Ask any mother. They will tell you. They can be in the deepest sleep and if their baby makes even the slightest noise, they are immediately wide-awake. When it's a murder case I feel my brain is always processing information. Sometimes I'm aware that I'm dreaming about it. Sometimes my subconscious wakes me up with a new insight or possibility clear in my mind. When that happens I write it down. That's what the notepad is for. I can't trust that I will remember it in the morning.'

The sleeping Peter rolled onto his left side. There was a notepad and pen on the bedside table next to him. The dvd – the *dream* – continued.

'You almost certainly will remember it,' Marcus said. 'You just might not be able to recall it. Some scientists believe that the human brain actually stores every memory, that it houses a perfect record of everything that we have ever experienced. So we are technically wrong whenever we say that we have a bad memory. Our memory bank is faultless and complete. What is flawed, in most of us, is our ability to recall.'

'We actually have perfect memories? Wow!' Nic shook his head in amazement.

'No.' A look of impatience crossed Marcus's face. 'That's not what I said! Pay attention! We store memories perfectly, but the memories we actually store are far from perfect. Usually they are distorted and twisted by unhelpful beliefs or fear. Often they are deep and dark and dangerous. Memories can kill us and they can lead us to kill others. You know that Peter, don't you? You know that the most powerful memories, particularly the dark ones, present a challenge to anyone. Even to a magician like me.' Marcus laughed suddenly and harshly; his teeth showed jagged and sharp.

Despite himself Peter recoiled from the unexpected aggression and threat. Marcus turned towards him, his head down, his chin low over his throat. He made Peter think of an alpha wolf asserting its authority, a split-second away from launching a devastating attack. He found himself surrendering completely. He sat back in his chair, his hands raised and open, his neck exposed.

'Those memories, the really bad ones, are the price I pay for doing my job. I keep them secret,' Peter said. 'I've never even shared them with you.'

'Of course you have!' Marcus laughed. The sound was at once cold, harsh and excited. 'You share everything with me, whether you mean to or not. No one can hide when I look at them! I see more than just your thoughts – I see your darkest memories!'

'And what are they?'

'Shadows.' The voice belonged to Nic not Marcus. Peter swivelled to face him. He felt the blood drain from his face. His partner had changed, lost his identity, turned into a faceless black human form. 'And those shadows surround me, too, because you bring them home with you. You breathe them into me. I see them. I feel them. Every time you get out of our bed in the middle of the night and drive away to another crime, you leave me alone with the shadows. Don't you realise that? Don't you understand how they are drawing the life out of me? How they threaten us?'

'He's right. You carry the shadows everywhere and they cling to your home.' This time it was Marcus who spoke. Only when Peter looked to him he found himself suddenly transported in to Marcus's garden. Now he was standing in front of the weeping willow. The shadows surrounded the light. Peter turned a slow, tight circle, staring into the impenetrable darkness. His right foot caught against an unexpected object. He looked down. The earth had been disturbed. A grave had been dug. It held his partner.

'Help me! Get me out!' Nic's voice, faint and desperate beyond measure, choked off abruptly as the earth began filling his throat.

Peter dropped to his knees and began clawing frantically at the soil with both hands, like a dog searching for a hidden treasure. 'Nic! I'm here! I will save you!'

The willow shook, its lowest branches rustling against the grass. The shadows closed in. Peter dug frantically. 'Just hold on!'

He threw the soil behind him, felt some hitting his own chest and thighs as he increased his efforts. Only the more he dug the deeper and darker the hole became, just a shadow within the earth with no sign of his lover inside it.

'Nic!' Peter heard the terror in his own voice, saliva spraying from his mouth, his tears blurring his vision. 'Nic!'

There was no reply. Peter screamed. His hands closed around an object and he pulled it from the soil. It was the branch from the willow tree, painted purple, trembling in his grasp as if gulping in air. The earth-shadow released itself and soared heavenward. Peter fell backwards, dropping the branch.

'Nic!'

'Help me! Get me out!' The desperate voice again. Peter pushed himself to his knees and began to dig some more, going ever deeper.

And so the nightmare held him. Repeating itself. Increasing his sense of hope and desperation in equal measure. A nightmare that refused to end.

Whilst Peter slept, the killer reviewed the lessons he had learnt from his second killing.

28.

The next morning was unusually bright and clear for the time of year. The sky was cloudless and blue, promising warmth it did not deliver. At 9.25am Simon Westbury, protégé of Marcus Kline, walked into the Cross Keys public house less than two hundred and fifty metres from the offices where he worked. He smiled and waved a greeting to Cassandra, the dark haired half-Italian twenty three year old who served him breakfast here most mornings. She was behind the bar talking on the phone. She returned both the smile and the wave before mouthing 'Usual?' whilst listening to the voice on the other end of the line. Simon nodded and took his preferred seat at the corner table by the window.

He liked this place. It was what he and his friends referred to as a 'proper pub'. It was a phrase that brought out even more sarcasm than usual from his boss, who argued that neither Simon nor any of his friends were old enough to remember what proper pubs used to be like. What Simon actually liked about the place was the old-fashioned wooden floors in the bar, the large windows that looked out onto a road that was now dominated by the tramline, the fine selection of ales and, most important of all, Cassandra.

She had started working there, doing the morning shift, three months ago. That was when Simon had decided that it was the best place in town for a spot of breakfast.

'It's all about location,' he had explained once to Marcus and Emma when they had taken an unexpected interest in his early morning habit. 'Breakfast is the most important meal of the day and it makes sense to take it somewhere close to the office.'

The other two had looked at each other and smiled. 'You don't even need to be him,' Emma gestured towards her boss, 'to know that you're lying your head off. Any girl could see that you are not going there for the eggs benedict.'

Marcus had nodded his head in appreciation. 'I'll tell you what then Emma, you tell me why he's going there and I'll do my best to go one better.'

'There's no charity donation involved in this one is there?'

'None at all. This is all just practice and fun.'

'Practice and fun and the chance to show off again,' Simon couldn't help himself. 'And, of course, the chance to be right again, to win when there wasn't even a competition there in the first place.'

'Everything is a competition,' Marcus countered. 'One of the keys to being a great strategist and a successful businessman is to recognise what the nature of the competition is before anyone else does. That's how you get a head start. That's how, sometimes, you even get to influence the rules.'

'Enough of this competitive nonsense!' Emma spoke quickly, before Simon could counter again. 'The simple fact of the matter is that you, Mr Westbury, are going to the Cross Keys because there is a girl there that you fancy. And the way you have just started blushing confirms it!'

Emma giggled both at Simon's embarrassment and her own success. She looked triumphantly at Marcus. 'How are you going to be beat that then?'

'By telling you about the girl.' Marcus looked intently into Simon's face. 'I'm going to ask you some questions about her, just the usual stuff you would expect. You know the sort of thing. All I want you to do is answer my questions silently in your mind. Say nothing out loud. Don't even try to visualise her until I ask you to. And certainly don't think about her name, or even....' His voice trailed off. He turned his attention back to Emma. 'That didn't take long, then.'

'But you haven't even started yet, you haven't asked him anything!'

'Actually, I've finished. I now know at least as much as young Simon here about this dark-haired beauty.'

'That's not possible!' Emma turned to Simon for support, but he was already looking down at the floor, shaking his head in disbelief.

'Dark-haired could just be a lucky guess,' he mumbled.

'Only you don't believe that it is,' Marcus said. 'And when I also tell you that she is of Italian descent, has not been working in the pub for very long, is twenty three years old and is the sort of expressive person who will almost always wave a greeting as well as a goodbye, then you will know that there is no luck involved.'

'Tell me he's wrong!' Emma demanded of Simon.

'Wish I could,' Simon pursed his lips and exhaled forcefully. 'At least he couldn't tell me her name.'

'Cassandra,' Marcus said without hesitation. 'Can't think it can be anything else.'

'Oh God, I hate this man!' Simon groaned. 'I'm going back into my office. If anyone needs to contact me, tell them to send thought waves to the boss and that he'll pass them on.'

'I'm not your secretary,' Marcus said as his protégé turned to walk away. 'And before you go anywhere, ask me the question.'

Simon halted. 'What question?'

'*The* question.'

Simon looked to Emma for help. He shrugged helplessly. 'I don't know what *the* question is.'

Emma took pity. 'He wants you to ask him how he did it.'

'What if I don't want to know right now?'

'There is no time like the present.' Marcus smiled. 'But, still, if you don't want to know the Magician's secrets, perhaps you do Emma?'

'I certainly do.' Emma matched Marcus's smile. 'I think learning can only ever be beneficial.'

'I think you deserve a migraine each!' Simon glared at the other two. 'C'mon then, let's get it over and done with. How did you do it? I'm guessing, though, before you answer, that you simply read micro-expressions on my face as you forced me to think of Cassandra by telling me not to.'

'You think that doing something like that is simple?' It was Marcus's turn to shake his head in disbelief. 'Wow! How can anyone – let alone you – think that something that requires such incredible skill is simple?'

'Alright then! That's how you did it and I acknowledge that only you can do it because you are a genius!"

Simon raised his open palms in submission. 'Can I please go now?'

'Not quite yet.'

'Oh, come on! This is torture! Emma, please make him stop.'

'I don't know how to, I'm only the secretary. You're the future Marcus Kline, you're going to be the new, improved version. That's what you always say after a couple of drinks. So if you can't stop him what chance have I got?' Emma's eyes twinkled with delight.

'A single migraine is not good enough for you,' Simon growled. Then he straightened and looked Marcus full in the face. 'Come on then, what else do I need to know?'

'That I didn't get that information by reading the expressions on your face. I knew that you would recognise the covert commands I gave you, but on this occasion they were just a form of misdirection. I used them to steer you towards an incorrect conclusion.'

'But if you didn't read my face, how did you do it?

'By very good fortune, I had a couple of drinks in the pub last night. Cassandra and I had a very pleasant chat.' Marcus beamed. 'She told me that she usually served you breakfast.'

'That's... that's cheating!' Simon exploded as Emma burst out in a fit of laughter.

'That's not cheating at all. It's just an example of how to create and control a competition. And also how to recognise and take advantage of opportunities when they come your way.'

'But...but you're not supposed to misdirect people! You are supposed to help to them change things for the best!'

Marcus waited until Emma had regained control

before replying. 'Misdirection is an important tool. It's an essential part of the Magician's armoury. Misdirection limits opposition and hides your real intention. Sometimes we will even use it to keep our behaviours secret. I don't always need people to know what I have done, or what I am doing. Sometimes the outcome is all that matters. Even for me. The learning point Simon, is that if you want to become a master of influence you need to master the fine art of misdirection...'

Simon looked out of the pub windows and watched idly as a tram moved passed, heading into the city centre. It was hard to get Marcus Kline out of your head once he had found a way in – or, as in Simon's case, once you had invited him in.

Could he really one day become a better and improved version of his boss? Was that really possible, or was it a young man's bravado? Perhaps bravado was needed, Simon considered, if he was to have any chance of superseding his mentor. Perhaps courage and self-belief were as important as a willingness to work hard? And yet, if he possessed those qualities why hadn't he asked Cassandra out? After all, for a man who didn't believe in love at first sight, he had come pretty close to it the first time he saw her.

Simon looked instinctively for Cassandra behind the bar. She was not to be seen. In all likelihood she was collecting his breakfast. In a minute she would be back, smiling her smile as she placed his coffee and egg and bacon ciabatta in front of him. In a minute he would have the chance, once again, to suggest a drink together, or a visit to the cinema, or a dinner, or any combination she liked. Or anything else, for that matter. Only right now probably wasn't the right time. Even if Marcus's voice in his head was saying, 'The clue is in the words, *Right* and *Now*. Just take the Bard's advice, *Screw your courage to the sticking post and you'll not fail.*'

Yeah, right. Easy enough for Shakespeare to write and Marcus Kline to say – and, actually, even if it wasn't easy for either of them, what the hell did they know? Apart from just about everything to do with words and influence...

Simon sighed. He had never hesitated about something so much before. He was the guy who always volunteered first, who accepted the challenge ahead of everyone else, because he knew that was the right thing to do if you wanted to become the best. So what was stopping him now? Realistically, what was the worst that could happen? Simon shook his head. That was a question he didn't want to answer. He turned his attention instead to the television on the wall to his right.

The presenter on the local BBC news programme was reporting a murder in the city, the second she said in less than week. The images that appeared next were of a detached house in the suburbs transformed into a crime scene. Simon was only mildly interested and his interest disappeared completely when Cassandra appeared carrying his breakfast. He watched her walking across the bar. He marvelled at her smile and tried not to stare. He heard Marcus Kline's words of encouragement whisper in his mind. He felt his stomach tense and his appetite disappear. And then she was next to him.

Simon Westbury didn't hear the news presenter revealing the name of the victim, the man who had lived for over twenty years in that detached house, who was, according to his neighbours, a vital part of their community, a man

who helped others, a man with many friends and no
obvious enemies. If Simon had heard the name the shock
would have distracted him even from Cassandra.

29.

A street changes when a murder occurs within it. The change isn't the result of just the event itself, nor the unwanted police activity, nor the sometimes welcomed and enjoyed media spotlight. These all play their part, but they are finite in nature. They come eventually to be viewed by residents as the markers of a form of psychological no man's land; those activities and the period of time sandwiched between the killing itself and the establishment and acceptance of a new, forever altered reality.

A street changes inexorably and in silence when a murder occurs.

Even if the killer is never identified, this change is the greatest secret connected to such a crime. It is never discussed nor openly acknowledged by any who live there.

Yet all feel it.

It is as if the emotional intensity of a killing, the anger, the hatred, the fear, the violence, seeps into the very soul of the street, into the pavement and the brickwork, into the hedges and the gardens. It hangs in the air and is breathed in by the entire community. It clings to the darkness of night, penetrating every home.

Whenever people drive slowly by a fatal traffic accident they often say to themselves or their passengers, 'There but for the grace of God go I'. When people see a news report about a murder on a street, they never think to offer the same heartfelt thanks. Peter knew they would if they realised just how the murder of one human being kills a street.

Peter had recognised this change long ago. He believed that it was as sure as death itself. He knew the damage that it caused. He knew that he was powerless to prevent it. And he gave it no more attention than a casual glance. It was a reality he was neither paid nor trained to manage.

In Peter's experience every event rippled out through a wider community than one would ever expect. From his perspective there were usually far less than six degrees of separation between cause and effect, between one individual and a seemingly random other. That was why, as a detective, he started his enquiries within the victim's most immediate social circle, casting his net gradually wider only if the answers he sought were not forthcoming.

Peter had been called to this killing in a suburban street only minutes after he had woken up. It was everything he had been secretly dreading. And more. In life this new victim had been nothing like Derrick Smith, the small-time criminal who had been killed only four days before.

Was that all it was?

Only four days?

In one sense it seemed to Peter to have been, quite literally, a lifetime ago. And yet now, now that a second person had been killed in exactly the same way, it felt like a hand on his shoulder, as close as his own shadow and as impossible to pin down.

The second victim seemed as far removed from Derrick Smith as it was possible to be. He was a legitimate and successful businessman – on no grand scale admittedly, but first impressions suggested that he had done well enough to create the sort of life that many would aspire to.

He had been married to the same woman for twenty six years. They had lived in this house for more than two decades. They holidayed in France twice every year. They were solvent and apparently secure. They were likeable and appropriate neighbours, friendly without being too intrusive, quiet without seeming remote. They were a well-established part of the street.

The victim's wife had been visiting her sister in Durham for the last few days. She had been informed by the local constabulary and was now being driven back to Nottingham by her sister and husband. Although she didn't know it yet, she would choose to leave the street; sooner rather than later, Peter guessed.

Today she would feel the change rippling out to greet her long before she arrived in her neighbourhood. And when she did, she would see everything differently, hear everything differently, and feel her awareness locked inside her. She would be isolated from the inside out. She would be unable to put into words the way her world seemed to her now. She would become convinced that her only option was to move away, to find a street that had not been changed.

The tragedy, Peter knew, was that wherever she went she would carry the stain from this street with her.

Peter Jones, the man, the everyday human being who knew what it meant to be in love, to have dreams, to care for others, wanted to wait for this woman to return.

He wanted to hold her and let her cry against his chest, to promise that he would catch the person responsible, to offer some form of reassurance about the essential goodness of humanity, to create some form of hope – however false.

However, Peter Jones *the man* had not been called to this street. The person who now walked out of the house towards his car, grim-faced and purposeful, was Detective Chief Inspector Peter Jones. He had no emotional energy to spare on the victim's family or friends. He looked through eyes that searched only for clues. He saw only pieces in a jigsaw. He felt nothing.

That, Peter reminded himself, was what it meant to be a professional, to be driven by purpose and results, to be detached from the human situation. This is how he was able to make the connections that led him to his quarry, whether it began with six degrees of separation or not. And he had seen something of enormous significance in the victim's study. Pages of handwritten notes, with clear sub-headings and arrows connecting one sentence or passage to another as the writer made their own internal connections, as they sought to create clarity from their thoughts. The pages were as obvious to Peter as a signpost.

Which is why he knew precisely where to go when he left the street. It was also the reason why Detective Chief Inspector Peter Jones was fighting an unexpected internal conflict with Peter Jones the man.

As he drove away from the street, despite his emotionless face, the detective's heart was hammering inside his chest.

30.

Simon Westbury was making no attempt to hide the way he was feeling. He knew that Emma would instantly see the delight and triumph etched across his face. And, for once, he was very happy for her to know just what was going on inside his head.

'Morning!' Simon greeted. 'How are you today?'

Emma looked up from her computer and glanced at the clock on the wall. 'You are even later than normal.'

'I always make up for it at the end of the day, and I'm never late if I have a morning meeting. And you're not my boss, so it's none of your business.'

'That's true. I guess that also means that the reason why you're late is none of my business either.' Emma looked back at her computer screen.

'No! That's more personal than it is professional, so you can ask me about that.'

'What if I don't want to?'

'If I were you, I'd want to.'

'Not necessarily. If you were me you'd only want to do what I would want to do.'

'You know what I meant!'

'I know that you are looking extremely pleased with yourself and, at this time of day, that can only mean one thing: Cassandra has finally asked you out.'

'I asked her out!'

'You might have plucked up the courage to say the actual words but, trust me, she is the one who first decided that today was going to be the day. That's the way we women work. We make the decisions and then let you guys think that you are in control.' Emma winked. 'She will even have decided where the first date is going to be, and she will have known for sure that you would give her the choice.'

'Actually, she said didn't mind where we go.'

'And then?'

Simon shrugged. 'She suggested we meet for a drink in The Orange Tree and then take it from there.'

'In woman-speak that translates as "then she will take you wherever she plans to go". Still, I'm pleased for you, now you've got a great boss while you're at work and, by the sound of things, an even better one when you're not.'

'I don't need to be bossed around all the time! I'm an independent spirit – and remember, one day I'm going to be the boss round here! Besides, Cass isn't like that. She –'

Simon was cut short by the unexpected arrival of Peter Jones.

'Inspector.' Emma stood up instinctively as she spoke. She had met the policeman twice before. Once in a nearby bar at an early evening drinks celebration for Marcus's most recent birthday and then again, a few weeks later, when she had almost literally bumped into him in one of the city's larger department stores. She had been surprised – and impressed – on this second occasion, not only by the fact that he had remembered her name but even more so by the many details about her that he clearly recalled. When she had commented on it he had chuckled and replied dryly, 'A forgetful policeman is really not going to be very good at their job, now are they?'

Today, though, there was no sign of humour in his countenance.

'Inspector,' Emma said again, glancing at her diary for the day. 'Is, er, Marcus expecting you?'

'No. But I need to speak with him.'

Simon couldn't help but notice that the detective's tone was firm, his inflection lowering at the end of the sentence denoting a command rather than a request.

'He's in his office, 'Emma said. 'Should I let him know that you're here?'

'It's OK. I'll see myself in.'

Peter crossed the reception area without waiting for a reply. A curt knock on Marcus's office door and he stepped inside.

The consultant was sitting with his feet crossed at the ankles on top of his large, walnut desk. He was leaning back in the brown leather chair, squeezing a tennis ball in his right hand, looking up at the ceiling as if lost in thought. Only his eyes moved as Peter stepped into the office.

'It's that bad, is it?' Marcus let only the briefest frown cross his face.

'You could say that.' Peter crossed the room in three strides.

Marcus dropped the ball. He swung his feet to the floor and leaned forwards, both of his forearms resting on the desk. He entwined his hands. 'Has he killed again, already?

Peter nodded and sat on the other side of the desk. 'We've still got to go through all the usual stuff, but there can be no doubt. The M.O. is exactly the same. Taped in a chair, scalped, top of the head removed.'

'Two in less than a week,' Marcus pursed his lips. 'He is urgent. The question is, why is he?'

Peter shook his head. 'That is a question. It isn't the most important one.'

Marcus's gaze returned to the ceiling. He was silent for several seconds only. 'Sometimes I hate being right,' he whispered. Then he looked back at Peter. 'The most important question is "Who has he killed?" And the answer to that, the answer that makes it even more significant than normal, is that there is some connection between the victim and me. That's it, isn't it?

'Looks that way.' Peter said nothing more. Instead he watched Marcus closely. He saw the slight, uncontrolled intake of breath followed by the swallow as the adrenaline hit. Peter waited, forcing the question.

'So what's the connection?'

'I'm guessing he is – was – a current client of yours. There were notes in his house that he wrote over the last few days. It's clear that he was writing them in preparation for his next meeting with you.'

It took barely a second for Marcus to realise the answer. 'Paul Clusker?' Marcus's eyes widened. 'Is that who you found?'

Peter nodded. It seemed to him that Marcus's face had lost some of its natural colour. Once again he remained silent. This time the pause lasted longer. Peter felt the unspoken competition stretching the silence. He automatically relaxed his shoulders and his hands.

He didn't care if Marcus noticed. Right now it didn't matter what Marcus saw. This was a competition the detective had played many times before and he had always won. The only difference here was that the person opposite him was acknowledged as a genius at understanding and influencing others and was also his best friend.

But not when I'm at work, Peter reminded himself. *DCI Jones is the best at what he does and he doesn't have friends. He just has a job to do.*

'You're looking at me as if I'm a suspect,' Marcus said finally.

'You're connected. That's all.'

'At the moment! That's what you thought and didn't say. I'm connected *at the moment*. Meaning that you don't know where the connection will lead. Meaning that you have an open mind. Meaning that you have already considered the possibility that I might have killed him. And, by extension, that I also killed Derrick Smith.'

'I didn't tell you his name. When I showed you the film, you never asked.'

'I didn't ask because I'd already seen it in the newspapers.' Marcus's smile lacked warmth. 'So this is what you look like when you are in front of a suspect.'

'When I am in front of someone who is connected.'

'I guess you're not going to ask me to watch the film of this crime scene?'

'I'm going to ask you to tell me everything you know about Paul Clusker.'

'Hmm. It's normally me who asks the questions. How weird is this?'

'It's not weird at all. When I'm investigating a murder – in this case a series of murders – it's always me who asks the questions.'

'Wow! Has Nic ever seen you like this?'

'That's your first and last personal reference in this conversation. Now, tell me about Clusker.'

Marcus hesitated. He gathered his thoughts. 'He was a nice guy. He came to me to help him rejuvenate his business. It's a small therapy centre, called "Health Matters". Paul knew that he needed to change so that his business could, only he didn't know how to go about it. I was teaching him.'

'When did you last see him?'

'The same day that Derrick Smith was killed.'

Peter's phone rang. He took it out of his pocket, checked the caller ID and ignored it. 'Tell me again how you interpreted the purple branch. What was the take-home message for you?'

'I didn't have to take it home. It was already at my home.' Neither man smiled. 'To me it was as personal and as obvious as a phone call. And even more direct and deliberate, because a caller can claim they've dialled the wrong number.. Whoever did that to the willow tree didn't make a mistake. They were going out of their way to point me out. And they were telling me something about themselves too. They were telling me how smart they are. Or at least how smart they think they are. And they did that because they were laying down a form of challenge. Albeit a silent one.' Marcus looked briefly into Peter's eyes and then continued. 'In one way or another they are trying to take me on. It's like a communications joust.'

'If the person who did that is actually the killer, it's far more than a joust.'

'So you are considering that possibility now, are you?'

'I'm considering all possibilities.'

'Then you have to consider that Paul's connection to me could just be a coincidence.'

'I don't believe in coincidences in the workplace any more than you do. And where this case is concerned there are very few individuals who have the right, the power, or the experience to tell me what I should or shouldn't consider.'

'Prickly.'

'Professional.'

The silence fell and stretched again. The nightmare, the thought of Nic buried alive, tried to force its way unexpectedly back into Peter's mind. He refused it entry, using the anger he felt for letting the memory resurface as a weapon. The Detective Chief Inspector suddenly heard himself speak.

'Did Clusker say anything to you that indicated he felt he was facing any sort of personal threat? Did he mention any problems he was having with anyone? Did he talk about anything out of the ordinary that he had experienced recently?'

Marcus shook his head. 'Nothing like that. The notes I asked him to write were designed to help him reconnect with himself and his business. That was the only topic we discussed. I've no doubt that everything else in his life was safe, secure and very much to his liking. This was a man who wanted to revitalise himself through his business before he went off into the sunset with his wife.'

'Into the sunset?'

'I suspect that they had plans to retire abroad. Europe definitely. France most likely.'

'Did he tell you that?'

'Nope.'

'And you have never been to his house or talked to his wife?'

'Of course not.'

'Then how do you know?

Marcus spread his hands. 'It is still me you're talking to. I did spend some considerable time looking at him very closely. He wasn't that difficult to work out.'

Peter nodded, his face emotionless.

To Marcus the implication was clear. 'Have I just made myself even more connected?'

The Detective Chief Inspector ignored the question. Deep inside, Peter Jones wished that he could ignore certain connections just as easily.

The meeting did not end well.

31.

Anne-Marie felt as if she was meeting familiar – in many cases loved – faces and scenes for the very first time. It was, she acknowledged, in one sense true and in one sense not. Like most things. In the very final analysis, life was a matter of perspective. Open to interpretation. Rarely clear-cut.

Life, she considered, was a word people used to describe a constant, unpredictable state of flux. Life was like the ocean with its hidden currents, its shifting moods, its beauty and threat – interchangeable and, ultimately, uncontrollable.

Sure, sometimes people played the winds, used the current, steered their intended path. Sometimes, though, the ocean took you as its plaything and, no matter whom you were, it did whatever it chose. In such times it taught you a lesson that was easy to miss when surrounded by the city and supported by your own success. It taught you how *small* you really were. How weak compared to nature's whim. It taught you that the ocean could swallow you up – completely and utterly – without even noticing that it had.

Anne-Marie was looking at the photos she kept on her iPhone. They were not the carefully created, professionally thought-out images that she was famous for. Rather, they were scenes from her life. They were each, in their own time and in their own way, driven by a common need to capture an experience and guarantee, in part at least, the accuracy of the memory.

Truthfully, though, Anne-Marie had never placed such importance on them before. The long-term need, whilst evident, had been more subconscious than explicit. Indeed, the more she thought about it, the more Anne-Marie was forced to accept the fact that she had taken these photos because everyone else did. It was fashionable to use your phone to record every social encounter. It was a social trend so powerful that it was almost compulsory to do so. And then, of course, the trend was to share them on Facebook with hundreds, possibly even thousands, of people you had never spoken to, let alone met, who were all labelled as 'friends.'

Anne-Marie wondered how her many friends, virtual and otherwise, would respond to her planned new Facebook page titled *Far from the Shore: The Life and Death of an Ovarian Cancer.*

She would use it, along with her blog and Twitter account, to alert as many women as possible to the danger of feeling immortal, of the need for regular health checks, of just what it was like to find yourself suddenly – terrifyingly! – far, far out of your depth. And, whether the cancer died first or she did, the publicity she attracted would help others and also, of course, help to disseminate her photographic essay. The most significant unknown in that regard was who, precisely, would take the final photo in the series?

Anne-Marie shivered as she contemplated the answer. The photos on her phone had now assumed a personal significance she could never before have imagined. The pictures she used to flick through occasionally when in a bar waiting for a friend, or when suddenly reminded of a past event, were suddenly vibrant and powerful and rich with emotion.

Yet distant.

They seemed so remote. And the danger was that they would become even more so. Much as she felt compelled to return to these pictures, Anne-Marie felt a force, a current, trying to pull her away from the normality she had been used to; away from those taken-for-granted things that were, she realised with a mixture of regret, shame and anger, the reflection of a happy life.

Anne-Marie looked at each photo, spending many minutes over each one, reminding herself as much as she possibly could about everything that went before and after, recreating the associated emotions as if they were a form of medication more powerful than any consultant's offering.

Cancer, she was going to tell the world, threatened to kill more than just a body.

In fact, the body was the very last thing a cancer killed. Before it managed to do that, cancer tried to destroy your connections with everyone and everything you held dear. Its devilish trick was to make you realise just how selfish and short-sighted you had been, how you had failed to appreciate how lucky you were, how you had failed to recognise the beauty in so many things, For Anne-Marie, a professional photographer who had prided herself on her ability to *see*, this awareness was at once a condemnation and a revelation. And, along with fighting the cancer, she found herself fighting a sense of self-disgust.

Why had it taken *this* to open her eyes?

It was the sort of question that could only be addressed from an emotional distance and creating any sort of emotional distance from anything was almost impossible for Anne-Marie right now. So, she had realised, it was essential that the emotions she created were as positive as possible. To do anything else would be to fuel the cancer, to give it precisely what it needed to grow.

That was not an option.

Anne-Marie was determined to use her learning, her new insights, to make herself stronger. She could – *would* – survive this. Then the new, improved, Anne-Marie, the one who had lost her fear, left behind her self-disgust, the one who for the first time ever truly understood the nature and importance of gratitude, would take even better photographs. And – far more importantly – see her world very differently and build even better relationships.

At the very heart of this would be rebuilding her relationship with Marcus. They had both been so intent over the years on developing their careers, and so supportive of each other in doing so, that they had slowly drifted apart. She still loved Marcus as much as she ever had, and she believed he loved her too, but there was a gap between them now that hadn't been there at the beginning. It was a gap, she feared, that would only widen if they – *she* – didn't address it and manage it and create for them both the opportunity to seal it with love.

The first step in this process would be returning home and telling him of her illness. Some secrets, she believed, actually helped a relationship to blossom, whilst some risked destroying it. She had to tell Marcus the truth about this. It wasn't just that she owed him that much; she owed *them* that much. And then she had to ask him for his help. Whilst the medical consultant focused on surgery and drugs, Anne-Marie knew that her mental state was at least as important in the battle ahead. She just happened to live with, and love, a man who was the best in the world at influencing and changing peoples' minds.

Strangely, alone in the cottage on the edge of the moor, Anne-Marie couldn't help but wonder if that was a blessing or a curse.

32.

Paul Clusker had not known when he kissed his wife goodbye that he would never see her again; that his life would soon be ended. He couldn't have known. Most people never know which is to be their last day on earth. In fact, during his last few hours of life – at least those hours before the killer visited him – Paul Clusker had been looking forward to the future.

For the first time in years he had felt truly invigorated, as if the energy he had known as a young man was suddenly returning. He had a sense that he could now breathe new life into his business. More than that, Paul felt that he would be reasserting his presence in the world and, significantly, escaping some of the ghosts of his past, finally silencing his father's whisperings, his own self-doubt.

'I, Paul Clusker, am going to control time: the past, the present and the future,' he had told himself out loud just a second before his doorbell rang.

Paul hadn't been expecting any visitors and he instinctively glanced at his watch as he made his way into the hall. Through the frosted glass in the front door he could make out a single figure, standing motionless. It was impossible to see any features, but from the size and shape Paul presumed it was a man and there was something undeniably familiar about him.

Paul opened the door, smiling a welcome as he always did. His smile broadened as familiarity turned into recognition. 'Well! This is an unexpected surprise!' He said. 'Please, come in.'

Paul stepped to one side, gesturing towards the hall with his left arm. The killer accepted the invitation, regarding it silently as the first of several offerings. He walked without hesitation into the dining room. Paul closed the front door and followed, unsure whether he should be excited or concerned.

'Are you going to have to change our schedule?' He asked. 'Is that why you're here?'

The killer shook his head. 'Not at all. In fact, nothing could be further from the truth.'

'Oh.' Paul didn't quite understand what the other man meant, but decided swiftly against asking for clarification; he didn't want to appear stupid. 'Can I get you a drink?'

The killer shook his head for a second time. 'There's something very important that I want to share with you,' he said. 'I think it will really help you to gain clarity. And we both know the value of that.'

Paul sat down on one of the dining room chairs. He thought it strange that his visitor had walked into this room and not the lounge. More than that, however, he really wanted to know what was so important that it couldn't wait until their next planned meeting. As he trusted the other man's expertise completely he found himself agreeing willingly and easily. 'Yes. Yes, of course. I'm all ears.'

The killer laughed and Paul tried to follow suit, his confusion deepening. 'Trust me,' the killer said, 'you are far more than that.' He paused, looking out for a moment through the window at the beautifully tended garden. 'Nature in the winter,' he whispered. 'Sharing so much colour, daring us to look. If only you knew how.' The killer shook his head a third time, only now it seemed to Paul that he was reflecting on a mystery rather than answering a question.

'I see the colours in the garden,' the killer said. 'The colours that are invisible to you, the colours that move, the colours with scent. I see them as clearly as I see your confusion. And when your confusion turns into realisation, then disbelief and then, inevitably, into fear, I will see the colours change. My experience will be so very different from yours.'

'Why...why should I become afraid?'

'Because you are human. Because, so far, your understanding of your own mortality is intellectual. You know that sooner or later there will come a day when you will die. You know that no one lives forever. You know that your body and brain must eventually perish. You know this and yet you live in denial because your intellect, your conscious mind, cannot truly imagine its own non-existence. Its need for facts and proof and so-called logic is ignored conveniently in the face of this, its own ultimate limitation. Its arrogance is at once appalling and appealing in the most perverse of ways. You see, Paul, your conscious mind believes it is the master of creation, the greatest force in the universe. And it is so very, very wrong. It is the silence behind the conscious mind that is the source of our power – of *all* power. It is within the silence of the subconscious that we truly live and die.'

'Why are you telling me this? How does it help with –'

'Ssshh!' The killer raised the index finger of his right hand to his lips. 'Be silent. It is the first step towards becoming the silence. And true insight – the most profound insight – can only be achieved when we move beyond being silent and *become* the silence.' The killer nodded an affirmation and Paul followed suit automatically. 'Your future, Paul, is in sight.' The killer's voice softened, becoming as warm and inviting as a favourite bed. 'At least, it is within my sight. And it cannot be avoided. So, as you sit here listening to me now just give yourself permission to wander inwards into the silence that is waiting for you, that is you, that is everything and everywhere. Just follow your in-breath, easily, naturally, letting it lead you, carry you, support you. Just trust what you are feeling now. Let your eyes close, easily, naturally…That's the way…And follow it now…Breathe in…Deeper….And deeper still…Let the different parts of you come together in the deepening silence…Becoming one…That's the way…Just breathe in…Just follow…'

Two hours later the killer had completed everything he had to do. He had finished *looking*.

He ended Paul Clusker's life swiftly and painlessly.

In his final seconds, as his heart stopped and his body began to close down, Paul thought that he heard in the deepest recess of his mind a single, faint, voice, distanced by the silence that was now as tangible, pervasive and dense as the thickest fog. He thought he heard the voice of Diane, his wife, calling his name.

33.

Peter Jones had never before felt the two parts of his *self* come face-to-face, let alone in a way that threatened to become confrontational. But, then, he had never before been in charge of an investigation to which his best friend was connected. Which meant that until the evidence proved otherwise, Marcus was a potential suspect.

For Peter Jones, the *man*, that was an impossible thought. Marcus was undoubtedly an arrogant, self-assured expert; the sort who provided solutions when no one else could, even though he did so in a way that made him almost unbearable. Of course, the people he helped were always grateful and usually amazed by his ability. They just rarely liked him.

Peter agreed wholeheartedly with Marcus's analogy. From Peter's perspective Marcus was like the world's greatest surgeon. He was precisely the sort of person you wanted to have working for you when you were facing a significant and specific threat. However, you were unconscious when your surgeon did his or her most important work. You had to actually engage – *cope* – with Marcus when he did his.

It had always been a source of amusement, confusion and concern for Peter that his friend, the world's greatest communications expert, failed to communicate personally in ways that made people like him.

Perhaps, Peter thought, *being fully aware and in control of one's own self-image is an even greater challenge than helping others with seemingly unsolvable problems?*

As a detective, Peter Jones helped others as a consequence of what he did, not because helping others was his primary concern. Only now, as Peter Jones the detective felt himself challenged by Peter Jones the man, he found himself wondering just what that meant.

Was he actually as remote from others, as distanced and detached, as Marcus? After all, he felt nothing – *nothing* – when addressing even the most violent and perverse of crimes, other than a desire to identify and apprehend the perpetrator, to win the game.

Yet for the victim, their family and friends, even their neighbours, this was anything but a game. This was the most terrifying of all possibilities. For them, this was life and death, raw and unwelcome and so shockingly invasive it cast an inescapable shadow over their lives.

For Peter it was his job. Nothing more. Admittedly, it was often all consuming, but that wasn't because of the detective's sense of humanity, rather because of his need to succeed.

Interesting, Peter thought as he headed down the corridor towards the meeting room and his waiting team, *all these years of knowing how I operate, how I function in my role, and I've never thought to question it before.*

That's because it's a futile question, a pointless challenge, the detective replied instantly. *The only thing that matters is that you get the right result as quickly as possible. Stop comparing yourself to Marcus. He can afford to create a caring persona if he wants to. He has that luxury. If he chooses to ignore it, that's up to him. You, however, don't. You don't have any luxuries. You just have a purpose. So shut the fuck up and do what you do best.*

Peter nodded as he opened the door and stepped into the room to greet his team. 'Everyone here?' He glanced left and right as he moved to the front of the room. His question was met with some grunts of acknowledgement mingling with a chorus of 'Yes, Boss.'

'Good. Let's make this short, sharp and to the point. Effectiveness and efficiency are as important as they've ever been in this case.' Peter looked at each member of his team briefly and deliberately. Everyone was present: both detective sergeants and all eight detective constables. They were his. Some had been with him for years, others only months, but they had all made a commitment to him and he to them. They would stay with him, he knew, until a better option came along. For these men and women that would mean only one thing: promotion and the chance to move up the career ladder. In their current roles they were part of the best team possible. They all knew that.

Peter asked key individuals to provide a brief summary of their most recent enquiries. This was the formal activity at the heart of their daily routine. Any significant discoveries were relayed to him instantly as the enquiry progressed. However it was vitally important that the team met regularly, that everyone heard what was happening, that they all felt an important part of the process, that they were reminded constantly why their individual work mattered.

Everyone in the team knew exactly what Peter required. They all knew that anything less would lead to a sharp put-down. When you worked with the best you followed their instructions to the letter, you adopted their procedures, you met their requirements. There was no alternative, not if you wanted to stay on the team, not if you wanted to learn.

Peter listened to the updates. He asked questions even when he already knew the answers. He made sure that his team felt connected to each other and to him. He had learnt a long time ago that he couldn't win the game on his own. He knew that the greatest paradox was that the people in his team were there because of him and yet he was nothing without them. As he had said once to Nic, 'It's funny, I'm the leader and the teacher and the people I lead and teach don't realise that if they walk away, I'm neither.' Nic had chuckled and replied, 'It's a pity that Marcus doesn't understand that. If he did, he would be even more amazing.'

Now, though, Peter had something of his own that he wanted to share – and ask – the team. And he would take their response seriously. Whenever he asked them a question he was always willing to be influenced by their reply, everyone in the room knew that, it was one of his characteristics that drew them to him. In an organisation that required and created confident, often arrogant leaders, Jonah was an alpha male of the highest order. His most special skill was that he made every member of his team feel valued even though they knew that he called the tune.

'Right,' Peter said, 'I want to talk to you about Marcus Kline. He's connected to this case.'

Everyone knew the name. Those who had been with Peter the longest exchanged glances, aware of the friendship between the two men. Peter's voice was emotionless as he spoke. 'There's a very clear association between Marcus Kline and Paul Clusker, our latest victim. Not only that, Marcus Kline contacted me last night with what he thought was evidence of a connection between himself and the killer. At the time I wasn't convinced. Now, though, we have to consider the possibility that he was right.'

'Are there any other possibilities that we ought to consider?' A young Detective Constable, new to the team, asked the question. The implication was clear: was Marcus Kline at risk or was he, in fact, a possible suspect?

Peter didn't hesitate. 'Marcus Kline's name goes on the board along with everyone else.' He gestured perfunctorily to the white board with its headlines, categories, names and parameters. It was the visual day-to-day summary of the investigation. 'And you all know that when someone's on the board all things are possible until we prove they are not. Once we have disproved everything else, what we are left with is what actually happened. So...' Peter took a breath, '...My question to you all is, should I tell the Boss about Marcus Kline or should we wait and see what else turns up?'

It was a genuine question. The others, especially the senior officers, knew that Peter would listen to their advice carefully. As the DCI, Peter was obliged to keep Detective Superintendent Michael Briggs informed of developments. He also had to make constant judgement calls about what he did or didn't report – and when. The sudden involvement of someone with whom Peter had a personal relationship was a delicate matter that would require careful handling. The room fell silent for several seconds as people considered the options and their possible implications. This time the younger officers waited for their more seasoned colleagues to reply.

'Not yet.' DS Kevin McNeill offered the answer. 'The only reason to do so at this stage would be because of your connection to Kline – it's not as if we have any real reason to think that he's a significant factor in all of this – and no one here or outside the team doubts your professionalism Boss. Given that, I don't think it needs to go any higher. Not yet, anyway.'

The conclusion was greeted by several nods that were matched by one from Peter. 'That's my instinct too, to be honest with you Kev. We'll keep it amongst ourselves for now then.'

'And we'll keep our fingers crossed that he stays on the edge of the investigation.' It was the young DC who had spoken earlier. 'That'll be best for all.'

'You can't do detective work with your fingers crossed,' Peter replied sharply. 'You have to get your fingers into everything and follow where the evidence leads. If you want to spend your time doing wishful thinking, go home, put some porn on, and imagine that you're right in the middle of it.'

'Or that your cock's as big as the bloke's in the film!' McNeill roared with laughter and everyone joined in.

Peter let them all laugh, giving them a moment to reinforce their sense of hierarchy and camaraderie, giving himself a moment to gather his thoughts; to make sure that his own fingers weren't crossed.

34.

Nicholas Evans was concerned. The most important person in his life was behaving in a way that he had never experienced before.

Nic always felt a significant degree of stress whenever Peter was involved in a major investigation. He always wondered how his partner was able to shoulder the burden without any obvious sign of effort. He always then reminded himself that it was possible because he, Nic, silently and inevitably took the weight of Peter's world on his own shoulders, too. Now, though, despite the fact that Nic was taking even more of the strain than normal, Peter was clearly feeling a pressure that was unprecedented.

Last night, maybe half an hour after Marcus left, Peter had received a phone call and gone out immediately without a single word of explanation. When he returned Nic had pretended to be asleep. He had sensed the tension gripping Peter's body as he lay next to him. Later Nic had watched with ever growing concern, as a nightmare rumbled through Peter's sleep like a violent storm.

Twice Nic had tried to wake Peter, saying his name, shaking him gently by the shoulder. It had been futile.

The nightmare was all consuming. Even when Nic thought that it had passed and that Peter was freed from its grip, the nightmare reached out again and drew him back in. Nic felt stranded on the periphery, desperate to help but not knowing how without becoming even more assertive than the dream that was raging. And of that he was incapable.

So the night passed with Nic doing everything in his power to stay awake, to watch over his lover. Occasionally he fell asleep despite his best efforts not to, but an instinct even greater than the need for rest kept forcing him back to consciousness.

The morning brought no respite. News of the second murder released a visible tremble of adrenaline through Peter's body. It was followed by a setting of his features and a change in his eyes as if some invisible, impenetrable filter had coated them; preparing him for whatever he had to look at, creating both a distance and a perspective from which he would operate until the investigation was over.

Nic had never seen Peter like this before. The difference was reinforced some hours later. Peter's voicemail response to Nic's simple question, 'Are you OK?' had been a shocking revelation.

It wasn't just what Peter had said that sent shivers through Nic. Rather it was the cold, *cold* tone of his voice, the sound of a man steeling himself to face the unimaginable.

'Am I OK?' Peter had repeated the question and followed it with a brief, harsh laugh. 'I'm better than some I can think of. Nobody's bagged me yet.' A slight pause and then, 'Possibilities my love. Sometimes I think that life keeps us busy so that we don't have time to consider all the possibilities. That's how it stops us from going mad.

Even if we've got everything we could possibly want, we are still only ever hanging on by a thread.' Another pause. 'I explore possibilities. It's what I'm trained to do. No matter what.'

The message had ended without warning. Nic had stared, motionless, at the phone in his hand. He knew Peter better than anyone else on the planet, better even in many ways than Marcus Kline. Nic knew Peter the way only a true lover, a soul mate, can know someone. He could read Peter's mind and mood so swiftly and easily it felt intuitive. And he had never before heard such a mix of emotion in his partner's voice. It was a mixture of resolute intent, fear and uncertainty – of not knowing – that made Nic think of an explorer committed to walking a previously untrodden path that was fraught with danger. Moreover, it was the voice of a man walking the path alone.

Suddenly Nic felt helpless. He didn't know how to carry a burden he couldn't identify. He didn't how to support Peter when it felt as if he was being deliberately left behind in a way that he never had been before.

When the pair had first realised that their relationship had the potential to be the special one, the subject of Peter's commitment to his job had been the topic of much discussion. Nic had been shocked to learn that in the 1960s the police contract had included a clause that stated that the job was more important than family. By the time Peter had joined the force, years later, the clause had been removed. The job, however, had not needed a contract to capture Peter's physical and emotional energy. As he had risen through the ranks his focus had grown commensurately.

Nic had made it clear from the beginning that he wasn't prepared to take second place to Peter's work. Peter had assured him that he wouldn't. It was only as the years passed that Nic had come to realise that his demand had been nonsensical and that Peter's assurance had been sincere, truly meant and, paradoxically, irrelevant.

Peter *was* a detective. It wasn't his job, it was *him*; fuelled by an innate, powerful and, at times, almost overwhelming need to win. Nic had learnt to accept that if you chose to live with a detective the question, 'Am I – are *we* – more important than your job?' was pointless. The honest answer, the one that no detective would ever give to their partner and which no partner would ever tolerate, was, 'Yes and no.'

In one sense it was like asking a parent which of their children they loved the most. The answer was all of them equally and differently.

That was Nic's understanding. Peter loved him more than anyone else. When he took phone calls in the middle of the night, when he worked an eighty hour week, when he cancelled dinner dates at the last minute because something had come up, he was just doing what the job demanded and, far more importantly, what he was trained to do. Nic had long since acknowledged the complex trade off that he was required to make to ensure that the most important relationship in both of their lives survived and grew.

Which was why Peter's voice message had been so upsetting. Peter was clearly dealing with something that was shockingly new and, given that he only ever shared carefully selected details with Nic, there was now a gap being created between them. Nic resolved to push Peter for as much information as possible – if only to watch Peter's response as he worked out just what to say. Before then, though, he had one other helpful source he could turn to. He phoned Marcus Kline.

The consultant listened in silence to Nic's concerns. Then he said, 'You have to let Peter go where this particular path takes him. Deep down you know that. That's why you're scared. I told you after I'd watched the film of the first crime scene that this case was going to turn into a nightmare –'

Nic flinched automatically at the word.

' – and it's one that you won't be able to share with him. To be frank, it's best that you don't even try. You are no more equipped to manage this than Peter is to present a lecture on the extent to which cinema reflects or creates society. If my sense of this is right, the only thing I would remind you of is that I recognised a feeling of urgency connected to the first killing, an imminent deadline. The fact that poor Paul Clusker was killed so soon after the first victim supports that.'

'So what are you saying, that it's going to be over soon?'

'One way or the other, yes.'

'What does that mean?' Nic's voice raised as anxiety squeezed his insides. His greatest, most secret fear had always been that in one case, one day, Peter would become the hunted rather than the hunter, that a killer would target his life-partner.

'It means that we can't know for certain how things are going to end.' Marcus replied calmly, as if he hadn't noticed the shift in Nic. 'We don't know who the killer is, or what his motive is. We don't know who the next victim will be, or if, indeed, there will be one. We don't know if Peter will be able to catch this man, or if he will just disappear.'

'Do you think that's possible?'

'Why not? Some people like to keep secrets. There can't be a much greater secret to keep than knowing that you are a killer who got away with it.'

'Do you think when it's over, that we will all be OK?'

'No. No, actually I don't.' Marcus's voice seemed suddenly far away. 'I fear that we will all be wiser – in ways that we wish we weren't.'

The certainty in Marcus's voice made Nic wish that he hadn't asked the question in the first place.

35.

Anne-Marie didn't want to keep her secret any longer. Just realising that fact made her feel lighter. The intellectual decision to return home and share her plight with Marcus had turned surprisingly quickly into a source of emotional comfort. From now on her photographic essay would include him as well as her, the two of them using their special relationship and their talents to share something with the world and, even more importantly, to save her life.

Alone in her cottage Anne-Marie had discovered that whilst she was understandably afraid of dying, she was also afraid of losing. She had never known that about herself before. But, then, she had never even come close to losing before. Not really. Not in anything that mattered. In fact, she had never really considered things in terms of winning and losing before. Throughout her life, whenever she had wanted something she had simply worked out – and worked at – the best way of getting it. It hadn't crossed her mind that in doing so she was possibly beating, or denying, someone else. She hadn't known that she was competitive. If asked, she would have simply said that she was 'goal focused'. Now she realised that was nonsense.

Anne-Marie wanted to *win*. She could feel the urge coursing through her system more clearly and powerfully than she had ever yet felt the cancer. She wanted to win not just to avoid the possible pain and fear of death, but also because she now had someone else in her life that she truly wanted to get to know a whole lot better.

That person was herself.

During the solitude of her last few days, Anne-Marie had come to understand that she had been living her life unaware of just who she really was. True, she knew – and was happy to know – Anne-Marie the partner to Marcus Kline, Anne-Marie the good and loyal friend to a chosen few and, of course, Anne-Marie the photographer. It was just that she had never encountered before the real, secret, silent Anne-Marie, the essence from which all those different parts of herself emanated.

Encountered?

God forbid, she had never even considered its – *her* – existence. And it wasn't as if she had come to the cottage, to the moor, searching for her hidden self. Truth be told, she had come here to escape; as if by changing the environment she could somehow miraculously change what was inside her.

No, the silent heart of Anne-Marie had made itself known unexpectedly, like a warm, caring neighbour introducing herself for the very first time.

It happened after she had decided to return home. She had been in the kitchen, sipping a peppermint tea, thinking for some reason about her garden, about the willow tree, about the fact that it would be there long after she and Marcus had left the house. Her thoughts meandered gently towards a simple insight: she didn't really own anything.

Not permanently. Not forever. She and Marcus both said that they owned the house – after all, the mortgage was paid – but the truth was it would be someone else's home one day. They certainly didn't own the willow tree. It belonged to the earth, or maybe the sky, or maybe both, but it was definitely beyond any form of human ownership. In one sense, Anne-Marie reflected, even her relationship with Marcus was on loan. She couldn't keep it forever. It had to end. One way or another.

The very unusual thing about this particular train of thought and the revelations it uncovered, was as much to do with where it seemed to be coming from as where it was leading. The thoughts seemed to be floating inside her, released from a previously unacknowledged source. It was as if they came from a part of her that was unaffected by everything that was going on in her life. A part of her that had waited until now before making itself known; a part that, unlike every other part of her, was freed rather than restricted by the cancer. Anne-Marie realised at one point that she was actually thinking about her lack of ownership -which, not so very long ago, would have signified to her a lack of power and control – with a genuine smile on her face.

How could that be possible?

'Perhaps,' Anne-Marie said suddenly, 'I'm going mad? Mad because I feel so alone right now, because I'm terrified of the illness, because I haven't had, and probably need, counselling.'

The thoughts that were floating beyond her conscious control seemed to dance with joy at the sound of the words. It appeared to Anne-Marie that the thoughts were listening and responding to a form of music rather than a despairing question. How could that be? And who are you – exactly – if you can hear your own fear and find within it a reason for celebration? The innermost Anne-Marie responded by releasing another thought in front of her, encouraging her to follow. Although she couldn't hear it in the usual way, couldn't turn it into words in her conscious mind, Anne-Marie sensed the answer; more accurately, she felt a *connection* she had never experienced before.

It was not just a connection between question and answer. No, it was far more significant than that, far more complete. It was a seamless connection with everything around her. It was, she would write in her diary later, the nearest thing she could imagine to a state of bliss.

Anne-Marie was unsure how long the experience lasted. Inevitably, though, her mind considered the possibility that the state could not continue indefinitely and then she felt an urgency to maintain it and then, of course, the state just disappeared. Almost at once her conscious mind reminded her of the cancer...

Anne-Marie stood up from the kitchen chair. She looked out of the window. She needed to see the willow tree. She needed to re-connect with Marcus. She would win, she told herself, because now more than ever before she had a purpose, a reason, an overwhelming need to meet her true self again.

Anne-Marie had another even more significant insight: she had just had the most profound experience of her life. And it hadn't crossed her mind, not once, to try and take a photo of it.

36.

Marcus Kline had cancelled all of his scheduled meetings after Peter's visit to his office. He spoke to no one from the moment Peter left until Nic's phone call. He spent the time simply replaying the conversation – the *interview* – with Peter over and over in his mind.

'What you need to remember is that I'm the detective here.' Peter had said towards the end. 'I neither need nor appreciate you trying to read my mind – '

'I'm not trying,' Marcus interjected.

' – And I certainly don't need you *trying* to assume control.'

The emphasis on the word and all that it implied marked the battleground as clearly as any geographical space ever had. The two men held each other's gaze. Neither moved. The contest of wills demanded all of their attention. Marcus saw a coldness in Peter's eyes that he never had before. The real man, he realised, was hiding behind the detective's obligation…To win, all Marcus had to do was tease him out.

Marcus wanted to win. The question he had to answer, however, was did he want to win a battle now or the war later? The response flashed into his mind almost immediately. He had invested too much into *this* to risk losing it because of an over-reaction now. He couldn't afford to push Peter too far. Not yet. There would be time enough for that later. Assuming the detective behaved as Marcus expected him to.

Marcus had blinked and looked down at his desktop. 'I am very clear about who is in control,' he said. He breathed high in his chest as he spoke, the unusual sensation making him swallow as he knew it would; making him look and sound nervous, giving out the signals of a man who was beaten. 'I didn't mean to question your role or your professionalism. You need to remember that this is a most unusual situation for me even though it isn't for you.'

Marcus had looked back up at the detective. He broke eye contact after only a few seconds. He was, he knew, demonstrating submission.

'Actually it's an unusual situation for both of us,' Peter replied in exactly the way Marcus expected him to. A smile flickered across Peter's face. For a moment it looked as if the friend was going to come to the fore. Then the detective reasserted himself. 'However unusual it is, though, it's one that I'm paid to manage. The fact that we are best friends and you have some insights into the investigation is neither here nor there. I do my job to the best of my ability regardless of who is involved.'

Marcus nodded thoughtfully, keeping his breathing high and shallow, sure that the time was right to make his final play. 'Intellectually I understand that, of course I do. I guess I just thought – hoped if I'm being honest – that you might not find it so easy to do. You know, with me.'

Peter frowned. 'Are you telling me that you couldn't, if

the roles were reversed?'

'How can I answer that? I could never do your job,' Marcus said. 'And I wouldn't want to, you know that. I'd hate having to be suspicious of everyone.'

Peter looked at him closely. 'Don't play games with me, Marcus. Not in this. There are lives at stake. Maybe yours.'

Marcus tipped his head. 'In more ways than one perhaps. Hmmm? As a victim or as the killer. That's what you're thinking, isn't it? We're back to where we started the interview.'

'It's been a conversation, not an interview.' Peter leant forwards, tapping the desktop with his fingertips. 'People who are connected to a serious investigation can either help or hinder our enquiry. Sometimes they help most by doing nothing at all. Remember that.'

Peter left without saying another word. Marcus saw the swirl of emotions inside the detective as he walked out of the office. He saw them and kept them at bay, aware of how they lapped against the edges of his disassociated state before turning back from whence they had come.

His reverie had been interrupted by Nic's unexpected phone call. It quickly became clear that Nic had no idea of Marcus's connection to the second killing, or of Peter's recent visit. Everything Nic said confirmed what the consultant had already determined about Peter's internal struggle. He responded to Nic in a way that he was sure Peter would find believable if Nic mentioned it to him. It was also, more importantly, in a way that would remind and reinforce with Nic that the situation was going to get a whole lot worse before it had any chance of getting better.

After Marcus's final review of Nic's phone call he was ready to move on. He called Simon into his office.

His protégé was there within seconds. He still had the shiny, bright air of a person who had just achieved a very significant emotional goal. Marcus didn't invite him to sit down and he didn't waste any time on preliminaries.

'It changes, doesn't it?' He said, without giving Simon any chance to unpack the question let alone reply. 'When we achieve something we didn't believe we could, something that really matters, we are given the very great opportunity to learn something about our own qualities. And if we grab hold of that learning and internalise it, we become instantly capable of achieving even greater things. You do understand that, don't you?'

Simon had no alternative but to nod in agreement. Marcus matched the movement and then went on, 'When Cassandra agreed to go on a date with you she was inadvertently teaching you a lesson. You see, sometimes we don't think that we are good enough. We don't believe that we are worthy of achieving our desired outcome. However, the inescapable truth is that someone has to be that successful. Someone has to be the best in any given domain. Someone has to live the life of their dreams. Someone has to become the calm centre of the storm that is raging around them. Sometimes they have to be the calm centre of the story they create.'

Marcus relaxed back into his chair. He saw Simon relax, too. Marcus waited for a brief moment before speaking again, letting Simon follow his silent lead, waiting until Simon was completely in sync with him before saying, 'Those people who fail to achieve their potential – and that is most of the human race – do so because their negative personal beliefs blind them to the positive feedback they receive that not only challenges those beliefs, it actually proves the opposite to be true. You took so long to achieve this outcome with Cassandra because of your negative self-beliefs. That's OK, sort of, as long as you recognise the feedback, accept it, and change your behaviours accordingly. You do understand, don't you?'

Simon nodded again. Marcus remained silent until Simon felt obliged to ask, 'That's what I have to do, isn't it, if I want to become like you?'

'It's one of the things, yes. And it's one of the most important things. Everybody talks and writes about the need to get and learn from feedback. However, only the very best are willing, and know how, to really do this. To respond to feedback appropriately and powerfully means being willing to let go of things you have previously held dear. The paradox is that sometimes the feedback is flawed. So even though that feedback challenges our beliefs we have to ignore it. It requires as much training and skill to be able to deliver great feedback as it does to interpret and respond to feedback. If we seek to become great we need to know how to manage both. The person who gets the balance right rules the world.'

'You are one of those people.' Simon offered this as an acknowledgement rather than a question.

Marcus nodded. 'Yes. I can achieve anything I set my mind to.' He looked at Simon very differently to how he had looked at Peter. Now his breathing was low in his stomach. He felt as if he was living in his spine, from his coccyx to the back of his head. He was, he knew, creating a very different outcome. He said, 'Truthfully, no one is safe around me.'

They both understood that in different ways. They both smiled.

When Simon left work he felt more confident, more sure of himself and his future, than ever before.

The third killing changed everything completely and irreversibly.

PART THREE

Listening

37.

Everything changes. Always. That is the only certainty. Sometimes people learn because of change, sometimes they create change because of what they have learnt. Change is inevitable. Learning is not. I learn through the changes I am creating.

I am so very different from the herd. The herd is made up of individuals who have forgotten – actually, they never realised nor went in search of – their own potential. Instead they chose to lose themselves in the wasteland of conformity. The herd is made up of pack animals. They hope, individually, that they won't be noticed, that they won't stand out. They make noise, they talk as if they know how everything should be and yet, at the same time, they explain how they would do it all differently if they could have their time again. They tell themselves and everyone who will listen what they would do, what others should do, whilst they only follow the herd.

They speak only to hear their words reinforced. They have no idea how to truly listen to the sounds around them or the sounds they create. They do not know that listening is the greatest and most challenging art. One cannot look deeply and with true insight until one has learnt how to listen, how to see the brightness, the variety, in sound.

Despite the significance of what I am doing – of what I am going to do – none of you will see clearly. Despite the way my actions will echo throughout time, none of you will hear clearly.

Most people fear losing their sight more than they do their hearing. Those people are wrong. The other senses compensate for loss of sight far more readily and easily than they do for loss of hearing. That is because there is no compensation for loss of hearing.

The tragedy is that most people are deaf and they don't even realise it.

Most people – people like you – keep their gaze down and their ears tuned in to the collective murmur of the herd.

I am not a pack animal, a member of the herd. I am a predator simply because I seek to learn. I am successful because I have mastered the art of listening. That is why I see with such clarity the things that others do not. That is why I am ready to see what no one else ever has.

If you wish to step away from the herd and begin your own development, you need to understand this one thing:

Creation begins with sound.

In the beginning was the Word – and that only had power because it could be heard. That is the secret meaning in the writing. Words don't have power if they can't resonate. That requires a receptacle, a listener.

I am that listener.

I select my prey with care. I talk to them so that I can listen. I listen so that I can see.

You cannot imagine what it is like to live behind my eyes.

You cannot imagine how colourful my hearing is.

And don't ever think – don't you dare ever think – that you hear me now. Don't you dare ever think that I either want or need you to. I know the breadth of your failings. I know who I am communicating with.

You don't.

38.

Peter Jones was standing in the private garden at the rear of Harts Hotel. He was looking out over The Park where Marcus Kline lived, and beyond as far as Ratcliffe on Soar Power Station. He was sipping a glass of sparkling mineral water, trying to make sense of what was going on inside his head. He had decided that he wouldn't have another glass of red wine, or any other alcohol for that matter, until the investigation was over. He needed to be mentally alert, at his very best, day and night for as long as it took.

Only he didn't feel at his best. He felt as if he was being pulled in different directions. He was angry with Marcus, annoyed with himself, scared about what was going to happen next, and all too aware of the mounting political pressure the case was creating. All he had, the source of his strength, was his sense of professionalism and process, his belief in what it meant to be a detective, his trust in his team and his determination to win.

In the past that had always been enough – more than enough. Now, though, Peter was feeling more emotional pressure than ever before. After all, Marcus was a person of interest in the investigation. Dammit! He was a possible suspect. He was a potential victim. He was a man who could read your face, your mind, like it was an open book. Peter knew that however skilled he was as a detective, he couldn't hope to beat Marcus in a war of words. He couldn't possibly interview, influence or negotiate with him successfully.

So what should he do?

Peter drank from his glass and took in the view. He felt as if he was above the noise of the city. Below him, and for as far as he could see, thousands of lives played out their span oblivious to the challenges he faced; oblivious often, he suspected, to the challenges they faced.

Peter came here whenever he needed to get an overview of a complex investigation. He had never needed it more than he did now. Only now the power of Marcus Kline, his relationship with Marcus Kline, was blurring his vision. He was finding it almost impossible to dismiss Marcus's voice from his mind. And he needed to.

Peter looked out to the distant horizon and let his mind wander. His thoughts drifted back to the first time he had knowingly put his life at risk in pursuit of a criminal.

Karl Brent had been in charge of a major drugs empire. Clever enough to have built a successful legitimate business, Brent had chosen a very different endeavour and lifestyle. A calculating, ruthless and determined professional criminal of the old school, Brent had shared Peter's understanding of the game the two men were engaged in. They had treated each other with what could only have been described as a form of mutual respect, and yet both recognised they were playing for the very highest stakes.

Peter knew with the right evidence and a skilled barrister Brent would be facing at least twenty five years in prison. He also knew that Brent wanted him dead.

The game between them had gone on for over two years, a constant and dominant thread running through their working lives. During that time Peter investigated and solved several other significant cases, but his patient information gathering and, at times, deliberate baiting of Brent continued throughout.

Sometimes he would make a point of having a drink in Brent's local pub. Sometimes he would visit the criminal at his home. Whenever the two men were face-to-face, they each shared a silent promise with the other and neither man blinked. Peter came to know Brent's face better than he knew his own.

Such was the acknowledged level of risk that Peter and every member of his team had a panic alarm fitted in their homes. If pressed it would automatically summon an armed response unit. Peter had downplayed the threat with Nic. Indeed, he had actually believed his own line that, 'Brent would only come after me as a last resort. He's a top-rate professional. He knows that I'm only doing my job, just as he believes that he's only doing his. And he knows the heat that would come down on him, and stay down on him, if something happened to me.'

Nic had not been reassured. 'How am I supposed to stay calm during this?' He had asked.

Peter's initial reply, 'Try using it creatively; write it up as a film script,' had not been well received. The two years had been an increasingly testing time for their relationship. They had made it through though, and it had helped them realise they could get through anything together.

It had been vital, of course, that Peter win the game. And he did. Brent's trial had been a high security affair, with armed police escorting the criminal to and from the courtroom, stopping traffic en route to ensure a clear path, whilst a helicopter stayed overhead observing everything that was happening. Armed police guards stood outside the court throughout the trial and armed detectives sat in the actual courtroom. The evidence against Brent had been compelling. The security measures served not only to deter any attempt to break Brent free, they also told the jurors in no uncertain terms that this was a significantly dangerous criminal. Both factors combined to ensure a guilty verdict. The expected twenty five years were duly administered.

Peter's reputation as a fearless and unrelenting detective was established as a consequence. He also learnt something important about himself. He could manage challenging new experiences as if he had encountered them before. The secret, he realised, was to always act as if you are doing something for the second, third, fourth or even fifth time, but never as if for the first. That way you never show vulnerability and you inspire confidence in those around you.

It was one of the secrets upon which he had built his success.

Now, as he looked over the treetops to the grey, threatening clouds that spewed from the power station's unrelenting towers, Peter asked himself the necessary question, *'Just what would I do with this situation, with Marcus Kline, if I had experienced it before?'*

The answer popped into his mind with surprising ease. *'Be his friend, not a detective. Whenever you are with Marcus forget that he is a person of interest. Never consider that, God forbid, he might be the killer or the next victim. You cannot hide your thoughts from him, so don't try. Just be his best friend – which, after all, you are. Let your team investigate Marcus and make them do so, wherever possible, from long-distance. That way he has nothing to interpret and no one to influence. That's how you win this game.'*

Peter nodded. The smoke from the power station was blowing to the east, away from the city. Patches of blue sky were showing through the November cloud. Peter found the hint of colour somehow reassuring. He was ready to go back to work. He had a way forward now. He finished his drink and saluted the horizon.

Peter was right, from his vantage point he was above the noise of the city. He was right about the many lives playing out below and beyond him. He was right about the need to do new things as if they had been experienced before. Ultimately, though, despite his skill as a detective and the many lessons he had learned over the years, he still couldn't see or hear the detail of what was happening.

He didn't know that the killer was killing again.

He didn't know that the challenge he was about to face was going to make everything that had gone before seem simple by comparison.

39.

Simon Westbury lived alone in a two bedroomed third floor apartment in Castle Quays, a contemporary development less than a thirty minute walk from the offices of **Influence.** From his balcony Simon had views onto the canal and, even when the weather was chill, he would drink his first and last coffees of the day standing outside enjoying the view. He found that he experienced both a sense of calm and a sense of achievement looking down on the water, observing how it attracted life to its constant, gentle flow.

Simon was not usually on his balcony in the middle of a workday. He was usually in the office. Today, though, Marcus had given him the unexpected task of preparing a hypothetical workshop for Dean Harrison and his senior management team and, even more surprisingly, he had told him that he could work on it at home. Simon had been embarrassed by the fact that Harrison knew his phone call of a few days ago had been both over-enthusiastic and inappropriate. He wondered if this so-called hypothetical workshop might lead eventually to him actually delivering it. He found it hard to imagine that Marcus did not have a plan and purpose of his own connected to the activity.

Simon had been working on it non-stop since before 9am and he was now taking a ten minute break, watching people walk along the canal path, smiling to himself at the sheer optimism of the solitary and, presumably, very cold fisherman who sat unmoving, fixed on the subtle interplay between his line and the water.

It didn't take much, Simon considered, for people to feel that they had managed to get away from it all. For his own part all he had to do was stand on his balcony and watch the world go by. Or in the case of the fisherman, going nowhere.

Just associations and influence, he reminded himself. Just like Marcus Kline says. We create associations with places, people, objects – sometimes without even realising that we are doing it – and then they shape our lives. The canal has always been more than just a routeway. It means so many different things to so many different people. It influences without even trying...

Below him, the fisherman reached into his bag, took out a flask and poured himself a drink. It seemed to Simon that he did it all without once taking his eyes off the water. The young consultant found himself hoping that the fisherman's optimism and commitment were rewarded – and that, in turn, he released his catch back to the canal's dark water.

Simon believed in the value of win-win resolutions. Of course, he wanted to make his mark in the world – he wanted to change it, to be a world leader – but he was sure that could be achieved through creativity and cooperation rather than domination and destruction.

"Communicating for a Change" had been the title of Marcus Kline's first international corporate training programme and third best seller. Simon loved both the sentiment and the word play in the title. He had subsequently committed his life to communicating for a change. He wanted to be a warrior of words. He wanted to fight for the things he believed in, to empower people, to improve the quality of their relationships and their achievements through world-class communication. And he intended to do it without ever becoming as arrogant as his mentor. Marcus was a genius and in many ways Simon adored him. He just wanted to be, well, better than his teacher and...*softer*...too. He shared Marcus's belief that there was nothing more important in the world than the quality of peoples' communication. The difference between them was he also appreciated there were many other really significant things people could do that he couldn't. The world was filled with talented people, capable of doing all sorts of amazing things. Sometimes experts like Marcus Kline forgot how to appreciate and value the abilities of people beyond their domain.

Simon turned his back on the canal and the fisherman and stepped into his open plan lounge and kitchen. The killer was stretched out across the two-seater settee, his left leg extended over the second cushion. He looked incredibly relaxed and completely at home, waiting with the calm patience of a man who knew the inevitability of what was about to happen.

Simon should have been shocked, scared, outraged. Only he felt none of these emotions. Instead he felt as comfortable as the killer looked. And because of this he didn't ask any of the questions, or take any of the actions, one might expect. Rather, he simply forgot everything he had been observing and everything he was planning to do and gave himself up to the silent, calm, irresistible lead of the intruder.

Because his conscious mind had been completely stilled, Simon wasn't able to acknowledge to himself that he was now in the grip of a masterful communicator and influencer. He wasn't able to think about the amazing skill being demonstrated, about the fact that this was precisely the level he aspired to.

Nor was he able to identify – and this was a blessing that only some people would come to realise and appreciate later – that this was the first stage in the communication of a change that would end his life.

40.

'Why don't you sit down.' The killer gestured to Simon's modern, minimalistic, aluminium framed armchair.

The young man did as instructed. An outsider looking in would have commented on how completely relaxed he looked. Simon was unaware.

As he sank into the chair his state deepened.

The killer nodded his approval. He stood up, crossed the room and closed the glass door that opened out onto the balcony. Then he slowly and deliberately pulled the curtain across it.

The room darkened.

Simon blinked. He looked at his hands, resting on the thin metal arms of the chair. He was comfortable with the fact that they were distant, that he could neither feel nor move them. He felt a warmth in his chest and stomach. It recreated the feeling he experienced often before, when tired at the end of a very long day. It was the feeling that came with being satisfied with himself and with life, with needing to sleep – knowing it was close – but wanting to stay awake for just a few minutes more to enjoy the wonderfully soothing mixture of achievement, relaxation and security.

'It feels fabulous, doesn't it?' The killer said.

Simon smiled. At least he believed he was smiling. He couldn't actually tell whether the muscles in his face were moving or not.

'That's OK,' the killer said. 'It's what is happening on the inside that is most important. Sadly – tragically – there is too often a massive disconnect, between what people say and what they are actually feeling inside. You know that as well as I do. The tragedy is not that they try to hide it from experts like us, it's that they actually hide it from themselves. Tell me, how can they ever expect to be happy?'

Simon looked at the intruder. In his mind he said, 'It isn't their fault. Everyone wants to be happy. We are all searching for happiness. We just don't always know how to share ourselves – how to communicate – well with others. Most people don't understand the power they have to influence. They don't know how easy it is to hurt themselves as well as those around them.'

The killer watched and waited until Simon had finished. Then he said, 'They all have the opportunity to learn. The truth is they don't want to. Even those who say they do – even many of those who teach others – don't really want to make the effort needed to become truly skilled. They think they know how to look and listen because physically they can, because they were born biologically capable. In my eyes they are no more worthy of emotion than rats that are caged and used by scientists.'

Simon felt himself tense with anger and then abruptly tremble with fear as the absolute conviction of the other man hit him like a powerful wave. This man's certainty came out of the very pores of his skin. His *presence* was overwhelming.

Simon realised at that moment that he would never speak again. He knew that his home had become someone else's laboratory. He thought instinctively of Cassandra and his mind conjured a series of fast-playing images, as if flicking at high-speed through a private photograph album, showing the life they could have created together.

Simon watched the images, amazed that in the deepest recesses of his subconscious he had already imagined the rest of his life with her. Then the sequencing slowed. The images began to move away from him, floating into space, shrinking, losing their colour; leaving him forever.

Simon didn't feel the tears running down his face.

The killer saw it all. He felt nothing. When the images had disappeared he said, 'You are alone, Simon. We are all alone. Alone with our own peculiar perspectives. Alone with our own terrifying fears. What, I wonder, are yours?'

Simon's mind couldn't resist the question. He thought immediately of his parents dying, of his younger sister living with an abusive partner. He thought of his failure to change the world. He thought – tried to think – of what this man was going to do with him. And, worst of all, he thought of this man alone with Cassandra.

'You should always put yourself first,' the killer said. 'If you don't, you can never hope to be able to look after others. It's a lesson that is irrelevant for you now, but learning never stops. So why not learn something even if you will never be able to apply it?'

The killer nodded again, this time in support of his own argument.

Simon was completely unable to move.

He could feel nothing.

Not even his fear.

Simon was alive and yet he was, he knew, close to death. The strange comfort-blanket of absolute certainty was wrapping ever more tightly around him. The thought that he should have been feeling despair was like the faintest cloud on a very distant horizon.

Then, for the first time, Simon saw the brown leather holdall the killer had placed on the floor. His hands automatically tightened their grip on the slim, aluminium arms of the chair. He didn't notice.

The killer did.

'It is time', he said. 'We are both ready.'

It was true. Simon had never been so sure of anything in his life.

It seemed to him that what happened next took place in slow motion.

41.

The killer opened the bag and removed a variety of tools, placing them in neat lines on the carpet. He took out a bright red jigsaw, a drill, a hammer and chisel, forceps, a scalpel, cotton thread and gauze. Then a white laboratory coat and thin, surgical gloves. Finally, he took out some brown, heavy-duty adhesive tape. He used that to silently and swiftly secure Simon to the chair. That done, he picked up the cotton thread and placed it in one of his coat pockets.

'To carry out this procedure most people – even highly trained surgeons – would need at least one very bright light to ensure they could see everything clearly,' he said. 'I, however, do not. Although the margins of error are very fine, my eyesight is even more acute. You can rest assured that I will not make a mistake.'

The killer put on the lab coat and the gloves. Then he picked up the scalpel. He pushed the razor-sharp point into Simon's head, a little more than one centimetre above his right temple. He pushed until the tip of the blade scraped against Simon's skull. Blood began to flow down his face. The killer was unconcerned. 'I have to scalp you first,'

he said. 'Because of the state you are in you will feel
no pain. You won't even feel the blood. You will see it
though. In a few moments it will be spurting from you.
You can give yourself permission to be surprised by its
force. You can even enjoy the show if you choose. It
will be brief, but it might make you wonder why life
abandons us with such enthusiasm. Because I need to you
to continue for some time yet I will stem the blood flow
and tie up the necessary arteries. Unlike the vast majority
of others who have suffered this fate, scalping will not
be the death of you.'

The killer forced the scalpel in a circular line around
Simon's head. At times the blade scratched bone. It took
only one minute to return to the original starting point.
Blood flooded down. The scalp was still not fully free. The
killer reversed the scalpel, using the handle to force apart
the occasional sticky, fibrous tissue that was holding it in
place. With that done, he dropped the scalpel to the floor
and used the fingers of his right hand to complete the task.
When Simon's scalp came away the killer lifted it clear and
dropped it next to the scalpel.

Blood was firing from the arteries he had severed. Some
even hit the curtains. Simon's head was such a bloody mess
that it was difficult to see the precise points of leakage.
The killer calmly picked up the gauze and the forceps.
Blood sprayed his white lab coat. He didn't respond to
it. Instead he used the gauze to apply pressure. Once the
blood was under control, he placed the forceps around the
end of a damaged artery and pinched tight. Maintaining
the pressure he reached into his pocket took out the thread
and tied it off. He repeated the process with a second
artery. The blood spurts stopped.

The killer stepped back for a moment as if admiring his handiwork. Simon was still conscious. The killer could see that his heartbeat was still strong. The trance was protecting him from the physical trauma. It was time for the second part of the procedure.

The killer didn't speak. He simply picked up the drill and made a hole through Simon's skull in precisely the same place he had started cutting. When he felt he had gone in far enough, he put the drill down and took up the jigsaw.

Simon heard the saw buzz into life. He felt its teeth against his skull. He was aware of the pressure and the movement. He was back in time. He was reminded of a woodwork class at school. He knew the sound. In his mind's eye he could see dust clouds and splinters.

The killer could see the same. Only the dust and the splinters were bone.

It took him ten minutes to saw around Simon's skull. When he stopped it was clear that he had not sawn to the required depth in every place. And, as with the scalp, some fibrous tissue was still helping to hold the cranium in place. That is why he had brought the hammer and chisel. The killer used both to complete his work. He was methodical and unhurried. Simon noticed the dull, flat sound as the chisel tore through the remaining tissue. He felt an unusual coldness as the killer removed the top of his skull. He didn't see it being placed on the floor next to his scalp. His eyes had been closed for what seemed like forever.

The killer looked at the white, ridged tissue of Simon's brain, at the fibrous membrane that covered it, at the clear spinal fluid below. He felt a sudden surge of excitement and anticipation. He controlled it instantly. Now he had to deepen Simon's trance even more. Now their communication would move on to a completely different level.

To do that he had to access a trance of his own. He had to move partway at least towards the place where Simon was. Then, and only then, could he create the experience he sought.

The killer prepared himself. Simon's brain looked as if it was pulsing in readiness. The killer breathed a gentle breath onto the right hemisphere.

Listen to me now, he whispered. *Feel my influence. Show yourself...*

Thirty minutes later the killer left the apartment as quietly as he had entered it. Outside the water of the canal was already darkening as the winter sky lowered and drew itself together. The fisherman he had noticed on his arrival was nowhere to be seen. The killer wondered if he had caught anything at all.

42.

Marcus Kline believed in the value of fishing. It was one of his most powerful communication techniques. It was one of the ways he got under the skin of someone else, how he was able to make them reveal themselves to him, how he was able to see what they were really thinking, or feeling, or aspiring to at any given moment.

The key to understanding others was to get below the surface of whatever they were deliberately presenting and to hear what was left unsaid. Any half-decent educator, counsellor or, for that matter, politician, knew that. What very few people could do consistently and accurately was access that information. To do that you not only needed to be able to see and hear acutely, you also needed a method.

Marcus had created the method he called *fishing* early on in his career. Very simply, whenever Marcus went fishing he would provide a very deliberate stimulus to the person he was seeking to understand and then watch and listen to their responses. The stimulus would change according to the person and the context. It might be a story or a suggestion, or a challenge or critique. If necessary, he would simply repeat everything that he had already said in a previous meeting. What was common, though, no matter what the stimulus, was the relaxed intensity with which Marcus watched the often non-verbal responses. He had decided to think of it as *fishing* because it was the most appropriate metaphor he could conjure. The technique made him feel like a fisherman, selecting and offering the most appropriate bait, then sitting back and watching what happened next. The difference between himself and an actual fisherman was that they could very rarely see what was happening below the surface, whilst he always could.

As Marcus stood by the canal and looked into the dark water he thought back over the last few days and considered not for the first time whether or not he had got everything right.

Marcus had been fishing in his most recent meetings with Peter Jones. In fact, he had been doing very little else. If there had ever been a time when he needed to reel in the truth, this was most certainly it. Events were building to a head and, if he was going to see it through to his desired end outcome, he needed to be absolutely clear about what was happening at every level. That meant being absolutely clear about what was going on in Peter Jones's mind. Ideally, he had to be influencing Peter to think and act in the way that he, Marcus, wanted him to. Only that was not proving easy. Peter had his defences well and truly in place. They were both working to interconnected yet very different agendas. They were both highly skilled.

Marcus wondered what strategy Peter would employ next, whether he would explicitly use his professional role to exert power, to clearly redefine the nature of their interaction, or whether he would try to hide that away behind their friendship. Marcus let the canal help his mind drift, letting all of the possibilities and their associated pluses and minuses float before him. He settled, as he always did, for the conclusion that felt right.

It would be the latter, he decided. Peter would realise that his only chance of gaining the upper hand was to hide behind the truth. And the truth was they were best friends. Who for now just happened to be unstated adversaries.

Marcus had not been in the office today. It was the first time he had ever let something take precedence over his work. But this was a situation unlike any other. Uncertain and dangerous, Marcus thought. And however hard the race had been so far, they were fast approaching the last lap.

The hardest part of the race.

He was sure that both he and Peter were prepared to do anything to win.

It was at that moment that Marcus's phone buzzed with the sound of an incoming text. He allowed himself to be distracted by it. It was a conscious decision; a simple reminder that he was still running his own mind. As further proof, he refused to let himself consider who might be texting. He doubted that Peter had such self-control.

The text was from Anne-Marie. It came as a complete shock. He had been keeping her out of his thoughts. Given the unparalleled stresses of the week and, if he was completely honest with himself, the decision he had made to end their marriage, he had found it easy to do.

He hesitated for a moment, waiting until he had regained his composure, before keying in his password and reading the message.

My Dearest Love, I hope you are safe and well. I am on my way home. I cannot tell you how much I need to see you again. There are important things we need to talk about, things we need to share. I am sorry for not having been completely honest with you. Since I have been away I have come to realise that together we can accomplish anything.

I will be with you soon, my Love!

PS I know now that you were right – it is impossible to capture a universal truth from behind a camera!

AM xx

Marcus read the text twice. He couldn't help but wonder in what way she had been dishonest and what had happened to change her philosophy as a photographer. More importantly he could feel her affection for him – her *love* – in a way that he hadn't for several years. The sensation tugged at his mind, wanting him to remember how it was when they first met, wanting him to relive the memories and the associated emotions, to feel the way he used to. It drew him back in time, reminding him of how he had described and thought of her when their love had first grown.

My Angel.

It had seemed such an apt description. Anne-Marie had been so understanding, so optimistic, so *bright*. Marcus had actually been surprised at himself when he had first thought of her in this way. For a man whose God was the power of the subconscious, it seemed an artificial, almost hypocritical, descriptor. Yet from the very beginning it had sounded and felt right. He had accepted it – been able to accept it – because he decided it was the perfect metaphor, another example of the power of words, a perfect representation. Nothing more.

As the memory strengthened Marcus suddenly recognised the danger it presented. He shook his head to clear it. This was the last thing he needed right now. After all he had made a decision. He *was* going to end their relationship. It had been the most difficult decision he had ever made, but he had made it. The full stop was in place. The time for internal chatter was over.

So why was the text affecting him so? Was it an indication that he had got the decision wrong? Was that possible?

Marcus returned the phone to his jacket pocket. For the first time since the murders had started, since Anne-Marie's departure, he felt his self-control waver. It ran from his mind to his body in a swift, seamless transition; easy as the tide coming in; just as dangerous.

Marcus knew that he couldn't afford to give ground. He couldn't afford to doubt his decision-making ability. Not now. Not with so much at stake. He needed instead to break his state. Fast.

To his right, on the ground floor of an apartment block, a young woman switched on her lounge light. Marcus glanced automatically in her direction. She was the distraction he needed.

The woman saw him look and closed the curtains in deliberate fashion. The material was thin. He could still see her outline through them as she moved, her shadow showing like a puppet in an Asian play. The difference, though, was that this was real life reduced to shadow. Marcus was sure that the woman didn't realise that she was still on show, faceless, lacking detail and depth. He was sure most people didn't.

For the briefest second the thought occurred to him that to be a shadow was perhaps to have the best of both worlds. Present and yet pain free. Associated and yet guiltless. The thought made him shiver. It was an argument for surrender, for choosing not to make decisions, for refusing to accept responsibility. It was a thought, an argument, he could not tolerate. Not with everything that was happening and was about to happen. If the coming battle was as difficult as he expected it to be, if the opposing force was truly as powerful as he believed, then responsibility might well be the deciding factor.

Responsibility will be King, Marcus told himself. *And I have to win. No matter what. No matter what the consequences. I have to win.*

Marcus turned to face the city centre and set off along the canal path. Behind him, in the ground floor apartment, the shadow was no longer visible against the curtain. Marcus didn't look back. It was too late for that. His decisions had been made. The verdict was in.

Associated and guilty as charged.

43.

The killer leaked the news of Simon Westbury's death to the national press within an hour of leaving the apartment. He simply phoned the switchboard of a prominent tabloid and said that he had an exclusive story regarding the Nottingham murders. He was given the mobile number of Dave Johnson, the reporter covering the killings, and he called him from a public phone box in a street that did not have CCTV cameras.

The reporter was at once curious and cautious. 'How do you know that someone else has been killed?' He asked. 'Convince me.'

'I know because I killed him. And I don't need to convince you. The very fact that we are having this conversation means that you will have to investigate what I tell you. Your Editor would go mad if you missed the opportunity of an exclusive just because you couldn't be bothered to leave the pub and go take a look.'

'How do you know I'm in the pub?'

'Background sounds.'

Johnson glanced around the empty snug he had been drinking in for the last couple of hours. He couldn't hear any pub sounds and he was sat there.

'What can you hear?' He asked, even though he knew that it bore no relevance to the main topic of conversation.

'Everything.' The killer smirked. 'Almost as loud as the sound of your cynicism. Now ask me something of more significance. You have one chance after which I will hang up and call one of your competitors.'

Johnson drained the final third of his pint of Guinness in one urgent gulp. 'How did you do it?' He asked. 'How did you kill him?'

'What makes you think it was a male?'

'Well, I, er, I just presumed that it was.'

'Presumption can get a person killed. You know that, don't you? It's a very sloppy way of thinking. It's a denial of our senses.'

'Are you telling me it was a woman? A child?'

'It disgusts me that you find those two options increasingly more appealing. It makes me want to punish you.' The killer sighed. 'But if I punished you because you are as dull as the basest metal, then I would have to punish so many others. It would be never-ending. And that isn't the plan. Do you understand?'

'Yes.' Johnson had absolutely no idea what the other man was talking about. In many ways the caller was offering the sort of nonsense every sad little fuck did who tried to claim responsibility for a high-profile crime. And in Johnson's experience, the world was absolutely littered with sad little fucks. Only he sensed something different about this guy. No matter how hard they tried, the SLF's always sounded needy. This guy didn't seem at all needy. In fact quite the opposite. He seemed composed. In control. As if he knew he held the winning hand.

'I do believe that you are the person responsible for the deaths,' Johnson said. 'I believe that if you chose to you could find and punish me and I really don't want you to do that. So please tell me whatever you want to about how you killed your latest victim. Do remember, though, that it will help me to tell your story – to promote you – if you give me some information, some details, that are not currently in the public domain.'

'I'm not seeking promotion,' the killer said. 'However, I will give you what you need. Are you ready?'

'Yes!' Johnson glanced at his empty glass and licked his lips. He was suddenly parched.

The killer heard the movement of Johnson's tongue and smiled to himself. The reporter was going to serve his purpose perfectly. 'Then listen,' the killer said.

For the next ten minutes he explained in absolute detail what he had done to Simon Westbury.

Johnson said nothing. He just listened and wrote. His mood shifted from one of self-congratulation – for this was most definitely the genuine killer – to a mixture of curious horror. There was nothing quite like being on the end of the phone talking with a murderer who was the focus of a police manhunt. It was at once exhilarating and terrifying, being so close to the bringer of death, knowing more than anyone else about what was happening, hearing the words, the *breath,* of a real killer.

Johnson's desire for another beer disappeared as the killer's words painted images in his mind, forcing him to see what had happened as clearly as if he was looking at photos of the scene. The images were utterly repulsive and yet he felt compelled to study them, powerless to prevent their creation. As he watched, the images came alive with movement and the killer's voice faded behind them. Now Johnson felt he was witnessing the killing through his own eyes, that he was in the room with them. The killer was unidentifiable however. Whenever the reporter tried to look at him directly it seemed as if a heat haze began shimmering around him, blurring his features. Johnson could see and hear what was happening to the poor victim, though, and it made his blood run cold.

He didn't notice when the killer stopped talking and hung up. The scene in his mind kept playing, repeating itself, repeating itself, *repeating itself*. Only when it finally dissolved did Johnson realise the call had ended.

He sat without moving, staring at his notes. He had stopped writing as soon as the images had appeared. He forced himself into action, picking up his pen, describing everything that he had heard, that he had *seen*. His hand was shaking. He struggled to control it. Despite that he wrote with an unusual urgency. He felt he was doing more than simply recording details. He felt he was writing to get something out of his system.

When he finished he drank two beers in quick succession and then began doing what he had to do.

44.

His call was put through to Detective Superintendent Mike Briggs as quickly as he knew it would be. His news was met with precisely the response that he expected.

'That's interesting. Any chance you can come in to talk about it?'

Johnson's reply was the next deliberate and measured part of what they both knew was a negotiation. 'Happy to.'

'Excellent. What phone did the informant call you on?

'My mobile.'

'And that is the number you are calling on now?'

'Yes.'

How long ago did he ring you?'

'Within the last thirty minutes.'

'Excellent. How soon can you be here.'

'Twenty minutes. I'm already on my way.'

'Excellent.' Briggs hung up. By the time Johnson arrived he had organised a trace of all the calls that had been made to the reporter's phone in the last two hours. He had also called Peter Jones in for the meeting.

The two detectives were not remotely surprised by Johnson's look and demeanour. He was a career journalist of the old school who had spent far too much of both his social and working life in the pub. It was clearly not his first time in a meeting of this nature. Unfortunately for him, it wasn't their first time either.

Briggs welcomed the reporter into his office, introduced Peter, and then got straight down to business.

'Mr Johnson, thank you for contacting us. I'm sure you appreciate the seriousness of the current situation and we certainly appreciate you coming here so promptly.'

'I'm always keen to help.'

'That's good to know,' Briggs replied with a straight face. 'Let's begin with the phone call. Tell us in as much detail as you can what the caller said to you.'

Johnson took out his notebook. He didn't need to, the images were still burning in his brain, but he knew that the detectives would expect him to refer to it. More importantly, for his own peace of mind he needed something to hold onto right now. If it couldn't be a pint glass, the notebook would have to do. If only the images could be contained and controlled within it. If only they disappeared whenever he closed the cover.

Johnson spoke for the next three minutes. His language was intense, emotive and rich in detail. It quickly became clear to the detectives that he was talking as if he had actually been present at the scene, rather than simply recalling the killer's words. They exchanged glances. They had not been expecting something that was more an eye witness account than a reporter's professionally taken notes. They sat back and observed in silence as Johnson progressed his story. By the time he had finished, his hands were shaking and there was a nervous, drained expression on his face.

Peter waited for Briggs to comment first. The DS made a point of simply looking at the reporter for what was intended to seem like a like long period of time before saying, 'You seem very personally involved in that account, Mr Johnson.'

'I, er, I feel that I am.'

'Oh? How so?'

Johnson realised the predicament he was creating for himself. It was easy to guess what these two detectives, desperate for any lead they could get, were thinking right now. Yet if he tried to tell them the truth – or, at least, as much of the experience as he was able to put into words – what the hell would they think then? Whatever they thought, it was better than thinking he was an accomplice to murder.

Johnson licked his lips, glanced from Briggs to Peter and back again, and said, 'This is going to sound really weird, but I swear to you it's what happened. When he talked it was as if he somehow transported me to the scene. In my head it felt like I was there. Not after the killing, you understand, but during it. That's why it seems so...so inside me. Like it's all trapped in here.' Johnson's right hand gestured briefly towards his head. He paused, hoping for a glimmer of understanding. The detectives offered nothing. 'I've never been hypnotised,' Johnson continued quickly. 'In fact before today I would have told you it was all a load of bollocks, but when he'd finished talking it felt like I was coming out of a trance. It was horrible. It was like he'd deliberately made me experience how he took control of his victim.' The reporter fell silent. He realised as he waited that he was chewing the inside of his cheek.

Peter studied the man opposite him. He didn't think for a minute that he was looking at either the killer or an accomplice. There was nothing about Johnson to suggest that he had either the subtlety or the skill to play this sort of game. Yet the information he had just shared matched so accurately the modus operandi of the other deaths that there could be no doubt it was genuine. The conclusion was straightforward and significant: the killer *had* contacted him.

Peter remembered his recent conversation with Marcus about hypnosis. The consultant had been adamant that a person couldn't be hypnotised into doing something they didn't want to. Whilst the reporter didn't believe in the power of hypnosis, he would have clearly wanted an exclusive. Perhaps that alone was enough to make him susceptible to a powerfully delivered suggestion? Perhaps – and this was the most unwelcome thought – Marcus was wrong and a truly great hypnotist *could* take control of another person's mind and behaviour no matter what?

'So what you are saying is the killer just talked to the victim and that alone was enough to keep the victim in place and prevent a struggle?' Peter pushed the point.

'Yes. It wasn't just that. It also seemed to stop the guy feeling any pain.' Johnson responded quickly, relieved that at least one of the detectives seemed to believe him.

'And despite the clarity of these images you couldn't see the killer's face?'

'No.'

'And you didn't recognise the victim?

'No. As I said to you he was just a young adult male. To be honest I tried not to look at him too closely once, you know, once *it* started.'

'Did you see or hear anything distinctive?'

'The room was clear even though the curtains had been drawn, but it was just a normal apartment. Nothing stood out.'

'Describe the curtains.'

'Dark green. Floor to ceiling. Maybe two metres across.'

Peter's heartbeat quickened instinctively. 'What else? Be specific! What else did you see in the room?'

'Erm, just a coffee table. And, erm…' Johnson's voice trailed off. The detective's sudden urgency had taken him by surprise. And although he wanted to help, and he really did need an exclusive, he didn't want to keep revisiting the images in his mind.

'Come on, man! What was on the table?'

Briggs recognised the change in Peter, too. He was a smart enough boss to know when to keep his mouth shut.

'Tell me about the table!' Peter demanded again. 'What was on it? What did it look like?'

'It was black metal, with a glass top. It had an empty mug on it and there were books. Several books.'

Another detail fitted into place. Peter knew someone who had green full-length curtains in their apartment and a black, glass-topped coffee table. More than ever before Peter's mind begged for this just to be a coincidence.

'The books! Look at them! Visualise them! Tell me what you see!'

'I've told you everything. I don't want to keep going back. I –'

'- Look!' Peter was out of his chair before he had even realised that he had moved. Briggs straightened, ready to intervene.

The image sprang into Johnson's vision. 'There were

three, three books. I can see the title of one. It's called
"Communicating for a Change". It's got the author's name
on the cover. His name is – '

'– Marcus Kline.' Peter was already leaving the office
as he spoke. He glanced over his shoulder at Briggs.
'Think I might have a lead, Sir,' he said, trying to sound
as dispassionate as he could. 'It's a long shot, but it's worth
following up on.'

'On you go, Chief Inspector.' Briggs waited for the door
to close behind Peter and then returned his attention to the
reporter. They both knew what had just happened. They
both knew that Peter had referred to the lead as a 'long
shot' purely for Johnson's benefit. They both knew that it
was obviously far, far more than that.

Detective Chief Inspector Jones stormed out of the
building, his mind in turmoil. How desperate was he?
Praying for a coincidence when no such thing existed. Was
that all he had got, a hope and a prayer? Was that the best
he could do?

Peter had visited Simon Westbury's canal side apartment once before. It was possible that the place Johnson
had described was not it. It was possible that another
young, aspiring executive had a very similar sense of
interior design to Simon. It was possible that this same
executive was a fan of Marcus Kline. It was all possible.

But only if you believed in coincidence.

Peter Jones's life was built on uncovering the truth even
if sometimes the truth was almost unbearable. Today it felt
as if it was scouring his insides. The truth he had already
accepted, the truth he knew was going to be reinforced
immeasurably in the coming hour, was simple and harsh
and relentless: his failure was costing lives. And it was all

coming far, far, too close to home.

Simon is dead. And it's because of me. The responsibility is mine.

Peter felt already as if it was tearing him apart. The most terrifying thing, though – worse even than the likelihood of Simon Westbury's death – was the fact that the game was far from over. Unless he could stop it there was worse to come. He was sure of it. He vowed silently that he would prevent at least that.

45.

Anne-Marie Wells was on her way home. It was proving to be a long, slow journey. Traffic on the M5 motorway had been horrific. As she queued in yet another traffic jam Anne-Marie felt time pulling at her gut. Why, she wondered, did time always seem to slow down when you didn't want it to and speed up whenever you were having a great experience that you wanted to last forever?

As she sat in her car, Anne-Marie tried once again to reconnect with the mysterious part of herself she had encountered whilst away. She had tried several times since the experience – the *revelation* – and all had ended in failure. Although she could remember with absolute clarity how the state felt, she had no idea how recreate it. It was like the best of all memories transferred from a living, breathing experience to the confines of the mind.

As a photographer Anne-Marie had often thought about the relationship between a photograph and a memory. Did the mind, she wondered, create and fix boundaries around memories in the way that she did around photos? Did it determine the focus and then influence the interpretation of a memory in the same way that she used lighting and colour and perspective to direct the viewer?

Before the cancer – before she had *known* about it – her interest had been only an intellectual, professional curiosity. It had been a subject for debate at dinner parties and a source of quiet introspection during shoots. Now it felt like a matter of life and death. Now Anne-Marie knew that how she viewed her past was as important to her survival as how she approached her future. Now she was aware of the most important truth:

How easily we trick ourselves.

Once upon a time Anne-Marie would have argued with conviction that she knew precisely who she was, that she knew precisely what it meant to be a photographer. More than that, she thought she knew what it meant to be a human being.

How misguided was that?

Only now, with death on her shoulder, had she started to wake up, to realise what really mattered.

And she had believed she could take photos that showed the truth!

Now that seemed like unbelievably naïve arrogance.

'You don't know anything about anything until you are dealing with your own death,' she said into the rear view mirror. 'And it's always on the move.'

In a matter of hours – she couldn't be sure how many because of the traffic – Anne-Marie would arrive home. Then she would have to tell Marcus about her cancer, about everything in fact. For a reason she didn't understand, it was a really frightening prospect. Anne-Marie tried to imagine how she would cope, how the conversation would go when she told him that she was facing death, that she needed him to...

The line of traffic began to inch its way forwards. Creeping towards the inevitable.

Anne-Marie knew that things had to change. Actually, they had already changed; it was just that she couldn't be sure of the outcome. One thing she did know for sure though, was that she wanted to share her life – *really* share her life – with Marcus. That meant she had to do things differently. Rather than simply trying to beat death, she had to focus on creating a new life for herself and for Marcus. However difficult it might be, she had to treat this as a time of creativity and growth. And with Marcus's help, with his love and his expertise, she truly believed she – *they* – could do that.

To begin with, she decided, she had to change some simple, everyday behaviours, break some patterns, have some simple indicators that things were not as they used to be. Before leaving the cottage, Anne-Marie had made a list of her daily habits, everything from the subconscious routines she followed first thing in the morning, to the previously unrealised ritual she undertook prior to going to bed. The list contained far more than she would have ever imagined. It revealed that her day was held together by a string of habits, with only the occasional unconstrained activity providing release. She was not the creative, free-flowing human being she had believed herself to be. Instead she had become a prisoner of her own routines! The behaviours she had introduced to make life easy, to free her up so that she could focus on the more important priorities, had actually taken over. And the result was that her thinking had become habitual, too.

It was time for all of that to stop.

Anne-Marie had made a second list of all the things she would do differently. She threw it away ten minutes later because it was, she realised, simply the very first step in establishing a new set of habits. Instead she had chosen to be guided by two of Marcus's favourite maxims:

'It starts before it starts,'

and

'It ends after it ends'.

Marcus had always claimed that one of his strengths was his willingness and ability to undertake extensive research ahead of every meeting, every interview, every presentation or debate, and to then access the necessary emotional and physical state before the event began. He likened it to the preparation a world champion sprinter would do before going out onto the track. He followed it up afterwards with a most thorough review of what had taken place, reviewing it from the different perspectives of all the key players involved, identifying and exploring the most likely implications of the outcome and deciding how he would respond to each. Most people, Marcus argued, started too late and stopped too soon. That was why their dreams were often too small and their level of influence too shallow.

Anne-Marie was definitely now going to dream bigger than she ever had and she was going to influence herself more completely and more positively than she would have once thought possible.

She would begin in the most simple of ways by doing something different before she even walked into the house. Just a simple everyday thing she had never, ever, done before. Just a symbolic act to show that change was already underway, that it had it had indeed started before it started.

She would park the car on the road rather than in the drive. That was all. Habit breaking didn't require extreme behaviour, she told herself. Just recognition and an appropriate response. In this case it also had a very positive knock-on effect. For whenever she parked in the drive and Marcus was home he would always open the front door for her or come out to greet her. Today Anne-Marie needed to enter her home on her own terms. The change needed to start before even Marcus Kline recognised that it had. Today she was going to let herself in.

'Perhaps I ought to take a photo of an open door,' she murmured. 'Make it symbolic. Perhaps it could be the first picture in the photo essay? Or perhaps it should be the last? Either way, what title would I give it?'

The traffic began to pick up speed. Home was getting closer.

46.

Having dealt with the most emotionally draining crime scene of his life, Peter Jones drove straight to the home of Marcus Kline. He arrived to find the lights on and the front door unlocked and open.

'Marcus?' He shouted as he leapt out of the Audi and raced inside, his heart pounding, his mind flooding with a wave of terrifying possibilities.

The consultant was standing in the kitchen, waiting for the kettle to boil. 'You were scared for me,' he said. 'I could hear it in your voice.'

'What!' Peter came to an abrupt halt; Marcus's opening comment, his immediate analysis, acting like an irresistible brake. And yet still two forces collided. Peter felt his fear crashing against the cold, hard wall of his suspicion. His intention to operate in front of Marcus as his best friend rather than as a Detective Chief Inspector was suddenly in danger of being derailed at the very first contact.

Peter's mind raced back over the last couple of hours. Marcus was bound to have seen the news reports about Simon's death. Surely he was not only feeling distraught about the tragic – *terrible* – murder of his protégé, but was also terrified for his own safety? Surely any normal human being would be in bits right now? And yet here he was, with the door open, playing his usual mind-games as if nothing had happened!

Marcus's voice cut through Peter's thoughts.

'I left the door open because I knew that you would be here soon enough. And when you saw it you were scared that something had happened to me like it did to Simon. I should have realised that's how you would react. I'm sorry. I'm not thinking straight.'

Peter licked his lips. He allowed himself to nod slowly and deliberately. He used the movement, the few seconds it gave him, to try to regroup. He said the most obvious thing first. 'You've seen the news.'

It was Marcus's turn to pause briefly before speaking. He ran the tip of his left index finger around the rim of the black mug that was standing on the granite kitchen worktop. He looked at it as he did so. 'How could anyone miss it? But that's how it was clearly meant to be. Leaking his own actions to the press was the killer's way of increasing the pressure on you. A powerful story like that released at the right time is like a forest fire. Once it's lit you don't even need to fan it. You just watch it spread and stand behind it. If you're lucky it becomes the main focus of everyone's attention. And even if it doesn't it still creates so much heat that no one can come straight through it. So, whilst they're fighting the flames, you can just get on and do whatever you've planned to do next.' Marcus sighed. 'How are you coping?'

'It's what I'm paid to do.' Peter shrugged. Marcus's interpretation was, of course, completely accurate. He was being as insightful as Peter would have expected him to be. *And he's saying precisely what he would say if he was the killer playing games with you.* The thought came unbidden and unwanted. Peter spoke quickly. 'The problem is sometimes they just don't pay me enough.' He forced a smile.

'You've been there, to the scene?'

'Yes.'

'How was he?' The kettle reached its crescendo and switched itself off. Marcus barked out a cold, dry laugh. He made no attempt to pour himself a drink. 'Listen to me with my stupid question! "How was he?" He was dead, Marcus, that's how he was. He had his cranium removed and then, eventually, he was killed. 'How was he?" Jesus! Is that the best I can do?'

Peter saw pain in his friend's face and body. He heard it in his voice. He believed it was genuine; a part of him, he knew, *needed* to believe that. Peter wanted to reach out. He was fully aware, though, that for a whole variety of very good reasons, he couldn't just change completely from how he had been in their last meeting. No matter how much Marcus was genuinely suffering, he would be at best confused and, more likely, immediately suspicious if Peter suddenly avoided his professional duty. The question, therefore, had to be asked. It had to be done in a way, however, that revealed Peter's empathy. 'I'm really sorry Marcus,' he said. 'I do understand how horrible this is for you right now, but I have to ask you – just how do you know those details?'

Marcus straightened, anger flashing in his eyes. 'How do I know? Well, there are two possible answers aren't there? The first one is that I know because you showed me a film of the first murder and you told me what happened in the second. So, being a fucking genius, I detected a pattern and guessed that it continued with poor Simon! Or, if you prefer, the second answer is that I know because I'm the guy doing the killing! Take your pick!'

'It's not a matter of choice. I am your friend first and foremost. The challenge I face – that we both face – is that I also have an obligation to fulfil my professional role. Actually, if you think about it, that's the best way I can help us both. Once I've asked you what I need to as a detective and you have answered me I can focus on our friendship. Then we can work our way through this together.'

'Is that so?' Marcus pushed the empty mug away. 'Let me tell you something Peter about the way human beings are constructed, and this applies to us psychologically, socially and physically. It's most relevant to our current situation. You see, as individuals we are essentially a collection of parts that are all connected and are, to a greater or lesser degree, aligned. For example, when we spend time together as friends we exercise and demonstrate those parts of ourselves that relate well to the other, that fit. It's an on-going process. There's actually no such thing as a relationship, there's only the process of relating. Friendship is a verb not a noun.'

Marcus paused, as if mentally reviewing what he was about to say. Peter waited, despite the desperate severity of the situation the detective knew better than to interrupt the lecture.

'However, we are made up of more parts than just those we share with our friends – or even our lovers. There are parts we only access in specific contexts. They can reflect our beliefs, religious or otherwise. They can underpin our sense of self. They can be developed and demonstrated only through our professional role. And that, of course, is most clearly true for both of us.

'When – *if* – the different parts are aligned, when a human being has all of these different parts working cohesively together, they inevitably feel a sense of purpose, of meaning, of value. They feel fulfilled or, at least, that they are working towards fulfilment. This, tragically, happens only rarely. Sadly, most people spend most of their time experiencing a continual internal struggle. They feel a battle raging inside. It is caused by the fact that the different parts of themselves are in conflict with each other. In cultures like ours this state has become an accepted part of the human condition. Hence we all accept without question the phrase, "Sooner the Devil we know than the Devil we don't." When, in fact, it would be far more appropriate to say, "Let's do away with all Devils and have only Angels instead."'

Marcus fell silent again. This time it seemed to Peter that his own words had forced an unintended moment of reflection. The consultant tapped his hand against the worktop and continued abruptly.

'It's interesting that even those who have realised the absurdity of religious belief, still use such language. The reason for that isn't relevant. What matters is that the most obvious conflict occurs when powerful, meaningful parts of different people clash. That's what we are experiencing right now. The professional you is thinking that it is obliged to interpret and influence the professional me. And both of us know that it can't...'

Peter ignored the bait.

Marcus continued, 'I'm saying this because I want you to remember that the current conflict is only between specific parts of us, parts of us that relate to this very unusual context. Our friendship will stay safe behind all of this as long as you remember that.'

'I understand that. I really do.' Peter felt the emotional power of Marcus's plea – or was it an argument? – enveloping him. He understood more than most the need to be able to compartmentalise situations and events. He knew that few people were able to do it.

Once, in the early stages of his career as a detective, a good friend had asked him, 'What would you do if I told you that I had committed a crime?' Peter's answer had been immediate, 'I would gather all the evidence I could to create the best chance of a conviction. Then I would arrest you and, if you were found guilty, I would visit you in prison on a regular basis and do everything possible to help make it easy for you.' His friend had been shocked by the reply. 'I...I thought we were close?' He said. 'We are,' Peter replied. 'That's why I would want to help you manage your time in prison.' Peter remembered how his friend had shaken his head in a mixture of outrage and dismay. 'If you did that to me,' he said, 'and then you tried to visit me in prison as if we were still mates, I'd tell you to fuck off.' The conversation had ended their relationship. *Parts clashing*, Peter mused. *It's what I have become used to.*

'We can manage this together,' Marcus's calm tone eased its way through Peter's thoughts. 'I truly believe that.'

'So do I.' Peter knew that he had to agree. He was trying to remember whether or not he had ever told Marcus the story about his friend. He couldn't be sure. Either way he had to match the sentiment if he was to have any chance of recreating rapport and persuading Marcus to do what he needed him to. Actually, it was easy to agree. A most significant part of him also believed that they could manage the situation successfully. He also believed that it was most likely to happen if Marcus let him take the lead. For two very important reasons he had to get Marcus's agreement for what he was about to propose. It was time, Peter decided, to go for that now. He considered the best way to begin.

'Why don't you just say what's on your mind,' Marcus prompted.

'I intend to. I just want to stress that I'm here tonight as your friend.'

'Once you have finished asking me what you need to as a policeman.'

'I have no more questions. For tonight at least.' Peter added the second line quickly. Marcus was giving him his undivided attention; to lie now would be to unravel his strategy before it had even begun. 'Instead I've got a recommendation that I would urge you to consider and act upon.'

Outside the light on the willow tree came on without warning. The large kitchen window framed the sudden brightness. Peter couldn't help but glance in its direction.

'It's on a timer,' Marcus said. 'Anne-Marie thinks the tree is far too magnificent to stay in the shadows. Personally, I didn't really agree with her. I didn't care about it to be honest. But now, well, I'm coming round to thinking that maybe she's always seen something that I've missed.'

'Now that's an admission.' It was a line that Peter regretted as soon as he said it.

'Who knows – perhaps the first of many?' Marcus raised an eyebrow.

Peter felt once again that his friend was toying with him, operating from behind a level of insight that was impenetrable and disconcerting. He couldn't afford to wait any longer, he realised. In this particular part of the game time was Marcus Kline's ally, not his.

'Who knows indeed?' Peter shrugged. 'But those answers are for the future. This is not the time for conjecture. Tonight there's something vitally important we need to do.'

'I'm listening.'

'Good.' Peter Jones tried to control his breathing. He looked at his friend and wondered just how he would respond next.

47.

'There are two things I need to achieve,' Peter said. 'Firstly, I need to catch the killer. Secondly, I need to keep you safe. For us to get through this together and for me to achieve what I need to, there's a basic, bottom line that I feel I'm operating to and you are not.'

'Really? And what would that be?'

'Ensuring your safety. As both your friend and as a detective I need to make sure of that. I admit that I wasn't originally convinced by what you told me about the purple branch. I didn't buy into your idea that it was a form of communication from the killer to you – '

' – And I didn't need my level of expertise to recognise that.'

'Of course.' Peter nodded his head slightly in acknowl-edgement and then went on. 'Now, though, I'm looking at a series of murders, a pattern, that seems to be centring around and getting ever closer to you.'

'So now you think he'll come after me?'

'It's a possibility that I can't ignore.

'Then what is your plan?' Marcus's voice was almost accusative.

Peter forced himself not to hesitate. 'The question is, how best do I keep you safe? There isn't actually a plan, only an answer to the question. It's straightforward. I keep you safe by putting you somewhere the killer can't get to you.'

'And you keep me there until the killer is caught?'

'Yes.'

Marcus looked out towards the willow tree. He nodded thoughtfully in what Peter regarded as a theatrical fashion. 'You,' Marcus said, 'Intend to put me somewhere and keep me there? You think that is an appropriate plan?'

'It's not a plan, it's a procedure. If you can't be found and you're protected, you are safe.'

'So I'm to be placed and protected?'

'You are the potential target of an active killer.'

'Not long ago I was a suspect.'

'You were a person of interest.'

'Past tense?' Marcus paused only briefly, just long enough to watch the play of emotions on Peter's face. 'Does that mean I've now become something else?'

'I think we should just focus on the danger you might be facing and not on clever word play.'

'I am focussing on what I perceive to be the realities of the situation. What you need to understand though Peter, is that I'm doing so from a totally different perspective to you. After all, I'm not under any professional or political pressure to achieve a result.'

'I'm not here because of media pressure. I'm offended that you think that.'

'How am I supposed to separate you, my friend, from the professional this situation requires you to be?'

'You're the last person in the world who can ask that

question!' Peter took a step forwards. 'When do you ever stop being Marcus Kline the expert? When do you ever step out from that shelter? Honestly, I don't know if words are your weapons or your defence.'

Marcus blinked. 'Why make them so combative?'

'Because you do.' Peter stepped back. 'Anyway, that conversation is for another day. When the killer is in prison and I know you are safe.'

'When you've won.'

'Dear God! I'm talking about your life!'

'Not in isolation!'

'Do you not think that you are under threat?'

'From whom?

'Fuck you!'

'Said the Detective Chief Inspector.'

Peter's fists clenched. 'Where are you Marcus? Honestly? Where are you – *who* are you – in all of this? We're the closest of friends, aren't we? Today my professional responsibilities and my personal desire overlap. It's as simple as that. So let me protect you, for God's sake!'

'No.'

The single syllable was delivered with a finality that Peter had never experienced before. He felt it resonate in his body. He willed himself to ignore it. 'Your life is potentially at risk and you need to move out of here into a safe place. My professional assessment is accurate and I urge you to act upon it!'

'No.'

Peter's fists clenched again. 'You could die!'

'We will all die sooner or later.'

Peter slammed the underside of his fist onto the granite work surface.

'I'm sure that could be interpreted as threatening behaviour.' Marcus frowned. 'It's certainly behaviour unbecoming of a person with your rank.'

'Why are you doing this?' Peter shouted, unable to control himself any longer.

Marcus didn't reply immediately. The silence was in marked contrast to the preceding escalation of pace and volume. It felt to Peter as if Marcus was somehow using the silence like a blanket to dampen the emotion that had been filling the room.

'You cannot force me to accept protective custody,' Marcus said eventually. 'Whatever your motives and concerns, the decision is ultimately mine. So I'm going to stay here. This is my home and now that it has a panic alarm fitted courtesy of your rather stern colleague, it's even more of a castle than it was.'

'That's your final answer?'

'This isn't a quiz show.'

'I really don't think you know what you are doing.'

'I really think that I do.'

'End of conversation then.'

'Sounds that way.'

Peter accepted defeat. 'Then I have to go.'

'You have someone to catch.'

'Yes.' Peter considered shaking Marcus's hand before he left, but decided against it. 'I'll be in touch.' He turned and walked away. When he reached the kitchen door he looked back. 'You were right, by the way.'

'What about?

'About my reaction when I arrived, when I saw that the front door was open. I was scared.'

Marcus's gaze returned to the window, to the willow

tree outside in its halo of light. It looked to Peter as if his eyes moistened. 'We are lucky, aren't we?' He said. 'Lucky that we are able to be afraid, to feel fear. Simon can't. And he never will again.'

48.

Fear has its own special colour. Everything does. The killer had known that – had seen it – for as long as he could remember. To him sounds were also as much a visual sensation as they were auditory. He knew, for example, the colour and vibration of a child's laughter. He knew how it thickened and dulled with age. He knew the blood red colour of anger, how it burst and shimmered like unbearable heat on a desert road. He knew the black cloud of the very last breath a living creature took. Many times he had watched it dissolve and fade as it travelled upwards.

The killer had known he was different from childhood. It had been impossible not to know. It had always amused him in a cold, hard way, growing up listening to his peers determinedly trying to create their own individuality. As if difference was the product of styling and carefully selected, self-promoting opinion. It was, the killer thought, the greatest and cruellest paradox of all: people had been tricked into believing individuality came from following fashion.

Society – just another name for the herd.

The herd had its own colour too. It was the colour of mud. The lifeless slurry that results when many colours are mixed and none are strong enough to dominate.

Without a leader, he reminded himself, the herd simply merges into a dull mass, unaware that life is being drained from them on a daily basis.

How could you feel sympathy for people who allowed that to happen? To be more accurate, for people who actively sought it out? He certainly couldn't.

Sympathy was an emotion he had never seen the colour of.

He had often wondered why it should remain beyond his vision, but he had considered it only in a disassociated way. In the same way that a cat considers a mouse as a potential plaything, a distraction, and nothing more no matter what the consequence. He had recognised as a teenager that some emotions, a limited few, were invisible to him. They remained so throughout his life, even as his skills and awareness continued to develop. He was sure that the emotions he could not see would also have their own colours. It was just that, for some reason, his eyes could not perceive them. He never felt diminished because of this. He knew there was no such thing as a perfect human being, just as he knew there was no such thing as a perfect colour.

The first time he had seen the colour of an emotion he had been nine years old. The family cat, Misty, had died of cancer. She had been adored by his mother; bought for her twelve years earlier by his father. His mother had always loved cats. When Misty died her grief was uncontrollable. The boy didn't share her emotion. Her anguish didn't touch him. Instead he had been captivated by an explosion of colour that emanated from her, surrounding her whenever she mourned her loss. He had shouted and pointed when he had first seen it, tugging at his mother's sleeve whilst she cried, reaching with his other hand – grabbing – into space in an attempt to pull the colours from the air. His mother had turned her shoulder to him abruptly. The boy had been shocked and confused. Why did she not reach for the colours herself? Surely she could see them? After all, they were hers.

The more he tried to tell her about them the angrier she became; the more the colours changed as her emotions did. His father ignored him, comforting his wife instead, promising her that everything would be all right.

That night, when the boy had gone to bed, his father had visited him to kiss him goodnight as usual. Before the kiss he whispered, 'I didn't see any colours, son. I believe that you did. I believe you are telling the truth. You see, I believe that Mother Nature has given people the capability to be more aware of the world than they ever realise. I think she has given you a very special gift.

'Do you know other people who can see the colours, Daddy?'

'No son, I don't know anyone, not even grown-ups, who can do it.'

'Am I poorly, like Misty?'

'Good heavens, no. In fact, I think you might be healthier than any other little boy you will ever meet...'

For the next few years the boy shared all of his increasing experiences of colour with his father. It became their secret. Within two months of starting comprehensive school, of being surrounded by a society of teachers and pupils, the boy stopped talking about his insights. His father stopped asking. From then on the boy's sense of isolation grew.

The killer grew to fill the space available to him. He didn't recognise how significantly he changed. He was aware of some elements but not the overall shift. However he was increasingly aware of how different he was from other people. He never considered that it was the result of the changes inside him.

He killed deliberately for the first time when he was fifteen. Not surprisingly, it was a cat. He wanted to see what he had missed when Misty had been taken to the vets for the last time. He saw the black cloud. He wondered dispassionately what happened to it when it dissolved. He wondered if he was breathing in the last breath of the dying animal.

Over time he lost such interest. Instead he became obsessed with the source of his gift. It came, he realised, from his subconscious. He didn't attempt to study it the way an academic would. Instead he sought to experience it, to delve into it deeply in the way a deep-sea diver would strive to go ever further down, to leave the light far behind.

As the years passed the killer's senses became more and more acute. He learnt how to see through darkness, how to hear even the slightest rhythm. He came to appreciate how wise his father was to believe in Nature. He found that he could see and hear the natural elements of the planet growing, dying and changing as the seasons passed. Nature, too, in all its many aspects had its colours. What it lacked as far as he could tell was a mind, a difference between conscious and subconscious. Nature did not have distinct ruling parts. Nature was a congruent system, without internal debate or doubt, at peace with itself, at odds only with man.

Although he pursued it for a time, killing animals became boring and pointless. No matter how sharp his senses, he couldn't see what he was looking for; he decided, therefore, that he was looking in the wrong places.

So he turned his attention to the herd, to those who, on the outside at least, were his own kind. He sought comparisons. He did not need to search to find an obvious leader. That was the easy part. He did have to give a little thought to the others. Not too much, though. It was simply a case of ensuring the correct progression. His purpose when killing amongst the herd was two-fold. He wanted to learn and he wanted to teach. It was time now to complete both.

The killer broke the light, plunging the tree into darkness, and walked to the side of the house. He sat with his back against the garage doors and waited. There was no urgency in either his movements or his breathing. He knew this place well. He knew what was going to happen. It was, he thought, as inevitable as daybreak.

Ten minutes passed before the front door opened and the man came out to investigate what had happened. He stood with his back to the garage. The killer rose and approached him silently. He didn't speak until he was close enough to whisper the man's name.

'Marcus.'

And with that the final lesson began.

49.

When Marcus saw that the light on the willow tree had suddenly gone out he felt a nervous tremor run through his body. His mind asked the obvious question even though he had already decided on the answer.

Was it a simple fault or a deliberate act?

Marcus didn't believe in coincidences any more than Peter Jones did. The removal and colouring of the purple branch could have been an act of mindless vandalism and the darkness could just be the result of a technical malfunction. Only he was sure that he had interpreted the first act correctly and that meant this was the development of a pattern rather than a coincidence. The darkness was a summons, a call to a meeting. It was the second direct communication from the killer.

However, as Marcus was fond of reminding his staff, it took two to make a conversation. He was not obliged to accept the meeting request. In fact, it would be downright stupid if he did. Only, if he was going to refuse now, why had he rejected Peter's offer of protection? He might as well have let the policeman put him in a safe room somewhere and acknowledged, at least to himself, that he was too scared to see this thing through.

Truth be told, he was more scared than he had ever been. The fear was almost paralysing in its intensity. He felt as if he had to actually force himself to make the most basic of movements, to think the most obvious thoughts. So why had he been so dismissive of Peter's concerns? Surely he could have admitted his own fear and still refused the offer of safety? Instead he had chosen to hide behind his skills, to seek shelter behind what he knew best. It was his de-fault position. He was used to being the boss, the expert, to getting his own way and having people do what he wanted. That was how he liked to live his life – how he had been living it for as long as he could remember.

Marcus looked into the darkness and wondered why he was only just realising this now. When he had taught others about the emotional and psychological filters they created through which they viewed all of their experiences, why hadn't he paused to consider his own? Why had he failed to recognise the feedback that would have told him loud and clear that he was too used to wielding power and seemingly incapable of accepting anyone else's? Why had it taken the death of Simon to open up this level of awareness?

And what else had he missed about himself?

Any other time that question would have consumed his thoughts. The paradox, of course, which he acknowledged readily, was that if it had been any other time, any other situation, he wouldn't have been asking himself the question. It would have been business as normal. He would have been too busy disassociating from everyone else, seeking to understand them well enough to create the desired influence, to have ever considered looking at and listening to himself. He knew how to create an emotional distance from others in order to help them. He knew how to avoid being dragged along by the current of their fears and concerns. He had loved being the expert, the master influencer. But at what cost? Who had he become? Perhaps even more importantly, who had he missed the opportunity to become?

Marcus suddenly wondered why he was planning to divorce Anne-Marie and not the other way round? He thought again of her recent text. He had decided that they should separate for his own selfish reasons. Now, though, he was forced to concede that she would be better off without him.

Perhaps if things went horribly wrong tonight she would be without him in a way that neither would ever have imagined.

Marcus thought of the panic button in the bedroom. It would take no more than twenty seconds to get to it and press it. Six minutes later, so he had been assured, a team of armed police would be on the premises.

The worst case scenario? He would look like an idiot if the lighting had suffered a simple electrical failure, and he would have also demonstrated to Peter just how very scared he was.

The best possible result? The killer would be arrested. Or shot.

Marcus shivered for the second time in as many minutes. Now it was his own thoughts that scared him. He had always argued against the availability, let alone the use of, the death penalty. He believed that society should only sanction killing in time of war. He supported the view that even the worst of criminals had rights and they had to be respected. If society failed to do that it became as bad as those it was punishing.

Only here and now he was thinking that it would be a great result if he summoned the police and someone – a man whom, presumably, would have to go home to his family afterwards – shot the killer dead. Because he was terrified, he, Marcus Kline, the man who had always been so sure about so much, was actually considering staying locked inside the safety of his home whilst the police killed on his behalf. How could he possibly justify that?

Simon.

That was the answer. The simple answer that under-pinned everything right now. Simon's death had not been a random act. His misfortune was not that he had been in the wrong place at the wrong time. His tragedy had been in knowing Marcus Kline. Being close to him. Marcus felt as responsible for Simon's death as he ever had about any-thing. In the past, though, he had only ever felt responsible for success. And he had always regarded it as his success, even if others had acted out the associated events.

Marcus had enjoyed his celebrity status, but he had chosen that deliberately. Whilst he recognised now that it had certainly satisfied and grown his ego, he had always believed that he made it happen purely as a means of promoting his business. After all, his first instinct had always been to operate in the shadows. He had never needed positive feedback from others to reassure him of his skill. He knew what he was capable of. He had always got a kick from helping someone change, making something happen, knowing that it was the direct result of his ability – and watching it all play out from the sidelines;

comfortable that only the key players knew who was responsible and who to thank for their success.

Now he felt responsible for the most tragic, terrible loss. And yet he was terrified of walking out into the shadows.

The truth was Simon's death could justify almost any decision he made right now. He could use it to justify locking himself in and calling the police or walking out to engage in the conflict he believed was waiting for him.

Perhaps I am just a fraud? Marcus heard the question and felt his head pound. *Perhaps when push comes to shove, I'd rather talk than push? Perhaps I really am out of my depth?*

Marcus stared down at his feet. They looked as if they were glued to the kitchen floor. He forced them to move. His breathing was ragged and fast. He had no idea how to control it. When he reached the front door, he opened it without hesitation. He knew that the slightest pause now and his determination would desert him forever. He found it impossible to make his mind work coherently. His body moved and he let it. Not because he had a plan, not because he was intending to influence, just because he had to.

He stepped out into the darkness and felt his right hand close the front door behind him. He heard the latch snick into place. It was a distant sound. He crossed the path and walked across the garden. His arms hung lifeless. His eyes were fixed on the willow tree. He was lost in a way he never had been before.

As he closed on the willow tree, Marcus Kline realised dimly that everything that had happened in the last few days, everything that was going to happen in the future, came down to an interaction right here and now between two people.

And he felt that he didn't know either of them.

50.

That feeling changed the instant the killer said his name.

'*Marcus.*'

Sometimes when alone in the dark the unexpected sound of a familiar voice brings with it a sense of safety and reassurance. Sometimes, the worst of times, it creates a very different response. As Marcus Kline heard and recognised the voice a mixture of outrage, confusion and despair swept through him. He stood still with his back to the killer, emotions swirling inside him, battling for supremacy.

They were equally matched.

He thought of the last time he had seen and talked to the person who had already killed three people. He thought of all the other times they had *communicated*. Why hadn't he *seen* something, *heard* something, that had offered some insight, revealed at least a glimpse into the true nature of the man? How had he, of all people, missed this?

'I know how to keep my colours hidden,' the killer said as if reading his thoughts. 'I have learnt how to make myself invisible.'

The words pulled at Marcus. He felt an almost irresistible urge to turn and confront his opponent. He fought it, doing everything in his power to keep any feelings of tension out of his back. He didn't want to show this man anything. He knew instinctively that he had to resist his influence. That he had to, quite literally, keep him out of his mind.

'It's only a matter of time,' the killer said.

Marcus laughed out loud. It was an unexpected reaction. He heard his laughter as if it was coming from someone else. He found it strangely reassuring. He felt it take his outrage, his anger, and move it out of him, travelling on his breath, revealed in the air as a fine, grey mist. He looked at it, watched it dissolve around him. It felt as if he now had an ally. He felt the anger give him strength.

'I see it more clearly than you,' the killer said. 'That is the difference between us. Even between you, the great Marcus Kline, and me. By my standards you live in a world that is only grey. I see your anger for what it really is. I see it vividly. Even in the dark. If I choose to, I can breathe into your anger and change it completely.'

There was something in the killer's voice, something more than his words, that changed Marcus's state. The anger and the associated feeling of strength disappeared. It was replaced by emptiness, a void that seemed endless and eternal, that offered nothing and made him feel insignificant and weak. As weak as a child unable to control the events he was involved in.

A memory played like a film in front of him. It was from his childhood. He was with his parents in the city. They were shopping in a crowded, bustling department store. He had become separated from them and in his panic had found his way out onto the street. Marcus, the young boy, had been swept away by the constant stream of people walking as only adults did with determination and significance and a focus that was fixed solely on their destination. No-one took any notice of the child being forced to walk at the pace fixed by the crowd, too fast for him, wanting to turn around, wanting to shout out for help, unable to do either, crying with increasing desperation as he became more and more lost.

Just as Marcus had felt the strength in his legs desert him, just as he was sure that he was about to fall and be trampled by the crowd, two strong hands reached down and scooped him up. He recognised his father's smell and touch instantly. He felt an incredible sense of freedom as he was lifted into the air, his father standing strong and secure with his back to the crowd, forcing it to separate and move around them. His father said nothing, using his thumb to gently wipe the boy's tears away. Marcus waited until he had finished, then buried his face against his father's shoulder and screamed his fear out.

The few, brief moments – for that's all it was – that Marcus spent being carried ever further away from his family stayed with him for the rest of his life. As the boy grew into a man he became increasingly committed to a simple philosophy. Never again was he going to be controlled by the crowd. He was going to control it. And he was also going to learn how to be comfortable being alone. He was going to be independent and strong, moving to his own rhythm, setting the pace, the flow, and the direction for others.

The recollection disappeared into the void and was replaced by a single question,

Whose rhythm are you moving to now?

Marcus knew the answer. The killer had been setting the pace from the very beginning. He hadn't realised that at the start because the killer hadn't wanted him to. The killer had been confident enough to simply direct the beat without anyone knowing he was doing so. This was a man so supremely self-assured that he was content to conduct the orchestra from the shadows. It was only as he had increased the tempo that he had been obliged to show his hand. And even then he had made sure that only Marcus recognised it.

So what else did Marcus know about the man standing behind him? Aside from his name and the nature of their relationship. The answer was, very little. The difficulty, even for Marcus, in hearing and uncovering anything more from the man's tone and pace of voice, from his language patterns, was that his conscious mind was getting in the way. It was still scrambling, trying to recover from the fact that he had known this man for years and had not recognised his true nature. He was truly shocked by his failure and, for the second time that night, he found himself wondering about his own capabilities and his relationships with the people around him. He wondered too about the skill of a man who could successfully remain in disguise around him for years. How was that possible? Before tonight Marcus would have said that it was not. That was another significant error on his part.

It would also be an error he realised to stand here in silence. He needed to engage, to communicate. After all, that was his strength.

Supposedly.

No! It was what he did best, better than anyone else on the planet.

Apart, perhaps, from one other.

No! Everyone had weaknesses. Even the killer. He just had to uncover and exploit them. This was going to be a battle of words, of insight and influence. How did he describe it when talking to Peter not so very long ago? *A communications joust.* Although he had deliberately understated it then, Marcus was now forced to accept the reality that the confrontation came with a pressure – potentially paralysing to both his body and his mind – that was far greater than he could have imagined.

To have any chance of beating this man Marcus needed his senses to be as sharp as they ever had been and his conscious mind to be silent as snowfall. He needed to recognise every detail and determine the most important communication patterns the other used. He needed to apply everything that he knew to his own advantage. He needed to regain control of the rhythm of this encounter. To do that he needed to seize the initiative and begin the next round of conversation.

Before he did Marcus remembered with a force that rocked him, the most important thing that he knew about the man standing behind him.

He had killed Simon.

It was that fact that was going to be the source of his power. It was the reason why he was going to win no matter what it took. Despite his recent doubts and shocking self-revelation, Marcus Kline realised that now, more than at any other time in his life, he needed to be the unbeatable genius. He owed Simon at least that much.

Perhaps, Marcus thought, as he readied himself for battle, *he isn't the only one I owe.*

51.

The press wanted the conference to be scheduled in time for them to get their reports out for the early evening news. Their agenda was not the same as Peter's. He needed to create damage limitation. He needed the story of Simon Westbury's death to go out later, when fewer people were bothered about what had happened during the day.

So he had announced that a press conference would be held at 5.30. Then he had put it back to 6pm and then again to 6.30. Everyone involved knew the game that he was playing. He knew that they did. And he didn't care. He had far greater responsibilities than satisfying the corporate and egotistical demands of newspaper editors.

More than that, he had an almost overwhelming concern for Marcus Kline thudding through his mind. It was threatening to extinguish his thinking and his skills.

Peter was in no doubt that Marcus's life was at risk. And rather than search for the source of that threat, he now had to waste time sitting in on a press conference that would reveal nothing, gain nothing, and serve no useful purpose in hunting the killer. Such was the job. And he was very good at doing his job. Only not now. Not when it was this personal. Right now he wanted to tell the journalists gathered in front of him to fuck off, and to keep out of his way until he had made Marcus safe.

Only he wasn't going to have to say a word, so there was no risk of him saying anything even remotely inappropriate. Actually, the Detective Chief Inspector knew that, ultimately, even if pushed, he wouldn't say a wrong word. It wasn't because of Peter's professional pride. It was because of his sense of identity. Much as he loved Marcus, it was something he daren't fracture.

Peter followed Robin Miles, the Assistant Chief Constable and Press Liaison Officer, and Detective Superintendent Mike Briggs into the staff dining area that had been turned into a temporary press conference room. They took their seats, with Miles in the centre. The journalists fell silent. Miles waited for a moment and then stood up. He held a copy of the brief, agreed statement in his left hand. The camera crews from the major TV networks went to work. The others had their pens poised. Not one of them expected a revelation. Their task was to force one. Miles knew that.

'Ladies and Gentlemen, welcome to Central Police Station,' Miles began. 'As I am sure you are all aware this is a very serious matter. Six days ago, the body of Derrick Smith was found in his home in the city. Four days later the body of Paul Clusker was discovered at his home in Wollaton. Today, the body of another adult male has been found. It appears that there are very obvious similarities between this and the previous two deaths. Because of the circumstances of this latest death it is not appropriate for me to take questions at this time.'

The journalists murmured their displeasure. They had, of course, expected Miles to say this. It was standard procedure in such situations. For their part, they had not the slightest intention of remaining silent.

'I'm sure you can at least tell us just how many officers are involved in the inquiry?' The question came from one of the older, more experienced journalists sitting on the back row. He knew that to have any chance at all of prying really useful information out of the officers at the table, the first few questions at least had to be non-threatening.

Miles recognised the ploy. He had to balance keeping the journalists onside without saying anything that could harm the investigation. He paused deliberately and then answered the question. 'There are over sixty officers working full-time, but because of the seriousness of the case all of the police family – and by that I mean officers, support staff, community support officers and specials – are looking for anything that will lead to the arrest of the offender.'

'And how much is it costing?' This from a different journalist, another experienced professional, keen to keep the momentum going, smart enough to keep circling the main issues.

'Cost is not an issue.' Miles said. 'We will spend whatever it takes.'

'Is this the third victim of the so-called Boiled Egg Killer?' The questioner was a young man sitting on the front row. He leaned forwards as he spoke. Behind him some of the less experienced journalists chuckled at the use of the title. Their more experienced colleagues frowned and shook their heads in anger. The question was too much, too soon, and they knew what Miles would do with it. One journalist, Dave Johnson, did neither. He simply closed his notebook and pressed down on it hard with the palm of his left hand, as if trying to keep something contained inside.

The Assistant Chief Constable listened to the question and hid his pleasure at being given a way out so easily. 'Nothing has been confirmed at this current time. We are asking everyone to remain vigilant until the perpetrator has been caught, although there is no reason to suspect that the general public are at risk.'

The young journalist seized on Mile's comment. 'Do you believe, then, that the killer is targeting specific people?'

'I don't believe anything. I wait until the evidence tells me what has happened and then I share that with you good people as and when it is appropriate to do so.' Miles raised an open palm, ending the interaction. He looked around the room. They all knew it was over. At least for today. 'I have nothing more to say at this time. If any of your viewers or readers have any information that they think might be relevant, I would ask that they contact us by calling Crimestoppers on 0800 555111 or by calling our switchboard directly using one of the following options.' None of the journalists wrote the numbers down. It didn't matter. He wasn't talking to them. He was talking to the millions of people who would watch this on their TV or hear it on their radio. When he had finished he offered the journalists in front of him a grim smile. 'Thank you all very much for your time. Good evening, ladies and gentlemen.'

Miles led Peter and Briggs out of the room. The conference had been as brief as possible. Peter nodded his thanks. 'Good job,' he murmured. Miles shook their hands and left the two detectives alone.

Briggs's face was hard. 'We need to start making headway on this really fast,' he said. 'Let's hope that our man contacts Johnson again, that we get the break we need through him.'

'Yes guv.' Even though it was easier, and quicker, to agree with his boss, Peter didn't really think that the reporter's involvement was going to make any difference to the eventual outcome. Things were moving too fast. Besides, his instinct was telling him that the killer was not genuinely compelled to share his story with the press. Instead, Peter felt that the killer had a very different reason for contacting Johnson. *Maybe he does just want to create a distraction*, Peter thought, *to start a forest fire as Marcus called it, to make sure that I waste some of my time managing that.*

If that had been his intention, the killer had certainly been successful. If there was one resource that Peter didn't have enough of right now, it was time. He quickened his pace as he left the building. He couldn't help but feel that despite all his best efforts he was, like everyone else, moving to the killer's beat.

52.

'We can't stand here all night,' Marcus Kline said to the man who had killed three people in less than a week.

'Yes we can. We could just stand here, learning true patience, waiting for the display when dawn breaks and night hands over to day. That's something I've done many times.'

'Where?'

'Right here, right where we are standing now.' The killer sighed. 'You didn't know that of course because your senses are not as bright as you think they are. You've missed more than you could ever possibly realise. All your life you have made the mistake of comparing yourself to the herd instead of seeking out those rare individuals who have truly learnt how to be different. You thought that by learning how to influence the herd you had somehow escaped from it. You thought that you were better than it. That is so stupid – I find it really annoying actually, for a man who is supposed to be so insightful. Dear God! You didn't even see me. And I have been so close to you for so many years.'

'You believe in God, do you?'

'Ha! All you need to know – no, all I am prepared to share with you – is that I can see a world you cannot. A world that most people cannot see. And it is our world. Just experienced more acutely. Anyway, enough of that, we will continue the lesson later. The truth is that I'm not planning for us to stay out here tonight.'

'And everything is happening according to plan, is it?'

'It is so far.'

'And what is the plan for the rest of tonight?'

'Can't you guess?'

Yes. All too easily, thought Marcus.

Marcus changed the subject again. 'For someone who sees everything so clearly, so much more clearly than I do at least, you have made one very basic mistake.'

'Oh? What would that be?'

'There is no such thing as the human herd. That's very lazy thinking for a man with your capabilities. When I stand alone in the city and watch people passing by I see individuals, not a collective. Whilst they might have some things in common, they are all different, too. If that wasn't the case, I wouldn't be able to do what I do.'

'Which is to be in control of them. To influence them. You do love that power, don't you?'

Marcus shrugged. 'I think I might have been seduced by it.'

'I find it amazing, the insights people achieve when they know they are close to death.' The killer's voice trailed off. Marcus sensed that he had become caught up in an unexpected memory. For his part, Marcus couldn't help but think again of Simon. He forced himself to ask another question.

'What insights do you gain when you are so close to

the deaths you cause?'

'So many things,' the killer replied, his voice sounding as if he was waking from a deep sleep. 'People reveal themselves most – *nature* reveals itself most – during times of transition. The more significant the transition, the greater the revelation. You must have seen that for yourself, surely?'

'I have watched the people I work with learn and grow and change for the better. I improve the quality of life. I don't take life. No one has the right to just take life!'

'See! The change in you is already beginning.' The killer's voice dropped to little more than a whisper. 'For as long as I have known you your arrogance has been vivid and obnoxious and impenetrable. Like an oil slick slashed with bright, abusive lines of colour. The same colours you would see if you put a shit-eating insect under a microscope. Your arrogance surrounded you. Even when you were silent it poured out of your skin. I hated being near you. I hated watching it reach out and draw people in. I hated the way it fed off the weakness of others. How could I not want to kill you? But now, already, it's starting to diminish, to pull apart. If only you could see it. If only you could have seen it. You would have spent every waking moment trying to scrub yourself clean, I promise you.'

Marcus rolled his shoulders involuntarily. He wanted to speak, to ask another question, but words seemed a long way away.

'I see the difference,' the killer continued. 'I see the difference between how you pretend to give something away and how nature truly does. I see how you fuel your own ego. I have actually seen it grow! And then I see the bright and gentle colours, the sharing and release every

morning when night hands over to day. So many people
travel to other places in the hope of seeing colours in the
sky, when all they need to do if they want to see the real
beauty of nature is know how to watch daybreak.

'Of course, if they could do that, they would see all
the other things, too. They would see you for what you
really are. They would feel repulsed at the thought of being
near you. They would vomit at the prospect of touching
you. I assure you, I am not being lazy when I merge you
altogether into the herd. I am protecting myself. When I
watch people passing by I see so many versions of you
that my senses can barely cope. I have to – had to – find a
way to dull you all down. Insight, real insight, is a painful
companion if you don't find a way to leave it behind. In
my lifetime I have had to learn how to *stop* looking and
listening. Whereas you, you pride yourself on your training
and skill and yet compared to me you are still blind. And if
you knew the truth, if you had my experience, you would
be grateful that you are.'

Marcus forced the breath up from his lower belly,
forced his mouth to move, prayed that the words would
come out as he needed them to. The sound of his voice
was like the most precious gift. He felt tears in his eyes
as he spoke.

'Insight is meant to be used to help people. Whatever
it is, however it's used, insight is the basis for all positive
change.'

'And still you sound like a consultant!' The killer snorted. 'What you fail to understand living in your clearly-de-
fined, simplistic world, is that when you really know how
to look you see the colours on the fly as easily as you
see the brightness of the sun. Only it doesn't make you

think the fly is beautiful – it gives you even more reason to destroy it.

'When I let myself look at you, at any of you, you have nowhere to hide. I see everything. There is nothing you can keep hidden. No thought, no desire, no experience. You have no secrets.' The killer paused to take breath. 'Can you imagine how disgusting you all look to me?

'Do you have any idea how you sound to me?'

'I have no interest. Your hearing is as poor as your vision.' The killer tapped Marcus on the right shoulder. The sudden physical contact sent a shockwave through his body. It stopped abruptly at his hips. Marcus gasped. The killer stepped back and waited, giving Marcus time to realise it for himself.

'My legs...I can't feel them.'

'And all the time you thought you were standing there, keeping your back to me, because you had decided to. I told you, everything is working according to my plan, not yours.'

Marcus shook his head in disbelief. Somehow this man had hypnotised him so subtly that he had not noticed it happening, and yet so powerfully that he could no longer move. And he had always believed – *always!* – that a person could not be hypnotised against their will.

'It can't be against your will if you don't know it's happening,' the killer said.

'No!' Marcus licked his lips. He was surprised how dry they felt. His stomach churned. He tried to hold back the growing tide of panic and despair threatening to overwhelm his gut. He needed to talk, to remind himself of who he was and what he knew. 'No, you cannot be reading my mind. That isn't possible. You can't tell what someone else is thinking without the aid of visual or auditory cues. Whatever else you are, you are not a mind reader – not in the way you want me to believe. You might have been able to fool others, but I'm not like them.'

'Of course you're not,' the killer's tone was deliberately patronising. 'And for once you are right. I'm not actually inside your mind. I'm simply standing here watching the colours change as your fear grows. Your thoughts have their own hue and they are as obvious to me – and more honest – than your words.'

'And what do you see of yourself? What insights do you find there?'

'I only ever look outwards. I have no desire for introspection. Explorers only ever look ahead.'

Marcus nodded. At least he had been right all along about the killer's motive. 'So you are searching?'

'You should try it. If you did you might realise something very close to home.'

'What?' The question came out before Marcus could stop it.

'Look down.'

The instruction was irresistible. Marcus looked at his legs and gasped. Blood was seeping from a wound in his right thigh. His trousers were sodden. The panic in his gut pulled low and then surged through him. He felt his insides twisting and turning uncontrollably as the panic raced upwards. Marcus vomited violently, spewing the contents of his stomach onto the lawn.

The killer waited until he finished retching. 'See? I punctured your thigh with a scalpel and you felt nothing. I used a point to make a point. Well, two actually. The first is that I am better than you. In every way. You will die tonight and I do want you to die knowing you were never the best. The good news is that you now know you will only feel pain if I want you to. And I promise you – even you – that no matter what I do to you I will not cause you pain unless you try to do something stupidly defiant. Much as I despise you I am not a sadist.'

Marcus spat once, twice, trying to rid his mouth of the vile taste. It took a moment before he was able to speak again. 'Is that how you are able to sleep at night?', he said at last 'By telling yourself that you are a pain-free murderer?'

'We both know that you are clutching at straws. It's a sign of the most extreme desperation when a person is grateful for even the most fragile support, just the briefest respite. We both know that, now don't we?'

Marcus blinked. He felt himself rocking on his heels.

'The truth is you can let go of everything,' the killer continued. 'Even the most recent of events can disappear beyond the horizon, and you can just float comfortably, supported by the power of your unconscious. Now or in a moment or two, or whenever you feel it most, you can just relax and float, feeling completely calm, letting the current drift you towards the one thing you can be sure of...'

Marcus blinked again. This time his eyes stayed closed. He felt them wanting to remain that way. He felt himself wanting to move into the darkness that was created. He forced them open.

'That's right,' the killer nodded his confirmation. 'I want you to keep your eyes open, to be able to see where you are going. Where *I* am going. You can drift down deeper later. For now just float on the surface and know that you will go deeper when I need you to. You do understand, don't you?'

Marcus nodded. His tongue was sticking to the roof of his mouth. The trance wrapped itself around him, protecting him from the chill night air. Because the killer had not deepened it fully, a part of Marcus's rational mind was still able to function. It was telling him that he would get one chance to break free – only one – and that he would have to take it if he was to have any hope of survival. The voice was faint. It kept drifting in and out of his awareness. It reminded him of the times he used to call Anne-Marie when she was abroad on photo shoots and how, in some places, the reception on the phone was always poor. It was a useful reminder. It was connected to so many things. *The complexity of life is all around you,* the voice said. *It is your lifeline. Hold onto it.*

If the killer heard the voice in Marcus's mind, he didn't comment on it. Instead he said, 'It's time to go inside now. We need to sit you down and move things along. Lead the way.'

Marcus did as he was instructed. He was able to walk without pain. He was vaguely aware that his thigh was damp and sticky. The voice in his mind threatened to break up completely as he moved towards the house. He strained to hear its final message. *Look and listen,* he heard, realising with a shock that it now *was* the voice of Anne-Marie. *And remember…*Her voice disappeared and then came back again. *Remember…*Now her words turned into muffled, indistinguishable sounds followed by silence as he opened the front door.

'Please,' he heard himself say as his tongue suddenly loosened from the roof of his mouth. 'Please!'

It was enough to restore the connection. If only for a second. Anne-Marie's final sentence was both a plea and an instruction. It reminded him of the most important thing of all. Of the one thing he was in danger of forgetting.

Remember that words are your weapon!

And then all contact with the outside world was lost.

53.

Marcus walked instinctively into the dining room. The killer placed a brown leather bag on the table. He pulled out a chair and gestured for Marcus to sit. He did. He realised that it was a chair he had never used before. Once sitting he felt that it was holding him in place. As if his body had been drained of the power to move. He considered it strange that he had never known this was the chair in which he was going to die.

He knew immediately that he could not allow himself to accept that.

He had no idea how to resist.

He wanted to speak, but he didn't know what to say.

Not yet.

The killer crossed to the window and casually pulled the curtains together until they were almost touching. Through the slight gap Marcus could see nothing but darkness. It served as just another layer of separation.

'I want you to see the darkness, just enough of it anyway,' the killer said. 'I think in your case it will be helpful.' He returned to Marcus's side and opened the bag, removing a roll of heavy duty, commercial adhesive tape. 'I need to wrap this around you,' he said. 'It's important for what I am going to do later that you really are very still.'

Marcus knew that now was the time to move. Before it became impossible to do so. Only it already felt impossible to do so. Even before the tape.

And then he realised that it didn't matter.

As long as he wasn't blindfolded or gagged he could still win this fight. Perhaps, though, he needed to frame it differently? Perhaps he had to stop thinking of this as a battle?

Yes! That was the key!

The thought raced through him like a slight but unmistakeable electric current. He had to define this on his own terms. Then he would be able to apply his skills; be resistant to whatever he saw or heard. For the first time the wound in his leg began to throb.

'Nottingham is built on caves,' the killer went on as he fastened Marcus in place. 'I'm sure you know that. Personally I love that fact. It seems so appropriate given that most peoples' lives are built on caves. Hollow. Empty. And they know it. They just choose to do nothing about it. That's the part I can't understand, that's what makes me despise them. They choose to waste this golden opportunity. You know this. After all, you are the one who works with them! All you ever do, though, is help them build an extra layer above the cave. That is at best only a temporary solution. It leaves them with so little substance when you dig just below the surface. Although, of course, deep below the cave it is a different matter. If you know how to look way, way beneath the cave, if you know how to reach the deepest places, then you will see the most glorious show. Well, I say "you" but I obviously mean myself. Even if I had taken you with me on my – what shall we call them? – research visits throughout this week, if I had let you stand next to me, if I had invited you to look, you would still only have seen the surface structure.'

Marcus forced himself to look and listen to the man who had killed Simon, who intended to kill him, as if he were a client.

He tried to force his sense of *self*, the place he was looking and listening from, to the very back of his head, as far away from his eyes as possible. He tried to get into that place from which he was always most aware, from which he always did his very best work. In his current state it was more than he could do to get there fully but he was, he recognised, closer to it than he had been since the encounter began; close enough at least to begin a response of his own.

'Let me tell you the mistake you are making in the way you think.' Marcus found his voice. 'And it is a mistake that I understand fully, one that I have been guilty of myself. It's simply this: however different you may be from the rest of us – and I accept that you are – you do inevitably share one thing in common. We are all built on caves. All of us. Even you. And I can see into you far more clearly than you can possibly believe, *Ethan*.'

Ethan Hall, the son of Samuel Hall, the man who had tended their garden and the willow tree for more years than they had lived in the house, stared down at him and bared his teeth in a harsh parody of a smile.

'Are you hoping to create the first semblance of rapport by using my name? Is that it? Are you thinking you can connect with me and weaken me as you begin your fragile counter-attack?'

'No. The caves inside you are far too dark and deep and dangerous for me to want to venture in.' Marcus paused, watching the other man's face intently, looking for every response no matter how minimal. He was starting the process of identifying patterns, of making associations. He was beginning to feel that he was moving out of the trance. 'Besides you are far too aware to be taken in by something so obvious.'

'So now you shift to flattery? What next, will you try and create in me a sense of obligation? Are you employing all those mundane tools they teach university students in an attempt to influence me?'

'Ethan, no one is ever going to flatter you. Whatever you think about yourself, however you process things differently, the rest of us – those few anyway who ever hear of you – will just think of you as part of a very specific herd.'

'Oh?'

'Yes. You're just an insane killer. That's the pack you belong to. In the grand scheme of things there's nothing very significant about what you do. You are not going to change the world. In fact you will be forgotten as soon as another one like you starts making headlines.'

'You are wrong!' Ethan screamed. He grabbed Marcus's hair suddenly, pulling his head back, exposing and stretching his throat, lowering his face over him, staring into his eyes. 'I can see and do what no one else can! I can see the colours of the universe in every movement, in every sound! I can taste your words! I can use space in ways that no one else does! I am –'

'– A synesthete.'

Marcus whispered the word. It was more than enough. Ethan released his grip and staggered back. He blinked two, three, four times before he was able to regain control.

'How – How did you know?' He stammered.

'Because you have made no attempt to hide it from me. You have talked about it, boasted about it even, sure that I have never heard about the condition.'

'It isn't a condition! It's a gift!'

'Synaesthesia is a neurological condition in which stimulation of one sensory or cognitive pathway automatically associates with and fires a second pathway. Or in some individuals even more. It's evident in your case that most of your senses are involved. You clearly make associations in ways that only a rare handful of people have ever done. You experience every interaction, including this one, in a powerful super-sensory way. I've been aware of synaesthesia for a long time, Ethan. Given what I do for a living and my area of expertise, how could you expect me not to be? How could you expect me to hear what you said about yourself in the garden and not realise eventually what that meant? Did you think I was lying when I said that I could see into you?'

Marcus studied Ethan's face and his body language. He could see the effect his words were having. He guessed that the younger man had never been exposed in this way before. He knew how very difficult it was to talk for the first time about a deeply held secret. He remained silent, watching the turmoil rage inside the man who had been born a synesthete, learning everything that he could, recognising all the things that he had missed from their time together in the past.

Marcus Kline had first met Ethan Hall when his father, Samuel, started bringing him to work. The fifteen-year-old boy had expressed a desire to become a gardener,

Samuel explained. He had a natural affinity with nature. For the next five or six years the pair had tended the garden together. The boy had been quiet and reserved. He had performed his tasks carefully and well. On occasions Marcus recalled him simply looking, unmoving for several minutes on end, at a flower, at the grass, at the willow tree. When asked what he found so fascinating, Ethan had simply shaken his head and gone back to work.

Suddenly and without warning, he had stopped coming. Samuel claimed that his son had taken the opportunity to work with a large and respected landscape gardening company in the South of England. Marcus had known that he was lying, but thought nothing more of it.

Now he was watching Samuel's son as intently as he had ever watched anyone in his entire life. His mind and senses were once again fully under his control.

Finally Ethan spoke. He turned his back on the gold framed mirror hanging on the dining room wall and looked down at the floor as he said, 'You cannot imagine what every day is like for me. Whenever I hear a sound – any sound – I see colours and firework shapes. They move in the air. Some fizz, some explode, some dance before they disappear. When I hear or read words I get a taste sensation on my tongue. A different taste for different word sounds. The associations are very specific. They never change. Number sequences exist in space around me. For example, the number four is always very close, to my right, just here,' his hand reached up to just in front of his right shoulder, 'whereas the number six is always several paces away directly in front of me. And I remember everything. Easily. I don't know how to forget.' He turned to face Marcus. 'Now do you understand why I think your skills are so limited compared to mine? Why I find your arrogance so despicable?'

Marcus saw for the first time the true nature of Ethan's experience. He saw it with a clarity that made his back straighten despite the tape that held him tight.

He said, 'What you have just described isn't a skill Ethan. It isn't a skill because you can't control it. Like all synesthetes, you experience automatic, involuntary responses. I've trained all my life to recognise patterns, to make or change associations deliberately. However acute your senses, they are the result of your genetic hardwiring, of some unique neural connections in your brain, not of training and study. Essentially, however you experience words or sounds or numbers, you suffer from a pronounced form of sensory overload. The clue is in the name, synaesthesia. It comes from the Greek for the words "together' and "sensation". You might be able to see and hear things in ways that most people cannot, but that doesn't make you a genius Ethan. When push comes to shove, you're just a killer who can see colours that others can't.'

'And you, for all of your clever words, are a man who is going to die tonight.' Ethan looked at his watch. 'Soon.'

He moved past Marcus and reached into his brown leather bag. Marcus twisted his head, desperate to watch what was happening. He couldn't turn far enough. He was able, though, to use the mirror. The sight of the tools and the clothing filled him with dread. He had never really considered before just how Ethan had gone about his work. The answer sent him scurrying back into the front of his mind, into the skin on his face, into his beating heart.

Marcus fought to regain control of his breathing. He reminded himself as the fear tried to scramble his thoughts that for words to have the desired influence they had to be delivered on the most appropriate breath. That breath had to be delivered from the most appropriate place. And it had to be controlled.

The weight of the drill as it thumped down onto the table top sent shock waves through him that, paradoxically, drew him into his flesh, pulled him into the very part of his being that was about to be broken apart.

Marcus knew that he had to get back into the deeper recesses of his mind, into the so-called reptilian brain. Into the one part of him that Ethan Hall could not touch. Marcus tried once again to shift himself there. It felt like he was trying to force himself through a dense, resistant fog.

And then he looked at the window, at the space between the curtains, and for a brief second he imagined that he saw Anne-Marie's terrified face peering in. He saw her as clearly as if she was really there. It was a pattern interrupt powerful enough to change his perspective, to let him rush suddenly into the safety of his subconscious.

Ethan said, 'The gulf is so wide, isn't it, between an intellectual understanding and the cold reality of metal?'

Marcus resisted the temptation to look at the chisel, at the razor-sharp scalpel delicate by comparison. Instead he eased a gentle smile across his face. 'You see my arrogance so easily, so completely, so do you not...' He took a deliberate and lengthy in-breath. He could see that Ethan was drawn in by the unfinished question and the unexpected calmness of his delivery. 'When you look into a mirror do you not see your own colours? After all, even an explorer must address his own reflection. So tell me, Ethan, do you not wish to explore the colours you create? Do they not repulse you at least as much as mine? Or are they more vile than even a shit-eating insect?'

Ethan's eyes flashed towards the mirror. It was only the briefest glance. It was enough to give Marcus hope.

'So they are unbearable,' he said. 'You do at least recognise yourself for what you are. You do at least –'

Marcus stopped abruptly, creating silence instead of completion. He watched Ethan struggle to ignore the question that had popped into his mind. Marcus waited until the precise instant he had managed to rid himself of it and then he spoke again, increasing his hold on the killer's attention.

'No wonder you have never been able to have a relationship with another human being. I guess the nearest you ever came to it was with your father. Only eventually you saw colours in him that you hated also, didn't you? That's why you had to leave. Isn't it?' Marcus saw confirmation in Ethan's face. He continued quickly. 'I wonder if nature sees you as clearly as you believe you can see Her? I wonder if animals recognise you for what you are? I wonder if the willow tree senses you somehow? If it screamed silently when you tore off the branch? I wonder these things Ethan. I wonder these things as I feel the mirror tugging on your shoulders, daring you to turn round and look deep inside. Don't you feel it, too, Ethan? Don't you? Feel the mirror pulling you round. Now.'

Ethan turned. He stared into the eyes of his reflection, his mouth opening and closing soundlessly.

Then the killer roared.

54.

Within five minutes of the press conference ending Peter Jones was in the Audi and heading home. He needed to freshen up, a quick wash and a change of shirt, before beginning what promised to be a very long evening.

Nic was in the kitchen when Peter walked in. He was making a pasta dish using tagliatelle, salmon, red chillies and tomatoes. It was clear at a glance that his heart was not in it.

'Didn't expect to see you tonight,' he said, his face registering briefly the unexpected pleasure he felt. It was replaced swiftly by the mixture of resignation and concern that had dominated his mood for the last few days. They hugged. Peter stepped back first. 'You look and feel stressed,' Nic said. 'Has it been a bad day?'

Peter nodded. 'So far, so bad. I'm going nowhere fast. That means I'm going backwards. Marcus is being, quite literally, immoveable. And, tragically, we have another victim.' Peter hesitated. It was clear from Nic's response that he hadn't seen or heard the news. Peter knew what effect Simon's death would have on his partner. Nic had met Simon several times and had taken an instinctive liking to the young man.

'It was Simon Westbury,' Peter said. 'Earlier today.'

Nic's mouth opened. He tried and failed to blink back tears.

Peter wanted to hold and comfort him. He wanted to cry, too. The DCI, however, didn't have time for either. 'I have to keep going,' he said. Before either could move, Peter's mobile phone rang. The very last person he expected a call from was Anne-Marie Wells.

'Sweetheart?'

'Peter! Oh, thank God! I don't know what I'd have done if you'd not answered! I can hardly...I'm so scared, I –'

'– It is me! You've got me!' Peter cut her short. 'Tell me what's happening!'

'Ok. Ok. Sorry.' Peter heard Anne-Marie fighting for control. 'It's Marcus. I came back. I parked the car on the street. I never do, but he always comes out and I needed to walk into the house by myself and so I parked on the street and walked up the drive and the curtains were pulled together and he never does that, not until the last thing at night, so I looked inside and he was there and so was Ethan and he was –'

'What's happened to Marcus?'

The tone in his voice cut through Anne-Marie's hysteria. She gasped and took a step back. The way Peter delivered his question – actually it felt more like a command that had reached through the phone and slapped her in the face – revealed a part of him she had never experienced before. Even in her current state Anne-Marie recognised that there was something frightening about the sudden absolute focus he had turned on her.

Nic saw it, too. He found it even more shocking. Log-ically he had always known that there had to be a part of

Peter's personality – the part that loved to hunt, challenge and confront dangerous criminals – he had never met. Logically it had to exist. Emotionally, Nic had trained himself to avoid thinking about it too much. Now he was encountering it for the first time. Even watching from the sidelines he could feel its power. He could actually see it growing as Peter listened to Anne-Marie. Her words were the catalyst for the transformation he was witnessing. Nic froze, every instinct he possessed telling him to keep still and to remain silent.

Suddenly Peter spoke again. It was to Anne-Marie first. 'You are absolutely certain that is what you saw? And no one saw you? You're sure of that? Right. So now I want you to keep your back to the house and walk to the end of the street, the end where the roundabout is. Do you understand? No! You only do what I tell you! Do anything else and you will get yourself and Marcus killed! Do you understand? Good! Then all you will do now is walk to the roundabout and stay there and a uniformed officer will be with you very quickly. From then on you just do whatever he tells you. Are you walking now? Then start! That's it. Good. Now repeat back to me what I've just told you to do. Good. Only do what I've just told you. Only that. I will know as soon as the officer is with you. And I will keep you safe. Yes, I will keep Marcus safe, too. Now I have to go. I'm going to hand my phone over to Nic. He will stay on the line with you until the officer arrives.'

The Peter-who-Nic-had-never-seen-before turned to face him. In that moment Nic knew that his instincts had been right. The man he loved was also someone else.

This.

A predator. Deliberate and irresistible once fixed on his target. The instant before Peter spoke again, Nic remembered a film he had seen of a giant komodo dragon walking along a beach towards its prey, its tongue flicking out checking the air for cues, its very being totally devoid of doubt.

'It all ends tonight,' Peter said, passing the phone to Nic. If he was at all aware of the way his partner was looking at him, he didn't show it. 'This is vital. Anne-Marie is on the phone. You will talk to her and make sure that she walks to where I just directed her. You will make sure that she stays there until an officer joins her and speaks to you. Before he does, you will get Anne-Marie to confirm that a uniformed officer is with her and no one else. Clear?'

Nic nodded. He raised the phone to his ear and said, 'Anne-Marie?' Even to him his voice sounded shaky.

Peter turned away and strode into the lounge. He used the house phone to call the Force Control Room. He knew the Duty Inspector. The two talked in the clipped, precise and functional language only ever used by professionals committed to working under the most extreme pressure.

The Force Control Room despatched firearms units to life-critical situations. A unit was about to be despatched to Marcus and Anne-Marie's home.

'A silent approach,' Peter instructed, meaning that neither sirens nor lights should be deployed.

'Absolutely.' The Inspector confirmed.

'Good. I'm on my way to the address as soon as we finish talking.'

'Of course. The team will do its job.'

'I know.' Peter hung up. He glanced briefly at Nic who was looking pale but was still on the phone. He nodded. His partner managed the weakest of smiles in return.

Peter set off towards his prey.

55.

Ethan Hall roared with a mixture of anger and hatred and fear. It came from the very deepest recesses of his stomach. It filled him with energy. It took him away from the mirror and back to the man he had saved until last.

Marcus Kline felt the killer's energy exploding out of him as a tangible force. He felt it rushing against his face and chest, crushing him briefly.

It was several seconds before either man was able to speak.

Ethan won the race.

'I taught myself how to hypnotise people,' he said. 'I didn't realise it is what I was doing at first. I just watched how my words influenced them, affected their mood, changed their colours. When you can actually see what works and what doesn't the learning process is so much faster. The end result is so much more powerful.

'Once I realised how easy it was for me, I began experimenting. I practiced changing their state without ever talking to them directly, or by whispering so quietly that their conscious mind didn't even realise I had penetrated it. I had to, you see. I had your example in front of me.

You showed me what my gift could be used for, what I was meant to be the best at. Only I learnt very quickly that I could never pretend to help them. What is the point of trying to change lives built on caves? There is none. Other than a desire for profit and reputation. And I need neither. I just need to continue my search.

'I will hypnotise you in a moment. Very deeply.' He gestured without looking towards the mirror, 'That was your last throw of the dice. Even though I could see what you were doing, for a few seconds you almost…Well, it was an interesting experience for me. Thank you.'

Marcus opened his mouth to speak. Ethan raised his left hand. 'No! No more words from you. No more words ever again. Do you understand? I promised I will kill you painlessly and I will. But if you utter even one more syllable I will break both of your hands with this.' He picked up the hammer. 'And that would be needless suffering. Clear?' Marcus nodded. 'Good. You don't need to ask your questions for me to know them. More than that, I will answer them for you now. It's appropriate don't you think that your final moments of consciousness should be spent listening?'

Ethan replaced the hammer on the table. He patted Marcus lightly on his right shoulder. Instantly he lost all sensation in his lower body.

'We'll move the loss of feeling upwards bit by bit,' Ethan said, 'Until it reaches right up to your scalp. A bit like the sea rolling in. That, of course, makes you my version of King Canute. Impotent and misguided.' He smiled. 'Now, let's bring this lesson to a close by telling you the final two things I want you to know. Firstly, let me explain about the others. As I'm sure you realised, after the first one – and he was a nobody, just a rehearsal – I selected them because I knew you would recognise the pattern, that we could have our private communication that no one else would either recognise or understand. Also, of course, I knew their deaths would hurt you. And whilst I have no desire to cause you physical pain I very much wanted to make you suffer psychologically. I wanted you to feel the pain of your responsibility in all of this. And you do feel that pain, don't you?'

Marcus nodded again. He couldn't feel his stomach. He was beginning to sweat.

'Good. However, it wasn't just malice on my part,' Ethan continued. 'You see, I knew Paul Clusker well. I had tended his garden for many years. I had in fact transformed it on his behalf. He told me that what I achieved was almost magical.' Ethan smiled. 'I needed to know if I understood him as well as I believed I did. So I had to look. Inside. I was pleased to find that my insight was accurate.

'Simon was an even more necessary part of my study. I had to explore him before you. As I told you earlier, I have seen our world – the most important depths of our world, the greatest power in our world – dancing before my very eyes. When I looked into their brains Marcus, I saw it! I saw the ultimate! I saw the subconscious! That's what I was looking for. Can you imagine that? I've seen the differences between people. I've seen the similarities, too. I've been able to compare, Marcus, and tonight I am going to compare them – Simon especially, after all you were training him – with you, with the man who preaches about the power of the subconscious, who claims to know and use it better than anyone else. I am going to see how different the genius is from his protégé!

'There. Now you know everything. Your lesson has simply been in understanding why I am doing this and in recognising how flawed you really are. Your lesson is now complete. My learning is just about to begin.'

It was over. Marcus knew that. His heart was still beating, but he couldn't feel his chest, arms or hands. The question, of course, was pulsing inside his head so hard that it hurt. He gritted his teeth and refused to let it out. It wasn't his fear of the hammer that stopped him from asking. It was pride. One last act of self-control. He had nothing else.

Marcus watched in silence as the younger man put on the lab coat and gloves.

'Even if you did ask me,' Ethan said, 'I wouldn't tell you. You want to know what the subconscious looks like. It never crossed your mind, or anyone else's, that it could be seen. Now you know that it can. By the right person. And you are desperate to know just what I saw. Of course you are. How could you not be?

'I could tell you simply that it is so amazing that words cannot do it justice. I could tell you that. Only why would I lie to you. I could talk to you now, paint you the pictures, and help you to see it in your mind's eye. Only why would I? You don't deserve it. Not you or anyone else. It's my prize and mine alone. I watched it change, Marcus, as I spoke to it. I watched it respond. I gave it permission to stop them living, to end their lives. I watched how it created and managed that great transition. Now I am going to see what you have to show me. This is my time now, not yours. I suggest you close your eyes. This is going to get very messy.'

Ethan picked up the scalpel. Marcus felt nothing. Either

inside or out. Ethan moved to his right shoulder. He placed the point of the scalpel on the skin just above Marcus's temple. Marcus kept looking straight ahead, at the gap between the curtains. At the sliver of darkness. Where he had last seen Anne-Marie.

'No more words from me now,' Ethan whispered. 'It ends in silence.'

Only it didn't.

The dining room door burst open and two armed police officers rushed in. They were both dressed in body armour and helmets. The lead officer traced the room in a fraction of a second. His pistol came to rest on Ethan.

'Armed police! Get on the floor!' The officer moved to his left as he shouted, allowing his colleague easy access. 'Get on the floor!'

Marcus heard Ethan growl. He saw him raise the scalpel and begin to move towards the officer. He saw the policeman take a step back.

'Get on the floor!'

Ethan kept moving forwards. The officer fired.

It ended noisily and abruptly.

It ends after it ends

A home changes when a killer visits and breathes his intention into it.

Anne-Marie and Marcus were both aware of the difference, of the sense that the very air in each room had been contaminated in a subtle but unmistakeable way, but they said nothing to each other. Instead they wondered if it was the result of the changes they were undergoing personally and of the things that still needed to be said.

Not surprisingly they came together to say those things in the kitchen, in view of the willow tree, almost exactly twenty-four hours after Peter Jones had stood there trying to persuade Marcus to move into a safe house.

When Marcus walked into the kitchen he had just finished a lengthy phone conversation in which his friend had updated him on events since the shooting of Ethan Hall.

'He's still in a coma,' Peter had said. 'To be honest, the doctor is surprised he's still alive. Given that he is, they are giving him a 50-50 chance of recovery. It seems that he has an incredibly strong system. Unusually resilient to shock is how the doctor described him.'

'Then he is well named,' Marcus replied.

'What?'

'Ethan. It's a biblical name symbolising 'a gift of the island'. It's derived from the Hebrew words for 'permanence' and 'strength'.'

'For an atheist you know an awful lot about religion.'

'For a public servant I've heard that you've got a very dominant phone manner.' They each heard the other chuckle briefly. 'Anyway,' Marcus continued, 'You know I'm not interested in religion; I'm interested in the power of human beliefs. For the most part they operate behind the curtain of the conscious and determine just about everything we say and do. Apart from that, names are just another example of how human beings can't resist creating meaning. You don't just give your child a name because you happen to like it. It has to mean something as well. Talking about naming your child, how's Samuel doing?

'He's in a state of absolute shock. He's always known that his boy could see colours when no one else could, that he had some special way of understanding and influencing others. He never thought for a moment that his son would turn into...into a madman. What parent would?'

'It's a good question. Parents have a blinkered way of thinking about and interacting with their children. They tend to mix a belief that they truly understand their offspring with a powerful love that produces hope and denial in equal measure. The result is the sort of relationship blindness that only operates when we are with the people we are closest to.'

'Thanks for the assessment. I was actually just asking a rhetorical question.'

'Even a rhetorical question has much more attached to it if you know how to listen.'

'You sound like the same old Marcus already.'

A brief pause; a slight intake of breath.

'I believe that the best way to overcome challenging times is to behave as if nothing has changed. To carry on as you always have, doing what you do best.'

'Do you feel like nothing has changed?'

Another pause; just a half-beat.

'I feel like everything has.'

'I understand that. Near-death experiences inevitably change people's perspective on life, even if only for a period of time. When the experience is caused by someone actually trying to kill you, well, its effect is even more pronounced.'

'Hmm.'

'So, tell me, how has your perspective changed?'

'You're not trying to turn into my counsellor, are you?'

'No. Just trying to re-establish myself as your friend.'

'There's no re-establishing needed. I know how difficult I made things for you. Truthfully, I can't imagine how stressful this whole situation must have been given the pressure on you.'

'Yeah. Right. I tell you, with friends like you...'

'What?'

'I really don't know. Anyway, we were talking about you.'

'Yes.'

The film played again, unbidden, in Marcus's mind. It was the film he had seen several times already of the moment he was saved and a young man was shot. He heard again the loud yet controlled voice of the armed policeman as he burst into the room followed by his colleague. He saw – he actually *felt* – the atmosphere shatter as a result of the sudden intrusion. It was as if they were all part of the same single sheet of glass that was fracturing from a central point, with lines running in different directions. Time slowed. Ethan turned towards the policemen. He took one step, then another. The first policeman shouted his command. His voice was like thunder. Marcus wondered if the sheet of glass would hold. Ethan raised his hands. The scalpel was a deadly weapon, but it seemed to Marcus that he had forgotten it temporarily, distracted by something that only he could see. He took another step, his mouth opening as if he was going to speak.

Marcus didn't see the policeman pull the trigger. He heard the sound of the two gunshots after he saw the wounds erupt in Ethan's chest. Then everything fell apart.

'I've never seen anyone shot before.' Marcus said finally. 'Whatever else it does to you, it reminds you more than anything that there are some things you can't take back.'

'Is that all it did – show you the difference between words and bullets?'

'Some words you can't take back either.' Marcus mused. 'But no, that's not all it did. It did something to me that I can't explain. I can feel...*it*. I just don't know what *it* is right now.'

'How does it feel?'

'Like a death. Like a part of me has died. I just don't know which part. What I do know for sure is that he – Ethan – could read people better than me. His senses were so much more finely tuned than mine. He had a natural ability that could have been so, so useful.'

'Only it turned him into a killer.'

'It wasn't his special ability that turned him into a killer. It was something else, something we will probably never understand.'

'If he lives we will need to establish a very clear motive. As for you though, you didn't really, secretly, think you were the very best did you?'

'Of course. Someone has to be. I thought it was me. I never made a secret of the fact.'

'I know you always said it. I just thought – maybe I always wanted to believe – that deep down you knew there had to be others out there who were at least as good as you and probably better. After all, the law of averages –'

'–Says that someone has to be the best.'

'But not forever.'

'No. You're right. Nothing's forever.' Marcus thought of the decisions he had made. He thought of one in particular. 'I was lucky,' he said. 'Lucky that Anne-Marie arrived home when she did. Lucky that she wanted to come home. Funny, I never used to believe in luck.'

'And do you now?'

Marcus considered briefly. 'I think the word is useful shorthand for a variety of complex, usually unplanned, interactions that take place beyond our control.'

'So luck is no more real than coincidence?'

'Who knows?'

'Obviously neither of us.' Peter considered for a moment. 'It's funny, though, isn't it? For everything the pair of us were trying to do, the whole thing was brought to a head by Anne-Marie looking in through a window.'

'It's a rare moment when fact and metaphor combine.'

'Is that another example of you carrying on as if nothing has changed, just doing what you do best?'

Marcus shrugged. 'I guess so. If I was a musician, I'd write a song about it.'

'I'm sure you would. I'm just happy that you both survived.'

The two men fell silent. For the first time in what seemed like a long time the silence held a natural warmth.

'Do you really think he could see the subconscious?' Peter asked eventually.

'I'm sure he believed it.'

'Many of his beliefs were wrong.'

'And many of the things he saw were real.' Marcus thought of the way Ethan had described his arrogance. He had showered several times in the last twenty four hours. The water hadn't helped.

'I have to go,' Marcus said. 'There's a conversation I need to have.'

'I know. I'm sure you will manage it brilliantly.'

'I can't be sure. What are you going to do now?'

'I'm going to spend the evening at home with Nic and the most excellent bottle or two of Rioja I can buy. We need to do some catching up.'

'Have a lovely night.'

'I intend to. Remember, just because you might not be the very best, you're still the best we've got.'

'I can live with that. I think.' Marcus ended the call.

Anne-Marie watched Marcus enter the kitchen through eyes he didn't quite recognise. He felt she was observing him rather than simply looking at him in the way she had for so many years. As Marcus returned her gaze it seemed that she was watching him through eyes that had found a new perspective.

'Peter is OK,' he said. 'He's got his result.'

'And what about you?'

Marcus shrugged. 'I honestly don't know what result I was aiming for. Not all of it. I was just trying to…' His voice trailed off. Anne-Marie waited for him to speak again. After a moment he said, 'Are you pleased to be home?'

They both recognised that the question worked on different levels.

After Ethan Hall had been shot the standby ambulance crew had rushed into the house. Peter Jones had arrived at exactly the same time. After a quick verbal debrief with Marcus and then Anne-Marie (who had been brought in by the police officer assigned to look after her), Peter had insisted that they both provide the most basic of written statements. He had then arranged for them to spend the night in the local Hilton hotel. Their home, he told them, was now his crime scene. He expected to be able to return it to them within twenty-four hours.

A family liaison officer had accompanied them to the hotel and taken all of Marcus's clothing back for forensic investigation. A uniformed officer had stayed outside their room throughout the night. Although they knew that the threat was over, they both found the police presence comforting. Anne-Marie knew better than to raise that fact in conversation.

Neither slept well. They both found it difficult to fall asleep and when they eventually did their sleep was so shallow that they woke repeatedly throughout the night, often at the same time. They made no attempt to talk to each other.

The next morning they tried unsuccessfully to eat breakfast. After that they provided their full and complete individual statements and Peter reassured them once again that their ordeal was over. As he had suggested they were back inside their own front door by late afternoon.

A home, they realised, changes once a killer has visited.

Which is why Marcus regretted his question as soon as he heard it. It had far more layers than he wanted his first question to have. It was, he noted, just one of many indicators that the so-called genius was currently not at his best.

'I needed to come home,' Anne-Marie said. 'And if I hadn't....'

'I'd be dead,' Marcus finished the sentence. 'Actually your voice helped keep me alive even before then.' He waved aside her question. 'And if you had not arrived when you did, if you had not phoned Peter, if you had panicked and made any sort of mistake, Ethan would have killed me and possibly you too.'

'Of course I panicked,' Anne-Marie spoke quickly. 'When I saw him with you, it wasn't that I didn't know what to think, I just couldn't think. And then when I remembered Peter, my hands were shaking so much I could barely work my mobile. I think...I think we were just lucky.'

That word again.

Marcus tried to ignore it. 'What do you mean when you say you *needed* to come home? Hadn't the photo shoot finished?'

Anne-Marie shook her head. This was it. The moment she had been preparing for over the last two days. Although the shockingly unexpected events of the previous night had pushed this moment both to the back of her mind and back in time, it had finally arrived. She took a deep breath and said, 'There wasn't a photo shoot. I just told you that because I knew you would accept it unquestioningly. The truth is, I needed to get away, to spend some time on my own, to do some thinking.'

'What about?'

'Me. Us. Everything.'

Marcus felt his heart miss a beat. 'Oh?'

'Yes. I'm sorry that I'm doing it now, like this, but it really can't wait. You see, there's something desperately important that I need to tell you. It's about our future.'

'I've been thinking about that, too.'

Really?' Anne-Marie's right hand fluttered over her stomach. 'What have you been thinking?'

'That you deserve someone better than me.'

Anne-Marie felt her breath tighten in her chest. 'No... No. I came home because I need *you*, not because I need to be *here*. It isn't the house I depend on.'

'Perhaps you feel that you depend on me simply because you are used to being with me? Because you have got used to tolerating me?'

'I don't tolerate you, I love you!'

'Really? Are you sure? To be honest with you, I don't know how anyone could love someone who has been as selfish and egotistical as me.'

'Don't say that! You do more good things for people than anyone else I know!'

'All on my own terms. Always for my own purpose.' Marcus looked down at the floor, away from *those* eyes that were now starting to fill with tears. 'I've realised something over the last few days. Actually, I've realised many things, but perhaps the most important is that for as many years as I can remember I've given the best of me to those who pay my wages – not to those who love me.

I'm so good at disassociating from people so that I can see and hear them clearly that I've forgotten what it's like to be close. I've spent my working life influencing others and in doing so I've lost touch with the most important influences in my life. With you. With Peter. With myself. I don't know who I am, Anne-Marie. Other than a cold-hearted bastard.'

'No! Please!' Anne-Marie fought to maintain her self-control. 'What are you saying? Marcus, what are you saying?'

'I'm saying that...erm...that I'm truly sorry for how I've been and I think...I think the best thing we can do, that the best thing for you is –'

'- I have cancer.'

She said it loudly. Partly because she could only say it that way, because she didn't yet know how to say those words in a controlled manner;   and partly – *mostly* – because she had to stop him from finishing his sentence.

She succeeded. The three words shocked Marcus more than anything that had happened in the previous days. Suddenly he felt a different type of fear altogether. Despite himself, he was drawn back to her eyes.

'What?'

'I have ovarian cancer. It's advanced. I need to have surgery, but there's still a very real chance that I'm going to die.' Anne-Marie trembled uncontrollably. 'You're the first person I've told. This is the first time I've said it out loud.'

'Is that why you...?'

'Why I went away? Yes. I needed to get my head around it. Now I'm home.'

Marcus felt Anne-Marie's fear and desperation filling the room. He felt it reach out and squeeze him hard. He waited for her to say whatever it was that she needed to say next.

'I need you to be with me. If I'm going to beat the cancer I need more than just great medical care. I need to *believe*. I need my mind – all of it – working together. Right now it isn't. I'm too…too scared…I'm too…too much of… of so many things. I need a genius to help my mind to work in the way that I know it can. Marcus, I need you to help me. To work with me. To love me.'

Marcus Kline looked closely at the woman who loved him, who depended upon him. No matter what decision he might have made, or what his intention had been, there was now only one answer he could give. It was the answer the consultant always gave when those with whom he shared his life asked for his help.

'Yes.' He said. 'Of course I will.' He took a deliberate step towards her to emphasise the reality and power of his commitment. 'I will keep you safe. I will make you well. I promise.' And then he added, because the phrase was in his mind and because he knew what influence it would have, '*My Angel*.'

Anne-Marie cried.

He held her.

The willow tree grew silently in the shadows. Its branches brushed the earth.

* * * * * * * * * *

Chris Parker began his study of interpersonal and intrapersonal communication in the 1970s. He is a highly experienced presenter, management trainer and consultant. He wrote his first novel in 1986. He has since written several books on communication and influence. He has more lines on his face than most and is afraid to read them.

Belief

The second book in the
Marcus Kline trilogy, is coming!

To keep updated and to learn more about
'Influence' and how to create it visit:

http://marcuskline.co.uk

Urbane Publications is dedicated to developing new author voices, and publishing fiction and non-fiction that challenges, thrills and fascinates. From page-turning novels to innovative reference books, our goal is to publish what YOU want to read. Find out more at

http://urbanepublications.com